HOLIDAY WARNING

Caprice turned toward the driver's side door of her Camaro. Grant started to say, "You be careful driving in this snow—"

He stopped mid-sentence and Caprice saw why.

"What are they?" he asked, puzzled.

Caprice could see that the sleigh bells from her door decoration were now hanging on the car door handle with a plastic twist tie. Snow was accumulating on them. She stepped closer and spied something wedged underneath the bells. A Ziplock bag. She pulled it out and as she did, she saw the note within.

In black marker on lined paper were the words— *Stop asking questions or your sleigh bells will never ring again . . .*

Books by Karen Rose Smith

STAGED TO DEATH

DEADLY DÉCOR

GILT BY ASSOCIATION

DRAPE EXPECTATIONS

SILENCE OF THE LAMPS

SHADES OF WRATH

SLAY BELLS RING

Published by Kensington Publishing Corporation

Slay Bells Ring

Karen Rose Smith

KENSINGTON PUBLISHING CORP.

http://www.kensingtonbooks.com

KENSINGTON BOOKS are published by

Kensington Publishing Corp.
119 West 40th Street
New York, NY 10018

All Kensington Titles, Imprints, and Distributed Lines are available at special quantity discounts for bulk purchases for sales promotions, premiums, fund-raising, and educational or institutional use. Special book excerpts or customized printings can also be created to fit specific needs. For details, write or phone the office of the Kensington special sales manager: Kensington Publishing Corp., 119 West 40th Street, New York, NY 10018, attn: Special Sales Department, Phone: 1-800-221-2647.

Kensington and the K logo Reg. U.S. Pat & TM Off.

ISBN-13: 978-1-4967-0977-6
ISBN-10: 1-4967-0977-2
First Kensington Mass Market Edition: November 2017

eISBN-13: 978-1-4967-0978-3
eISBN-10: 1-4967-0978-0
First Kensington Electronic Edition: November 2017

10 9 8 7 6 5 4 3 2 1

Printed in the United States of America

In memory of Agnes Ozminski,
who loved everything about Christmas:
the decorating, the presents, and the glitter.
She made my holidays brighter. I miss you.

Acknowledgments

I would like to thank Officer Greg Berry,
my law enforcement consultant,
who so patiently answers all my questions.
His input is invaluable.

Chapter One

"Your Christmas Delight theme for staging this house is perfect," Sara Merriweather told Caprice De Luca on the Sunday before Thanksgiving. Yet Sara's voice held forced cheerfulness and her eyes were troubled.

Caprice was enchanted with the 1918 historic Colonial on a side street in the oldest neighborhood in Kismet, Pennsylvania. But ever since she'd been putting the finishing touches on staging the house to sell, her client had looked worried.

Part of her job as house stager was to set up a house to sell quickly. The other part? Listening to homeowners' concerns, helping them declutter, and teaching them to show off their home in the best possible light. However, listening was her best asset.

"What do you have doubts about?" she asked Sara.

Her client glanced around the grand entry, the beautiful heart-pine floors under the oriental rugs, the wide entrance to the living room on the right, a hall leading back to the kitchen along the stairway, as well as the spacious parlor to the left.

"This house has been nothing but a delight for all the years we've lived here," Sara explained. "That's why I don't understand why Chris is so sure about selling it, about moving us into a condo in a retirement village. He insists I won't have stairs to climb, and we'll have less to maintain. But he's acting like we're eighty years old instead of sixty-six. I love this house, especially now with the way you've decorated it for Christmas. I just don't understand why he's pushing to sell fast."

"Maybe now that he's made the decision, he just wants to do it. He doesn't want to linger over the memories here as you do."

Sara shook her head as if she just couldn't understand her husband's thought process or lack of attachment. "Our children love this house too."

Caprice had used her red-and-white theme throughout the Colonial in addition to lots of brass. She'd chosen to keep the pine antiques in place as well as the huge sleigh bed in the master bedroom. This time of year, especially, with the house on the Historic Homes Tour, it could sell quickly. Still, she heard all of the doubts in Sara Merriweather's voice, none of which she'd heard from Christopher Merriweather when the couple had signed the contract to stage the home.

Pushing her straight, long, brown hair over her shoulder, she focused her attention on Sara and asked, "Do you want to have a cup of tea and talk about it?"

"Do you have time?"

Caprice made time for anything important to her. The Merriweathers weren't simply her clients. Christopher Merriweather was her dad's poker buddy. She knew her father was especially fond of Blitz, Chris's white Malamute, who usually attended the poker games too. As a favor to her dad, Caprice had spoken to Chris about staging the house to sell it more quickly, and he'd convinced Sara. Now Caprice wondered if that had been the best idea.

Sara led Caprice back the hall to the state-of-the-art chef's kitchen with its black granite eat-at counter, its custom-crafted walnut-finished cabinets, its high-end appliances. The terrazzo floor extended into a dining area where Caprice knew Sara and Chris had enjoyed many dinners with their children. The Merriweathers were proud of their family just as the De Lucas were.

Sara filled the copper teapot from the filtered-water spigot and set it on the burner. She turned on the stove and looked around the kitchen.

Chris's hobby was crafting toys in the workshop out back. Some of those toys Caprice had scattered behind the decorative spindle railing along the top of the cupboards. The toys were interspersed with sparkling flameless candles on timers. She'd switched them on to see how they'd look, and she liked the effect. The wooden toy train, the horse pull toy, and the assorted blocks accompanied the old-fashioned look of most of the house.

Sara motioned to the table, its gleaming polish reflecting the crystal vase that held pine boughs, white mums, red roses, and red Christmas balls. "You've really done a beautiful job with this staging,

Caprice. When you suggested we take a storage unit for the extras, I never thought we'd fill it, but we did. You've eliminated furniture that just wasn't necessary to make what *is* here really stand out."

Taking a seat at the eat-at counter, Caprice brushed the cuffs of her Bohemian top's flowing sleeves above her wrists. Her retro fashion sense was at work even over the holidays. Her hunter green, wide-legged slacks matched the swirls in her red-and-green blouse. She responded to Sara's statement with a smile. "That's what staging a house is all about. Nikki has a wonderful buffet planned. We'll go over it before the open house." Caprice's sister, who ran the catering business Catered Capers, helped make each open house a success with her layout of tempting dishes.

When the economy had hit a downturn and decorating houses and Caprice's design degree weren't in demand, she'd transformed her business into that of a home-staging company. Her reputation for coming up with unique themes for high-end clients had made the rounds of the surrounding area, even leading her to win a competition for designing a house on a cable TV show. That had garnered her even more clients.

Over the past few years, she'd learned the ins and outs of the business the hard way, by trial and error. She kept up with trends, but mostly went with the feel of the house. The idea of doing this Colonial, and an historic one at that, with the theme of Christmas Delight had been a no-brainer. After all, Chris Merriweather even played Santa Claus!

The tea kettle whistled, and Sara switched off the

burner. Her thoughts apparently running in the same direction as Caprice's, she said, "They moved the Santa cabin into the community park."

"I imagine Chris is looking forward to starting his Santa role after the parade next Sunday."

Children came from the surrounding areas to see Santa or drop off their letters to him. The downtown area would extend store hours between Thanksgiving and Christmas, and the park would be lit up with twinkle lights especially along Santa Lane, the path leading to the cabin-like structure.

"He looks forward to meeting with the children and reading their letters every year. I'm hoping his Santa duties a few evenings a week and on Saturdays will bring up his energy."

"He's been tired lately?"

"He's been taking shorter walks with Blitz. Ever since his yearly trip to D.C. with his friends, he's been quieter than usual, yet he won't slow down. This time of year, business really revs up at the craft shop, and Chris always feels as if he has to be on top of everything. Sometimes I think he needs to sell the business and retire. My memory isn't as great as it once was and neither is his. He keeps all the facts and figures in his head for inventory sheets and payroll."

Merriweather Crafts had been in business for at least the past twenty years. It was a craft shop that had changed with the times and done well. Caprice knew Sara helped out when they were busy, but she spent most of her time teaching scrapbooking and tole-painting classes as well as helping to keep the office in order.

"Is Chris at the craft store now?"

"Yes. He's getting ready for a rush on Christmas crafts when we open in the morning."

"Is Blitz with him?" Caprice missed the friendly presence of the Malamute.

"They're together. They're inseparable. And I suppose that's a good thing. We all need a friend who loves us unconditionally. That's what Blitz does for Chris."

After Sara pulled an old-fashioned, decorative tin from a cupboard and opened it, Caprice chose an orange cinnamon teabag and dipped it into the hot water in her porcelain teacup. Sara chose chamomile tea, and Caprice could see that she was stressed by the whole idea of selling the house. Maybe they should clarify something now.

As Sara sat with her and they let their tea cool a bit, Caprice said, "You're contracted with me to stage the house, and you're listed with Denise Langford to sell." Denise was a luxury real estate broker who handled many of Caprice's clients. "But maybe you should talk to Chris again about this. We can still cancel Saturday's open house, and you can back out of the listing."

Sara shook her head. "I hate to say it, but I think the only thing Chris is going to miss about this house is his workshop in the carriage house. There *is* nothing to talk about."

Except Sara's feelings, Caprice thought ruefully. "Is he going to continue to make hand-crafted toys if you sell?"

"He insists he can rent a space if he wants to continue. He seems to have everything worked out, yet I don't understand his thinking at all. Most of all, he doesn't seem happy.

A Vietnam veteran, Chris Merriweather was the jovial Santa-type at Christmas. Other times . . . oh, he was always pleasant and very kind, generous to his employees and friends. Yet over the years, even Caprice had seen shadows in Chris's eyes from the time he spent in Vietnam that he could probably never forget.

Caprice said, "I have a few finishing touches to make, then I'll be out of your hair—at least for now. I'd like to hang a heritage wreath on the spare-room door upstairs and add the spruce and pomegranate sachets to the bedrooms."

"That sounds nice. Those crystal nappies you found in my hutch to display them are perfect for all the bedrooms. Yes, I want you to go ahead with it. Do you really think this house will sell fast?"

"Oh, I do. It has the square footage and the polish and the charm. If it doesn't sell from the open house, think about how many people will be coming through for the Historic Homes Tour. There's no way to know for sure, but I would expect you to have a contract by the new year."

"This is really happening." Sara sank against the shiny wood of the chair back. Although well into her sixties, she looked closer to fifty. Her ash-blond hair was permed in sort of a pompadour, then trimmed snuggly to fit against her neck and around her ears. Her blue eyes were usually full of excitement and smiles. However, today, even dressed in a beautiful red, two-piece suit with a holly pin on the collar, she looked a bit weary. Maybe Chris wasn't the only one who was tired of working and juggling life.

Suddenly, a loud *bang bang bang* on the front door startled them both.

"Are you expecting someone?" Caprice asked. "Someone who doesn't know you have a beautiful-sounding doorbell?"

"Not expecting anyone. I'd better answer it before whoever it is breaks the door down."

Caprice could see down the hall to the front door as Sara hurried to open it. When she did, she faced a male who was about six two, with gelled black hair that wasn't exactly a mohawk but could have been. He was wearing a leather jacket, but Caprice spotted tattoos circling his neck. They were probably down his arms too. Caprice caught a glimpse of the man's face as he shifted from one booted foot to the other.

Sara remained calm, however, in the face of his scowl. "Can I help you, Boyd?" she asked politely.

"You certainly *can* help me. I received a phone call from the chief of police last night. Chief Powalski told me that if my band doesn't find another place to practice at night, we'll all be charged with disorderly conduct. I can't make a living if I can't practice."

Sara suggested, "Can't you practice at another band member's house?"

"No, we can't. I have the equipment, and I'm not lugging it all over town. If your husband knows what's good for him, he'll lay off calls to the cops or he'll be sorry."

Whew! Caprice thought. She wouldn't want that guy who was obviously a neighbor coming to *her* door.

When Sara returned to the kitchen, Caprice asked, "Who was that?"

"His name is Boyd Arkoff and he lives next door. Chris has enough trouble sleeping at night. I don't know if this band has Christmas gigs or what, but they've been practicing nightly right back there in Boyd's garage." She motioned toward the rear of their yard. "We have a wide property with the carriage house and the garage, so you can imagine how loud Boyd's band has to be for us to hear it in winter with the windows shut and furnace running. Chris couldn't take the noise anymore, and he asked Mack to make the call."

The chief of police, Mack Powalski, had been like a favorite uncle when Caprice and her siblings were growing up. He was a good friend of her dad's, and he was a friend of Chris's too. In fact, she remembered that he'd served in Vietnam with Chris. It only made sense that Chris might have asked Mack to do him a favor. Yet this one might have backfired.

"Do you know what Boyd means when he says Chris will be sorry?"

"Oh, just that he'll turn up the volume and play even more at night. I don't think he has the best attitude. I heard he dropped out of high school, got a GED, and has been playing music trying to become famous ever since. But his band mostly ends up in low-end lounges in Baltimore, D.C., Lancaster, York—wherever they can get a gig." Sara sighed. "I don't know where my manners are. I have some of that apple cinnamon loaf you gave me the recipe for. Would you like a slice?"

Caprice wondered if Sara really wanted a snack, or if she wanted to prolong their talk. Caprice checked her watch. She was fine on time.

Sara sliced each of them a piece of the apple cinnamon loaf and they enjoyed that while they talked about the neighbors in the area. When a house cost this much, $400,000 to $500,000—and Denise believed that's what it would go for—Caprice liked to be filled in on the neighbors. That was important information to have at the open house when interested parties wanted to know who they'd be living close to.

"If Boyd practices often, that's something we'll have to reveal," Caprice explained to Sara. "You don't want somebody putting a down payment on the house, living here a week, and deciding you didn't disclose something they can't live with."

"I know," Sara responded with a resigned expression. "That's why I hope we can get it worked out. Maybe Chris and Mack can visit Boyd together and help him see reason."

Caprice wasn't sure Boyd was in any mood to see reason.

They were eating their apple loaf and drinking tea, talking about festivities planned in the upcoming weeks for the holidays, when notes from "Joy to the World" came from Sara's pocket. She slipped her phone out, took a look at the screen, and then said to Caprice, "I'd better take this. It's my son-in-law."

But instead of staying at the table and having a

genial conversation, Sara stood with a frown creasing her brow and walked into the hall. She wasn't gone long, maybe five minutes, but when she returned Caprice could see she was upset.

"Is something wrong?"

"You know I promote a sense of family. I try to never say anything negative about one family member to another. But sometimes . . ." Her voice shook a little.

"Sometimes I imagine you need to vent."

"Yes. I just can't vent to the wrong person," Sara murmured.

Caprice waited.

"*You* could be objective," Sara decided.

"I can try to be."

"You know my daughter Maura."

"I do, though not well. She was older than me so we didn't run into each other in school very much. How is she?"

"She married about three years ago, and I'll admit Chris and I didn't approve of her choice. Reed Fitzgee is a car salesman, and that's fine. But he's been married twice before. Twice. We've tried to be supportive, but Reed borrowed money from us about a year after he married Maura to pay credit card debt that had gotten out of hand. To his credit, he did pay it back. But now Maura is pregnant, and Reed is asking us for money again to move to a bigger place. He wants us to help with the down payment. Chris has told him *no*, but Reed wants me to convince Chris otherwise. I told him I can't. The whole thing is upsetting, especially this time of year when I want peace and harmony around the table . . . when I just want to enjoy the idea of becoming a grandmother."

Caprice felt for Sara, and she certainly understood. Her own family had had its ups and downs. Her uncle had been separated from them for a dozen years, although recently he had reunited with them, and that was a good thing. But when daughters-in-law and sons-in-law were involved and parents didn't like them, that could be very sticky.

Caprice looked down at her engagement ring. Simply glancing at it made her smile. The diamond was a pink heart-shape with pink sapphires and diamonds alternating in a channel setting along both sides. It was the most beautiful ring she had ever seen, and Grant Weatherford, her brother's law partner, had picked it out all on his own.

Sara must have seen her looking at the ring. "When are you and Grant getting married?"

"We're not sure. We're waiting for Grant's annulment from his marriage to come through, but we're thinking spring."

"It's a good thing the Pope refined the rules or you could have been waiting a lot longer. Is the annulment process as complicated as before?"

"The complications arise in uprooting all the emotions and asking Grant's ex-wife to fill out a questionnaire too. His ex is willing. Thank goodness, they have an amicable relationship now or this could be much harder."

"I admire you standing up for what you believe in."

"Grant and I decided together that waiting for the annulment is what we want to do. Our faith is important to us, and we want to be married in the church."

"Chris and I were once active at St. Francis of Assisi. But that was before he went into the service. After he came back, he wouldn't even go to church. I kept going. Still, the past few years I've felt it's more important to spend time with him than to sit in a pew and listen to a sermon that's not much help in my daily life."

Caprice empathized that some sermons were helpful and others weren't. But she needed the spiritual connection Mass offered with or without a meaningful homily. She said truthfully, "Grant had been away from the church ever since he lost his daughter. But he's slowly come to realize he still needs faith in his life," Caprice admitted.

"We all need faith, hope, and love, especially this time of year," Sara agreed.

It was almost 4 p.m. when Caprice finished at the Merriweather home and climbed into her van, eager to pick up her cocker spaniel, Lady, at her parents' house, eager to see Grant later this evening. They had plans for him to bring his cocker spaniel, Patches, who was Lady's brother, over to her house. She'd made a casserole of lasagna to pop in the oven. They were going to light a fire and watch a movie.

She was about to switch on the ignition when the Beatles song "All I've Got to Do" played from her cell phone. She'd just set it on the stand on her dash in case she needed to talk hands-free.

Bella's photo appeared on the screen, and Caprice swiped her phone screen to accept the call. Bella was her younger sister, even though most of the time she acted like an older one, always ready to give out advice. Her pretty, heart-shaped face surrounded by a mass of black curls peered at Caprice from the phone screen.

"Hey, Bella. You caught me at a good time. I was just leaving the Merriweather—"

"Caprice, you've got to help me," Bella cut in. "I don't know what to do. The director of the Christmas pageant fell and broke her hip."

Not long ago, Bella, who'd earned a degree in fashion design, had started a kids' costume-making business. She also designed the most divine christening outfits. Because of her sewing skills, she'd volunteered to help with the community center's Christmas pageant, acting as assistant director.

"How can I help?" Caprice knew she shouldn't ask because her work schedule was demanding until Christmas. But if Bella really needed her . . .

"They've asked me to take over. Now I'm the director. I need you here yesterday. Can you come help?"

Caprice knew better than to ask Bella what she needed her to do. Bella could be overdramatic. If nothing else, Caprice could stop by the community center and maybe calm her down. Since Kismet was a small town, the Merriweathers' house, located not far from the downtown area, was less than a mile from the community center.

Caprice assured her sister, "I'll be there in five minutes, maybe ten at the most." She'd left plenty of kibble for her cats, Sophia and Mirabelle, before she'd left today, and Lady would be fine visiting at her mom's for a little while longer. Her mom, dad, and Nana—who lived in a separate suite in their house—liked having Lady around. Lady easily played with Nana's cat, Valentine, and her dad liked to take Lady on long walks. No worries there.

The Kismet Community Center was located up the street from the downtown area within walking distance of the stores, restaurants, and professional offices. The building had once been a warehouse, but it had been completely renovated twenty years ago, with some additional renovation last year. A chain-link fence surrounded the outside basketball court. Inside were a game room, an arts and crafts room, a couple of offices, and a meeting room. The pageant itself would be held at the Kismet Community Theater, but all the preparations were happening at the center. The sets would be transported to the theater the day before the pageant.

Caprice pulled into the parking lot, gazing across the street at the two complexes of low-income apartments, each consisting of about fifty units. This community center had saved many kids from roaming the streets, giving them a place to go and something to do. The wind buffeted Caprice, and she realized she should have worn something a little warmer than her sixties-style poncho with the fringe. November in Pennsylvania could turn bitterly cold. She hoped that wouldn't happen until at least after the holiday parade next Sunday. That would be Chris Merriweather's first appearance as Santa this year.

Caprice hurried to the game-room entrance of the center. It was her favorite room there. Not so long ago it had been given a fresh coat of beige paint. Then the teenagers had painted murals on the walls that were artistic and well-executed.

Caprice easily saw Bella trying to herd elementary-age kids, her children Timmy and Megan included, into the arts and crafts room. To Caprice's surprise she spotted her dad, along with her brother Vince, brother-in-law Joe, and two other parents. She also recognized the choir director from St. Francis of Assisi Church. Caprice waved to her and Dora Watkins waved back.

Bella spotted Caprice and came running into the game room. "I'm so glad you're here."

"What's Vince doing here? And Dad and Joe?"

"I need them to help with distributing scripts, choosing carols, designing sets, and constructing them. Nikki had a catering gig and couldn't come, and Mom's taking care of Lady and Benny. She said she'd come later and bring Benny. But I can't watch him and direct all of this too."

Caprice put her hand on Bella's shoulder. "Slow down. I'm sure Mom and Nikki will help when they can."

Bella's brow furrowed. "Hardly anything's been done, and now I've got it all to do."

"The first thing you need to do is to become organized," Caprice advised. "What's the pageant's theme?"

"Theme? It's Christmas."

"Bella, you need an idea about set construction.

What kind of sets are you going to use? You need a theme to tie it all together."

Caprice's dad came from the arts and crafts room into the game room. Nick De Luca was still a handsome man. His black hair was laced with gray. At almost six foot, his tight hugs and broad smile had always made Caprice feel safe and loved.

Now he shook his head and flung his arm around Bella's shoulders. "I told her she has to calm down. She just learned today she's the director. We still have time to make this a wonderful pageant. We'll all work together. You know that, honey."

Bella looked as if his kind words almost brought tears to her eyes. "I don't like to fail, Dad."

"No one does, and you won't."

"She needs a theme," Caprice said. "You can think about that tonight. In the meantime, we can figure out some basic set construction we know we're going to need. I assume you'll be doing a stable scene."

"Of course, I will. I already have the angels' wings made, and Mary and Joseph's costumes. I'm the only one who was ahead of the game."

"Since you're going to have a Nativity scene, the first part of our set construction can concern a few cut-out trees and a stable," their dad suggested. "Once you think of a theme we'll tie everything into that. But at least we can get started."

"Who's going to cut these out?" Bella asked, panic in her voice. "I don't know anything about woodworking."

Their father grinned. "You're in luck. I do know a lot about woodworking, and if I run into trouble, I have friends."

Nick was a brick mason who managed his own firm. He often executed home construction projects, and his friends helped him, so he knew a lot about construction besides masonry.

Her father added, "Chris Merriweather has a whole woodworking shop in his carriage house. If I pick up the plywood and whatever supplies I need, I'm sure he'll let me use his saws." Her father checked his watch. "Why don't I try to call him? I'll ask him to stop by. Santa Claus to the rescue again," her dad added with a wink.

Caprice hoped that was true—for Bella's sake and for the sake of the kids and the pageant.

Chapter Two

When Caprice checked her watch, she realized it was almost 8 p.m. She'd called Grant to tell him she'd be later than planned, and he'd said he'd wait for her at her house. Looking around, she caught sight of Bella, who was consulting with one of the parents adept at working behind the scenes since he also volunteered at the Kismet Community Theater. He was filling Bella in on the type of apparatuses they would need to slide the scenery on the stage.

Caprice glanced down at her electronic tablet, where she'd been making a list of necessary supplies. She thought her dad had said he was going into the storeroom with Vince to see if there was any paint back there that they could use.

Suddenly a male voice over her shoulder asked, "Caprice?" She turned to find Chris Merriweather. With his snow-white hair and twinkling blue eyes, he was a perfect stand-in for Santa Claus. But as her gaze met his now, she blinked in shock. He looked upset, but it wasn't only the frown lines on his face that troubled her. It was the cut above his eye and bruising on his jaw that caught her attention.

She recovered her composure quickly. "Hi, Chris. Have you been home to see the house?"

"I only stopped to drop Blitz off earlier. He needed his supper. So I didn't see much. But I like the garland around the door frame and the wreath takes me back to decorations I once saw in Williamsburg. Very tasteful."

"Thank you."

She couldn't help but notice that Chris's red down jacket had dirt streaks on it. He was wearing black cargo pants, which were usual for him. He'd told her more than once they came in handy when he was at the store and needed to fill his pockets with necessary items. But his disheveled appearance was out of character.

Just then her father came from the storeroom and strode toward them. But as soon as he stopped in front of Chris, he said, "What happened? You look like you've been in a brawl."

Chris's mouth twisted in a wry frown. "I had a disagreement with a box that fell from a high shelf at the store. It whacked me on the head and the jaw." However, his eyes didn't meet Caprice's or her dad's when he said it.

Caprice could easily see from her father's expression that he didn't believe a word of that explanation. Still, he and Chris were friends, and he didn't question him further. At least not now.

"I'm glad you stopped in," Nick said. "We could use your expertise, and maybe I need to borrow your workshop. We need to build some sets for the pageant. Is there a good time when I could use your saws? Or do you have everything set up for the toys you're making now?"

"I'm almost finished with toy making, believe it or not. I have plenty of trains and cars, all done in wood, of course, to use for angel gifts. I'm just finishing up some games and mostly that involves painting. Remember, I work on this all year, not just a couple of months before Christmas. I'd never have enough time if I did that. Not that I have enough time now," he said, smiling. "With Sara wanting to give dinner parties and the kids dropping in now and then, my free time gets eaten up."

"Your store is demanding this time of year," her dad offered.

"You're right about that, and sometimes I actually *feel* like Santa Claus when I'm in the store as well as when I'm in Santa's cabin. I've often thought of letting someone else take over the cabin, and I would just set up a corner of the store with Santa. But that cabin is intertwined in Kismet's history. It goes back twenty-six years, and finding a Santa who is committed isn't always that easy these days. Everybody's time is tight."

Returning to her dad's question, Chris asked, "Are you planning to use plywood for these sets?"

"That's something else I wanted to talk to you about. Vince thought maybe we could use a type of particle board."

Chris screwed up his face. "That's much harder to saw through."

"Why don't you come over here and talk to Vince about it. There's another guy here too, one of the dads who is going to help with the sets. If we all get on the same page, this whole project will come together quicker."

"I imagine that's true. Life's a lot easier when everybody is on the same page." Chris agreed as if he knew all about that concept.

It sounded to Caprice as if there was regret in Chris's voice.

But then he seemed to shake it off. "Speaking of being on the same page, are you both coming to the parade next Sunday?"

The Christmas parade was one of Kismet's biggest holiday events. Even the schools participated by building floats, so it wasn't just a matter of a fire engine driving through town. Santa had a float too.

"I wouldn't miss it," Caprice said. "We're all keeping our fingers crossed the weather is suitable and we don't freeze or get wet."

"I already checked the long-term forecast. We're supposed to have sunny skies. Did you hear about the elves?"

"What elves?" Caprice asked with a laugh.

"At the high school there was a group of kids caught cutting class, about six or eight of them. They thought going to a movie for the afternoon would be better than sitting in math. Anyway, to get out of a week's detention, or a suspension, they agreed to be elves at the parade and give out candy canes."

Nick laughed heartily. "You *are* kidding."

"Nope. I heard Sara talking to one of the teachers

at the store. Those new skinny jeans along with a few red tunics are all the costume they need, apparently. So, get ready for some real Christmas cheer." Chris unzipped his down jacket. "Let's go talk about that wood you want to buy. If you'd like, you can use my workshop tomorrow. I'll be going into the store early and will be tied up late. That's what holiday hours are like."

Vince was beckoning to Chris and her dad. Chris said, "I'll go see what he wants."

Caprice leaned close to her father. "Do you think he's all right? That bruise on his jaw looks nasty. There's a cut on his forehead. Do you know what's going on with him?"

"I'm not sure," her father answered. "At our poker game last week, his mind was on anything but the game. That's not like him. He's been distracted lately. Even when I talk to him, I get the feeling his mind is somewhere else. You spent much of the day with Sara. Did she mention anything?"

"Not exactly. She just said Chris seemed tired lately. But he's so busy with everything, and now with playing Santa he won't have any time to himself. You know, Dad, I don't think she wants to sell their house."

Her father looked thoughtful. "He's always taken her wishes into consideration. He's never been one of those men to just go do something without consulting his wife."

"I think they've talked about the sale plenty, but she's just not sold on the idea."

"At the game, he talked about it as if it's a done

deal. He thinks your staging is going to sell the house fast even before Christmas."

"It's a beautiful historic house. Just the carriage house on the grounds out back adds a lot of charm."

"Even in the winter?"

"Even in the winter. They have beautiful Norwegian pines and blue spruce. The brick patio almost looks like cobblestone and the path that leads to the carriage house is quaint. I can't imagine Chris without his workshop, and I don't think Sara can either."

"He can take his tools and supplies anywhere."

Caprice protested, "But the carriage house has charm, the outside of it with those huge double doors . . ."

"It's just a building, honey."

"But it's a building where he's made Christmas toys for years. I can't imagine there isn't sentiment attached to that. Memories are attaching Sara to the house. She remembers her kids when they were four and six and eight and ten . . . when they were teenagers bringing friends home. That house was, is, a real home. It's hard to leave something like that. I can't imagine you and Mom being any place but where you are."

"Even though we've made constant repairs for over thirty years?"

"Even though. I don't think you would have had it any other way. You've put yourself into that house, from patching plaster on the ceiling to building the brick fireplace outside."

"And that's the way it should be. Have you and

Grant talked about where you're going to live once you're married?"

"That's one of the discussions we still have to have. I think we're both afraid to move too fast because we don't know when the annulment will come through. So, we're just enjoying our engagement, not stressing out about anything."

Her father hung his arm around her shoulders and gave her a squeeze. "That sounds like the best plan. I'd better get over there before they decide something I don't approve of."

"I'm going to leave, Dad. I have to pick up Lady, and Grant is probably waiting at my place. In spite of work and other commitments, we always intend to make time for each other. I've seen you and Mom do it and know we can too."

"Tell Grant I said hello. How about if you meet me at Chris's workshop tomorrow morning around nine. If anything changes, I'll give you a call."

"Sounds good."

But as her focus again drifted to Chris where he was standing at a table speaking with Vince, she studied that bruise on his jaw. It was red and purple, not yellow or green like an older bruise. So it was possible a box had just tumbled onto him. Wasn't it?

The following morning, Caprice parked her re-stored yellow Camaro at the curb in front of the Merriweather house. She'd spotted her dad's truck in the driveway that led to the garage, and she didn't want to block him in. She realized the Merriweathers weren't at home. Both Sara and Chris would be at the store, ready for opening at nine o'clock on Monday morning.

Going around her car, Caprice opened the passenger door. Lady sat on the seat, studying her, her golden buff coat gleaming in the sunshine.

"I know you like this better than traveling in your cage in my van. But the cage really is safer."

Lady tilted her head and gave Caprice a look that said she knew that.

Caprice took Lady's fuchsia leash from the floor and attached it to her collar. "Come on, we'll see what Dad's up to in the workshop."

Lady happily jumped out of the car without any encouragement and trotted beside Caprice up the driveway that led to the garage beside the carriage house. The brick path and the patio added even more charm to the house. Caprice knew at night the twinkle lights on the evergreens almost made one want to sit out there even in the winter time. And she supposed they could, with the fire pit there.

Fire pits conjured up good memories for her. She and Grant had celebrated their engagement at the fire pit in Ace Richland's backyard. Ace was a rock legend they'd both come to know quite well. The night Grant had proposed, he'd commandeered Ace's estate. Caprice could still remember every minute of that evening vividly, and she never wanted to forget it.

She could hear the buzz of a saw as she stepped up to the carriage house door. Lady stopped and sat as if she wasn't sure they should go in. Lady was a lower pack dog, which meant she liked to please her mistress. But she had good instincts too, and the sound of a strange machine was enough to make her hesitate.

The buzzing suddenly stopped, and Caprice took advantage of that moment to open the door. When Lady spotted Caprice's dad, she eagerly went forward with Caprice and practically ran to him, even though he did look a bit strange in the goggles and woodcutting apron.

Immediately her dad pushed the goggles to the top of his head and hunkered down to give Lady a good ruffle around the ears. "How are you doing, girl?"

Lady barked as if to say *Just fine this morning, thank you.*

Her dad laughed then rose to his feet. "Chris got me started this morning before he left for the shop. I drove the plywood over in the company truck." Easily Caprice could see her dad had used the jigsaw to cut out two-dimensional fir trees.

"It looks as if you made progress. Bella will be pleased we have something to paint."

"I still have to attach the supports to the back so they stand up, but they should work wherever she wants to put them. After I'm finished with them, I'll take the circular saw to the community center. Chris said he's going to try to break free of work for a couple of hours this afternoon to cut out the stable for us."

"Does he really have time for that?"

Her father shrugged. "He said he'll make time. Apparently, he hired more help at the store this season, so neither he nor Sara would be overburdened. She wanted to take his toys to a couple of craft shows and sell them, simply because they're good for kids. He didn't want her to feel she should be two places at once. He knows she likes to be out and about in the community."

"You can't own a business like they do and not know practically everyone in a town the size of Kismet. Mom was talking about taking one of Sara's scrapbooking workshops and pulling boxes out of the attic so she could put all our childhood mementoes in order."

"According to Chris, scrapbooking has gained speed over the last five years, from die-cut adornments, to special papers, to making pop-up cards."

"Chris talks about this kind of thing?"

"After a few beers at the poker game. We ran out of sports scores."

This time Caprice laughed and let her gaze travel around the workshop. Her focus fell on a rocking horse that a three- or four-year-old might like to ride. It sported a string mane and a long string tail. The horse itself reminded her of a palomino, but the saddle was painted red. She went over to it and ran her hand over the workmanship. It was as smooth as silk and absolutely beautiful.

She saw a sled with the name *Jimmy* painted on it. "I guess Chris customizes some of his pieces."

"He does. He takes orders all year."

"I can't believe Thanksgiving is coming up on Thursday."

"Nana already started her preparations, and your mom bought her every grocery she'd probably need."

"How many are coming?"

"Too many to count," her dad said wryly. "Besides all of us, your mom asked Mack and his wife, and from what I hear, Nikki will be bringing Brett. Roz and Vince are coming as well as Dom and Dulcina. Do you think they're serious?"

Caprice's Uncle Dom had fallen on hard times and lived with her parents for a while. But now he'd opened his own pet sitting business and had started dating her neighbor Dulcina Mendez.

"They have kittens in common," Caprice said with a smile. Dulcina had taken in a stray cat Caprice and her uncle had captured, and that cat had been pregnant. Halo had had her kittens, and Dulcina had kept the firstborn, a dark tortoiseshell named Miss Paddington. Dom had taken the other two kittens, Tia and Mason, and they lived with him at his apartment.

"I guess animals can create common bonds. Look at you and Grant."

Yes, look at her and Grant. She'd taken in a pregnant cocker spaniel and kept one of the pups. Grant had taken another one and named him Patches.

"I haven't had a chance to talk to Roz for a while," Caprice said.

Her father frowned. "I think Vince is getting perturbed because Roz hasn't agreed to live with him."

"She has to be sure it's the right decision."

"You don't think it's just a matter of space, that both their places are too small?"

"That could be. Vince has been looking at houses, but I don't think they've found the right one."

"Are you still serving dinner on Thanksgiving Day at Everybody's Kitchen with Nikki, Bella, and Joe?" her dad asked.

"We hope to. I guess Megan, Timmy, and Ben will be staying with you?"

"We'll juggle the kids during all the prep. I'm sure it will be another Thanksgiving we can never forget."

Whenever the De Lucas got together, there were always unforgettable moments.

"If you have everything under control here, I have to scoot. I have a few video consultations this morning and orders to put in. Juan's coming over to discuss contracts for a new house staging." Juan Hidalgo was her assistant and she depended on him.

"I have everything under control here, I suppose."

The way her dad said it, Caprice wondered if he meant it. "What's wrong?"

"Chris still seemed out of sorts this morning. That cut on his forehead looked pretty sore, and his jaw didn't look any better. But he still insisted he'd just had a box fall on him at the store. He still wouldn't look at me when he said it, though, and that's not like him. I might ask Mack to tactfully have a conversation with him—not about his injuries, per se, but just to see if anything else is going on in his life. He's not his usual jolly self this time of year. There's got to be a reason for that."

Could her dad's friend use his detective skills to ferret out the truth?

That all depended on how much Chris Merriweather was willing to reveal.

* * *

Thanksgiving Day dawned crisp and full of sunshine. Caprice had baked a few loaves of bread the evening before. That morning she'd whipped up the filling for Nana's cannoli shells after she'd fed her pets and taken Lady out for a run. Now all she had to do was drop off Lady and the food at her parents' house and get herself to the soup kitchen in time to help finish cooking dinner and serve.

When she reached her parents' house, she found out Bella had already dropped off her sweet potato casserole, and Nikki had created antipasto platters. Her dad and Nana would be helping her mom with the turkey so all would be ready whenever everyone arrived in the evening.

Fifteen minutes later, Caprice parked her Camaro in the lot of Everybody's Kitchen and recognized Bella's red van and Nikki's cobalt blue sedan. They'd beaten her there. She'd dressed in a retro look today with a modern twist, wearing a houndstooth mini-dress with red trim over black leggings. Her red Mary Janes would make standing at the soup kitchen for a few hours comfortable yet add a bit of pizzazz. She'd topped her dress with a vintage baby-doll trench coat in gray, embossed with a black flower motif. It all worked together, and even Bella, who didn't appreciate Caprice's vintage style, shouldn't have anything disagreeable to say about it. After all, fashion history was fashion forward now. She'd been dressing in retro for years, but now it was suddenly *the* style.

As she walked through the dining area of

Everybody's Kitchen, she noticed the volunteers had spread the tables with white paper cloths in honor of the holiday. There was even a bright, autumnal flower arrangement on a table near the coatrack: spider mums along with yellow and cranberry daisy-looking mums filled the green ceramic vase. There would be an abundance of food here today from the donations. The food pantry side of Everybody's Kitchen had been delivering baskets all week, and Caprice hoped no one in Kismet would go hungry today . . . or on Christmas. For that holiday, angel gifts for children would be included in the baskets.

Joe gave Caprice a hug when he saw her. "Just in time to pull the turkeys out of the oven." He looked her over. "You'd better get rid of the coat and put an apron on, though."

"Will do."

Nikki and Bella were pouring cooked potatoes into a huge bowl for mashing with the electric beater. They stopped to give her a hug too, and she said hello to the other volunteers.

"What can I do?" she asked.

"Ask Mario," Nikki said, waving to Mario Ruiz who was cutting sheet cakes into squares.

"Hi, Caprice," he said with a smile.

She had come to know Mario in the summer when he'd made her suspect list for one of the murder investigations she'd become involved in. But he'd had nothing to do with it, even though he'd had motive. Now he was the managing director of Everybody's Kitchen. It was a paid position, and he seemed to enjoy doing it. A chef, he tried to make the meals more than edible. A good manager, he made sure the pantry ran smoothly.

He'd obviously heard what Caprice had asked. He motioned to Joe and another man who was helping him remove a huge turkey from the oven. "They're going to start carving. Can you put the fruit salad together? Begin with that gallon can of peaches and then add the fruit that's cut up in the refrigerator. Can you believe someone actually donated pineapple and melons? We're going to serve a good dinner here today, Caprice."

"You try to do that every day."

He gave her a wry grin. "I'm glad somebody notices."

"Everybody who eats here notices, Mario. You're doing a good thing."

Because of Mario's managerial skills, all of the volunteers seemed to know exactly what they had to do and were efficient about doing it. Most of them had been coming here for a long while. Her Nana volunteered one day a month, and so did her mom when she was off school for the summer. There was a schedule and everyone adhered to it. This was an important part of community service.

By the time Caprice finished stirring together the fruit salad and dumping it into a huge serving tray in the cafeteria-style lineup, she was surprised when a familiar voice at her shoulder asked, "Can I talk to you for a minute?"

She spun around to find her brother. "Vince! What are you doing here?"

"I thought you might need an extra hand or two for cleanup. But I need to ask you something first, before they open the door to the public. Can we talk?"

There was a seriousness to Vince's voice as well as in his dark brown eyes, so she said, "Sure." She motioned him to the back door. "Let's just step outside."

The kitchen was noisy and it would be hard to hear each other over the chatter and clanking.

Vince followed her lead, and they opened the back door and stepped outside. They were on a landing dock that ran from the kitchen over to the pantry side. Trucks unloaded donations there, but now the back lot was empty.

Caprice wrapped her arms around herself against the outside chill. "Is something wrong?"

Vince was wearing a sweater but no coat. His dark brown hair blew in the breeze. He looked at her in her long-sleeved dress and asked, "Are you going to be too cold?"

"I'll be fine for a few minutes. What's up?"

"I didn't want to discuss this at Mom's later because I didn't want Roz to overhear."

Caprice waited for her brother to go on.

"Will you go with me to look at a house tomorrow?"

Caprice studied her brother. "Why aren't you taking Roz?" Her straight dark hair blew against her cheek in the breeze.

"For several reasons. First off, I want your objective opinion. I think I want to buy this one. I went back to it twice, and I think it fits the bill. It's in your neighborhood. It's a split-level, stone on the bottom, blue siding on top."

"I know the one you mean. It's been for sale about six months."

"They just lowered the price. It has plenty of charm, from a stone fireplace to a family room to a renovated kitchen with quartz countertops."

"Then why aren't you taking Roz to see it?" she asked again.

"Because I want to buy it myself. I don't want Roz to put any money into it in case our relationship doesn't work out."

Caprice's brother was a lawyer, and he often thought in practical terms. She knew exactly what he was thinking. If he and Roz comingled their funds to buy the house and then their relationship didn't work, it would be a mess. On the other hand, though, not as much of a commitment was involved with his way of doing it. He'd been thinking about buying a house for a while and just hadn't made the move.

"You know I can't give you much input on structural soundness, just on design."

"I want your woman's opinion. I'll have one of Dad's contractor friends inspect it if I decide to put in an offer. I'm mostly worried that it's not bigger."

"Doesn't it have four bedrooms and a room that can be used as an office on the middle level?" She often went over real estate stats and had seen photos and video taken of the house on the sale site.

"It does. But Roz is rich. Would she want to live there? That's why I need your opinion. Also about how much work it might take to transform it into her taste."

"You're buying it but you want her taste."

"Of course, I do. I'm going to ask her to move in with me. We've been discussing it since summer, and I think she's close to a decision."

"As far as Roz being rich, yes, she is, and she likes nice things. But . . . she's living in a two-bedroom townhouse now and, if I remember correctly, that house has a nice-sized backyard that Dylan can run and play in." Roz's dog, Dylan, a fluff ball who was part Pomeranian and part Shih Tzu, would love a yard of his own.

Vince frowned. "It's a good thing Dylan's a small dog or we'd need a bigger yard."

Caprice put her hand on her brother's arm. "Do you like the house?"

"I do."

"Then calm down. Roz doesn't require a mansion to be happy. You know that what she needs has nothing to do with space or the color of the walls. You have to talk to her about this and use those lawyerly communication skills you're so proud of."

"I will. I just want your opinion first. Can you look at it with me tomorrow morning?"

"I can. Around ten?"

"Ten it is. I guess we'd better get back inside. They might start without you."

But before she opened the door to go inside, she asked him, "We have much to be thankful for, don't we?"

"We do," Vince agreed. "Roz is the best thing that's happened to me in my adult life."

"And Grant's the best thing that's happened to me." She raised her hand for a high five, and Vince matched the gesture vigorously.

Then they went into Everybody's Kitchen to start serving.

Chapter Three

When Caprice opened the door from the side
porch into her childhood home Thanksgiving
evening, she felt such a sense of welcome and roots.
That's what she wanted for her own family some-
day. This home held so many memories that they
bubbled up every time she walked into it. Tonight,
with Grant's arm around her, his other hand holding a leash with Patches, she felt true happiness.
She savored the moment. That elusive feeling wasn't
something you could capture just any time you
wanted it.

When they heard voices pour out from inside,
Grant looked down at her and she looked up at
him. "Just another De Luca gathering," he said
nonchalantly.

Grant had become accustomed to those. He'd
been her brother's roommate at law school and
often came home with Vince on weekends. Once a
month the De Luca family gathered from wherever
they'd scattered for a family dinner. Everyone
brought something.

Her parents always accepted Grant. He'd been out of their lives for a while after he and Vince had graduated . . . after Grant moved to Pittsburgh, met Naomi, married her, and made a life there. But tragedy had befallen him. He'd lost a child and his marriage. When he'd somewhat recovered, he moved to Kismet and became Vince's law partner. But it was really only in the last few months that he'd begun healing from the ghostly shadows of his past.

Last month, when he'd asked Caprice to marry him, she'd joyfully said yes. But since they were both Catholic, since her faith and her family's faith meant a lot to her, and his was beginning to mean more to him again too, they'd decided to go through the annulment proceedings for his first marriage. It wasn't that his marriage had never happened. Of course, it had. But they were hoping the church would agree that the sacramental part of the marriage hadn't been present. Naomi wasn't Catholic, and they'd been married by a justice of the peace. She'd been pregnant when they'd married. After the drowning death of their daughter, Naomi had an affair. All appropriate grounds for annulment, as Caprice's parish priest told them. Caprice hoped Father Gregory was right.

But if the annulment didn't come through?

They hadn't asked each other that question, but they knew in their hearts they loved each other. They knew what they wanted their lives to be. They shared the same values, and they *would* be together.

Entering the De Luca house, Grant released Patches from his leash and the cocker joined Lady, who was sitting in the living room to the left of the side entrance. Where Lady was a golden buff color, Grant's dog was cream-colored with brown ears, brown circles around his eyes and nose, as well as brown patches on his back and flank. His fur was curlier too.

Megan and Timmy, Bella's oldest children, immediately crouched down with the dogs, petting and talking to them. Joe was holding Benny, who was getting bigger day by day. At ten months, he was crawling as fast as Lady could run, and soon he'd be walking.

Caprice noticed Grant's gaze go to Benny and Joe, and she suspected the bittersweet feeling that was probably running through him. He desperately missed the child he'd lost. But he was looking forward to the future. So was she.

Her mother came to embrace her.

"Happy Thanksgiving, honey." Francesca De Luca gave Grant a hug too. Hugging as a family was an integral part of the De Luca legacy. Her mother said to Caprice, "I have to supervise in the kitchen. Nana's filling the cannoli with your cream. Come on in as soon as Dad takes your coats."

In the next second her dad was there, giving her a hug and kiss on the cheek and shaking Grant's hand. Then he took their coats and hung them in the foyer closet. Roz and Vince were settled in the living room talking with Dulcina and Uncle Dom as were Mack and his wife. They all waved and called hellos.

"Where's Nikki?" Caprice asked.

"Brett got held up at the station with some kind

of report, but she's with him and she texted," Bella informed them as she came into the foyer and gave them both a hug. "They should be here in about five minutes." She took Caprice's hand. "Come on. While we put everything on the table, I can tell you about my latest projects, and you can tell me about that historical house you're decorating. I hear it's fabulous."

When she was with Bella at the community center, Bella only had the pageant on her mind, and they had talked about little else.

Grant took her hand and gave it a squeeze. "I guess I'll see you at the dinner table."

When she looked at Grant with his black, wavy hair, his intense gray eyes, and his broad shoulders, she knew her attraction to him was much more than skin deep. It was soul deep. "At dinner," she said.

They hadn't had a chance to talk, either. They'd both pulled up outside at the same time. They'd kissed and hugged and then come up the walk together without saying anything. Words just hadn't seemed necessary. Sure, they did have a lot to discuss with plans for Christmas and plans for their wedding. But they'd get to it.

In the kitchen, Caprice hugged her Nana. "I hope you're not overdoing."

Nana gave Caprice a disgruntled look. "What overdoing? It's Thanksgiving. Of course, I'm going to overdo, and I'm going to overeat, and then I'll have to take medicine the doctors gave me. But I'm going to have a good time doing it."

And so it went, until Nikki and Brett arrived and they were all seated around the huge mahogany table in the dining room with the cuckoo clock striking six. Little Benny batted his fists against his high-chair tray. Bella was explaining to Megan and Timmy that the candlesticks holding the green tapers on the table were the same ones they'd used for Thanksgiving since she was a small girl.

Her father clinked his knife against his water goblet and stood. "We want to welcome all of you. We are grateful for so many things: that Nana celebrated her seventy-sixth birthday this month; that Caprice and Grant have announced their engagement; that Dom is already making a success of his pet-sitting business; that Nikki's business has picked up once more and she's busier than she's ever been. I know you all have blessings to be grateful for. So now let's bow our heads for just a few minutes and think of all those things."

They all did and even Benny was quiet, studying the adults and then his brother and sister, as if sensing something special was happening.

Finally, Nick De Luca said, "Let us all join hands." He then said the grace that Caprice had learned and recited since before she was in kindergarten.

Brett Carstead, Nikki's date and a detective on the Kismet police force, was seated next to Caprice. As she passed a bowl of stuffing to him, she asked, "Are things quiet down at the police department?"

"As quiet as they get for Kismet. I had a late call last night. A man tried to rob a convenience store, but he didn't try to take money. He was attempting to take food for his family."

"What happened?"

"Once in a while, when we think it's for the greater good, we bend the rules a little. No harm was done. It was shoplifting at its best, so to speak. The store manager took pity on the guy and gave him day-old bread and a canned ham. We took him down to the station though and tried to figure out his situation, not that I'm a social worker or anything. But we told him about the food pantry at Everybody's Kitchen. He had the convoluted idea that accepting help from them would hurt his pride more than stealing if he could get away with it. I talked to him for a while, and I think I finally made him see that for his family's sake—he has two kids—he needs to do more than shoplift."

"No job?"

"Not right now. He said he's willing to take anything, so I gave him the number of a temporary job counselor. I sure hope he uses it."

Although Brett Carstead was straight-laced and usually a by-the-book kind of guy, she could certainly see what Nikki saw in him. He was a good man. His work could be an impediment in their relationship, but that was for them to work out if they could. For now, Caprice was just glad he was here with Nikki.

Conversation ran around the table and leapt across it. The holidays were in the air, and there were side conversations from preparation of gifts to attending the parade on Sunday to figuring out a good time for Christmas dinner when Dom would be free from pet sitting. He was booked solid already and was hoping to make room for an hour for dinner with the family.

Right there at the table, he asked, "Dulcina, will you come back again with me for that holiday?"

Caprice's neighbor smiled at him shyly, ducked her head, and nodded. Caprice heard her say in a low voice, "You know I'd be glad to."

Dulcina, Roz, and Nikki said they'd ready the desserts and bring them in since everyone else had gotten the rest of the meal ready.

Grant leaned close to Caprice. "You know holidays like this are unusual for me. Whenever I had dinner with my parents and my brother, an argument always seemed to break out. Sometimes Holden and Dad would go at it. They could never just agree to disagree."

"And where did you step in?"

"I guess I tried to be the mediator. With Holden, I argued. But with Dad, I always just tried to make peace."

As Brett stood to help Nikki carry cups and saucers from the sideboard to the table, Grant took Caprice's hand under the table and settled it on his knee. His voice low, he said, "I got a phone call this morning from my parents. We wished each other happy Thanksgiving, of course, but they made a request. They'd like us to come to Vermont for a visit after the holidays. How do you feel about that? Can you take a few days off?"

"Can you?"

"I can manage it. I'd like you to see where I grew up. I can even teach you cross-country skiing. I'm not sure how successful my parents' visit was when they were here last month, but they'd like to see you again."

"I have to get to know your parents, Grant. Once I do, maybe we can get a little closer."

"My mom wants us to stay at the farmhouse. There really aren't many hotels in the area. In January, it's going to be drafty, but there *is* a fireplace and a woodstove."

"I'm not a hothouse flower," she teased. "And I do have good winter clothes. Do you think we can take the dogs?"

"I'll talk to them about that. There's plenty of room for them to roam, and they're fairly well behaved. I don't think Mom and Dad would object."

"Will your brother be there?"

"He's a medical systems rep, so he's often on the road. But it's possible he could be there."

"Will you be all right with that?"

"Why wouldn't I?" Grant asked, a bit defensively.

"Because sometimes I get the feeling you and your brother don't always get along . . . that maybe there's something between the two of you."

"Old stuff," Grant grumbled. "Old stuff that he doesn't want to let go of and always seems to come up. I keep hoping he'll grow out of it. Or grow up."

Caprice was wondering how she could help Grant when her cell phone in her pocket played "All I've Got to Do."

Grant glanced around the table where everyone seemed occupied with something. Mack was speaking with her dad and his wife had gone to the kitchen with Nana. Joe had taken Benny from his high chair, and Benny was crawling after Lady. Megan and Timmy had wandered into the kitchen just because they were tired of sitting. Caprice's mom was at the sideboard, sprinkling powdered sugar through a small strainer onto the cannoli.

"You probably have a few minutes," Grant suggested, "if you want to see who it is."

When Caprice pulled her phone from her pocket and checked the screen, she was surprised to see Sara's number. "It's Sara," she murmured. "I think I should take this." She swiped her screen and put her phone to her ear. "Sara? Is anything wrong?"

"Denise called. She thinks she has two couples interested in our home already, that the sale could happen fast. They're coming to the open house."

"And you don't think that's good news?"

"I don't know what I think. I'm still not sure we should sell. Even more sure now."

"Why is that?"

Sara hesitated, then she went on. "When I saw Chris this morning before he got out of bed, I realized he has bruises on his ribs and back. He'd come into bed after me the past few nights, so I didn't realize it before. When I questioned him, he just said it's nothing for me to worry about. Well, of course it *is*. I'm trying to convince him to go to the doctor, but he says he doesn't have time and he'll heal. After the parade, he wants to go looking at the condo units again and write a check for a down payment to hold one so we're ready to move when the house sells. I don't want to think about doing that over the holidays. But he's so insistent, Caprice."

"What would you like me to do?"

"I don't know. I just know I'm confused and not sure we're making the right decisions. Should I go through with the open house?"

Caprice had to consider her client's concerns. But Sara was only one-half of her client. Chris was the other half. She had both of their wishes to take into consideration, as well as the time and money involved. And Denise Langford had also put time and effort into getting the house ready to sell.

"Do you think selling the house is a possibility?"

Sara went silent, then finally she answered. "I agree with many of the points Chris has made. It's a lot for us to handle, and maintenance and gardening isn't getting easier. So yes, it's a possibility."

"I hate to see you stop this from happening now, causing more discord for you and Chris when it's something you might want to do. My advice is go through with the open house and see how it feels to look reality in the face. Imagine moving out and having someone else move in. Get a feel for the people who come to look at your home. Have Denise introduce you to the couples who are really interested. The point is, if a contract comes in and you still have doubts, or you've decided altogether not to sell, you do *not* have to accept it. You can pull out at any time. But I think you ought to give it a chance to work, and maybe Chris is right about looking at those condos. If you can see the life he wants to build with you, you might look at the whole process differently."

She heard Sara sigh. "I knew you could be reasonable about this and talk me down. And I know you're right. Everything's just been piling up and making us all ready to jump out of our skin."

"Do you want Dad to talk to Chris about going to the doctor?"

"I don't want to upset him any more than he is now, especially with the parade on Sunday. He looks forward to that so. After Sunday, after the parade and looking at the condos, I'll see how he is. Maybe we'll have another talk about him getting a checkup."

"That sounds like a good plan."

"Thank you, Caprice. I'm so sorry to interrupt your Thanksgiving."

"How was *your* Thanksgiving?"

"Despite the tension between Chris and me, I think our kids all had a good dinner. With Ryan and his wife Serena, Deanne, Maura and her husband, we had a quiet dinner but a nice one. They all left about two hours ago. Chris is out back in his workshop. I was just stewing about everything I can't fix."

"A mother and a wife's prerogative," Caprice agreed.

Sara actually laughed. "Put that way, it sounds absolutely silly. Thanks again, Caprice. Will you stop in tomorrow?"

"What time will you be there?"

"I'll be at the store in the morning, but I can be here in the afternoon."

"Then what if I stop over around two o'clock? Will that suit?"

"It sounds perfect. I'll see you then. Happy Thanksgiving."

After Caprice ended the call, Grant looked troubled. "A client who doesn't want to sell? Isn't it a little late for that?"

"It's never too late. Terms have been written into

the contracts that don't make them binding until everyone signs."

"I know there are always loopholes."

"I'm just hoping we don't need loopholes," Caprice responded.

Everyone was coming back to the table again. Grant pointed to the tray of cannoli and the pumpkin and apple pies. "I say we think about dessert now and worry later."

That was a philosophy she could live with . . . for today.

After another discussion with Chris, Sara decided to go through with the open house on Saturday. She'd taken everything into consideration and decided it was for the best. Besides, as she told Caprice, they might not even get an offer on the house.

Sara hadn't mentioned Chris's medical condition again, and Caprice wondered where his bruises had come from. It sounded as if someone had beaten him up, but he wasn't talking and apparently Sara wasn't pushing.

The open house started as any other. The servers had dressed in red satin blouses and black slacks. Nikki and Caprice had both decided not to go for a period theme even though it was a historic house. They believed a modern Christmas in a house full of charm and warmth was a better way to portray the house for a Christmas Delight theme.

As always, Nikki outdid herself with the food. After Caprice made sure the guest list prepared by real estate agents was in order, Nikki readied her dishes and warming trays and slow cookers. There was roast goose, glazed ham, and herb-encrusted prime rib. The Cornish hens with raspberry sauce called to Caprice as well as the spinach-mushroom lasagna. Side dishes ranged from roasted apples with carrots and parsnips to baked cheese and vegetable pastries, sautéed broccolini, and zucchini au gratin. The dessert bar carried everything from a peanut-butter and chocolate trifle to a peppermint-laced three-layer cake with fluffy white icing to an assortment of cookies—sand tarts, snowballs, and macaroons included.

As Caprice pulled a prosciutto, feta, and arugula wrap from the hors d'oeuvres tray and tasted it, Nikki shook her finger at her. "You can sample. Just don't mess up my star arrangement."

Nikki had arranged the hors d'oeuvres to form a star. Caprice rearranged the wraps so the star was in perfect shape again. "What did Brett think about Thanksgiving with the De Lucas?" She hadn't had a chance to talk to Nikki since the gathering.

"I think he was a little overwhelmed, but not in a bad way. He said he'd never seen so much food. Then again, I don't think he's really visited one of our open houses."

"You could have asked him to drop in."

"I could have. But it seems a little too soon for that. We're not immersed in each other's lives yet. I'm still not sure if I like the fact I'm dating a detective. Almost every time we have a date, he gets called in."

"As bad as dating a doctor," Caprice said. She'd

dated a doctor and had even thought he might be
Mr. Right. But then she and Grant had connected
again. For a while her world had been confusing
until she'd listened to her heart.

"Have you seen Sara?"

"She breezed through here a little while ago. I
think she said she was going into Chris's workshop.
Something about putting together more toys to box
up to take to Santa's cabin."

"I'll check on her," Caprice said. "If I'm not back
until Denise arrives, just tell her where I am."

"Will do," Nikki said as she spooned more raspberry sauce over the Cornish hens.

Caprice wound past Nikki's assistants working
in the kitchen and exited through the back door.
She took the brick path to the workshop. She'd
worn a midi-length skirt today, in cranberry. Her
cream blouse was reminiscent of the seventies,
with balloon sleeves and a bow at the neck. She'd
worn her hair in an upsweep, fastened with a gold
barrette. Her knee-high black boots rounded out
the outfit. She hadn't bothered to grab her coat
so she wrapped her arms around herself as she
walked.

The carriage door was partially open and Caprice
hurriedly slipped inside eager to get out of the
wind. But as soon as she did, she heard raised voices.

"I have to see him, and I need to see him *now*."

A tall, lean man towered over Sara. He looked
angry or maybe just upset. It was hard to tell.

To leave or to barge in?

Caprice wasn't known for backing away from

confrontation. She felt for her cell phone in her pocket. She liked clothes with pockets so she could always carry it. It had been her lifeline more than once.

She banged the carriage door closed so that both the man and Sara knew she was there. "Sara," she said with a bright smile approaching the two of them, "Nikki has the food ready and wanted you to taste it. Are you available to do that now? Denise will be arriving soon."

Okay, so a little white lie couldn't hurt. Sara had already tasted Nikki's samples of the food she was going to serve and had approved it.

Caprice got a better look at the man with Sara now. He looked to be about Chris's age. Whether he'd started to go bald or whether it was just the style, his head was shaved. It looked good on him. He wasn't dressed for the open house. He wore jeans and a red flannel runner's jacket. When he turned to look at Caprice, his green eyes were sharp and she could tell he wanted her to go away. She'd definitely interrupted something.

Next to the man, Sara looked like a princess in a red wool, calf-length dress with long sleeves and an A-line skirt. She wore pearls at her neck, and she could have passed for a present-day Mrs. Claus. To Caprice's eyes she seemed a little pale, but maybe that was because this man had cornered her.

Sara forced a plastic smile and moved toward Caprice and away from the man. "Caprice! Yes, of course. I can taste Nikki's food. And I'm sure Denise is going to want to talk to me. I can't wait to hear about the offers she might have for us."

Caprice's eyes widened a bit. So, Sara wanted to leave the carriage house too. But Caprice wanted to know who the man was. "I don't think we've met," she said to him, noticing a tattoo peeking out from the wrist of his jacket.

Now the man looked uncertain, as if he didn't know what to do. Still, he came forward and extended his hand.

"I'm Ray Gangloff, a friend of Chris's."

Sara explained, "They served in Vietnam together. Ray was interested in . . . interested in . . ." Sara grabbed for something, then she swung her hand around the workshop. "He's interested in the toys Chris makes. He might want to learn how to do some of it himself."

"That could be a rewarding pastime," Caprice agreed.

Ray seemed to find his composure. He focused on Sara again. "Please tell Chris to get back to me." Then the veteran said, "I won't keep you ladies. I know you have a party in the house."

He made the idea of a party sound like a crime.

After he'd left the workshop, Caprice went to the door and stared out. He'd moved quietly and fast and was no longer in sight. She turned back to Sara. "Is everything okay?"

"I don't know. I know Ray has PTSD that can cause him to be brusque, but today he was more than that. He was almost belligerent. He demanded to see Chris. I told him Chris was at the store, but he said he'd stopped there and he wasn't."

"Maybe he just stepped out for a few minutes. Maybe he went to the cabin to get it ready."

"But you and he had already gotten it ready yesterday."

Yes, she'd helped Chris make the cabin as cheery as it could be. They'd hung gingerbread men and she'd decorated a small tree. They'd made sure Candy Cane Lane with its sleigh and stacked pretend presents, its candy-cane lights and wooden candy canes lining the pathway to the little building, would draw children and adults alike.

"Have you tried to reach Chris on his cell?" Caprice asked.

"No, but I will now."

"You do that while I go greet Denise and any guests that might arrive early. Let me know if you find him."

"I will," Sara assured her. She touched Caprice's arm. "And Caprice, thank you. Thank you for walking in when you did. I've never been afraid of Ray, but something about him today just sent chills up my spine."

Caprice understood that feeling because she'd felt it herself. She just hoped whatever was happening with the Merriweathers could be resolved quickly and soon. Maybe selling their house would help do that. Maybe Chris talking to his wife would help do that.

It seemed to her he was hiding something . . . maybe more than *one* something.

Chapter Four

The Christmas parade was a big event in Kismet. In fact, some of the residents who lived downtown put out lawn chairs the night before to make sure they'd have a place to view it. The police department was used to the tradition and, for the most part, didn't mind. Keeping peace and having a few extra patrol officers on duty made sure there were no disputes if a neighbor tried to move a chair.

Today Grant had brought his SUV with crates for both Patches and Lady in the back, the safest way for them to travel. Since Vince lived downtown in a condo in an old school building that had been renovated, they were able to park in his guest spot and didn't have to worry about walking a few blocks or securing public parking. As they walked their dogs from the parking garage in back alongside of Vince's building to the main street, White Rose Way, Grant checked his watch.

"We have a little time before the parade begins," he noted.

"Let me text Dad and see where he is. Mom will

be on the high school's float, and I know he'll want to watch her pass by."

After she texted her dad, she received a quick response. "He said he's standing in front of Cherry on the Top, and he has Blitz with him. He's watching the dog for Chris until he finishes with the parade and goes back to the cabin."

"I bet the kids get a kick out of seeing a friendly, white Malamute as much as they do telling Santa what's on their list."

"I'm sure a few of them have dogs on their list. Blitz was a real find when Chris rescued him."

"I haven't heard the story," Grant said.

Caprice grew serious. "Someone chained him to a tree on the outskirts of town and left him there one December. Chris had gone out jogging and found him. He put an ad in the paper and phoned the area veterinarians, thinking a beautiful dog like that couldn't have been left behind. But no one claimed him, and Blitz claimed Chris. They've been inseparable ever since. That dog does seem magical in some ways. Everyone who comes in contact with him falls under his spell. He's so friendly. I think everybody in town knows him because they see him at Chris's store."

They made their way through the lineup of people along the sidewalk to Cherry on Top, Kismet's favorite ice-cream store. And there was her dad with Blitz. Lady and Patches trotted right up to Blitz. They all nosed each other. They'd been in contact before and were friends.

Caprice let Blitz smell her hand, then she ruffled

the fur on the side of his face and behind his ears. He leaned into her palm as if he were in bliss.

When she straightened, he sat at attention by her dad's side, looking toward the street.

"I think he knows he's going to see Chris in his sleigh," she joked.

"His concentration is better than mine," her dad said wryly. "Are you two going to be good standing through the whole parade? I can find us a couple of chairs."

"How about you?" Caprice asked. "Your knee was giving you trouble last week."

Her father brushed her concern away. "It's fine. I can't see a thing when I sit, and I want to make sure your mom sees me."

"I'm sorry Nana didn't come, but I know how the cold affects her bones. We could be in for some snow early this year," Caprice said.

"It's predicted for next week," Grant responded.

Patches and Lady sat smack up against each other, both looking all around at the people and at the street.

"I hear music," Caprice said with a smile, turning to look in the direction from where it was coming. "Who's the grand marshal this year?"

"The mayor dubbed Ray Butterworth from the Koffee Klatch to be grand marshal. He said Ray knows everything that goes on in this town, upside down and frontwards and backwards. So he could lead the parade. I think he's going to be driving a Buick convertible that his father restored."

The music was coming from the high-school band that was participating too. There would be

Girl Scout and Boy Scout troops, 4-H club, and anyone else who wanted to put a float together or walk in formation.

As the music grew louder, they caught sight of the Buick convertible slowly making its way down the street.

Suddenly a voice behind Caprice said, "I enjoyed this more when I was a kid. Being a grownup takes some of the fun out of it."

Caprice turned to see Vince and teased, "You'll *never* grow up."

"I made an offer on the house yesterday. It's serious grownup time."

She leaned closer to her brother. "You talked to Roz about it?"

"I did. She doesn't entirely like the idea that I want to buy it on my terms, but she's going to move in with me. We're going to do this, Caprice."

She gave her brother a huge hug. "You know I want this to work out for you. You took her to see the house?"

"Yesterday. She says it has plenty of room. I hope she's not just trying to placate me."

"Why would she do that? She tells you what she thinks."

"I suppose. I guess we're both a little nervous about moving in together."

"She has the shop open today, doesn't she?" Caprice asked.

All About You was a premier dress shop in Kismet. Roz's philosophy was that she wanted to fit any woman from petite to plus size. She carried the latest styles and classic ones too. She'd rented a two-story row house on Bristol Row, dubbed Restoration Row, an older section of town that had been refurbished. Bella worked at All About You part-time and, according to her, the shop was doing wonderfully.

Vince nodded. "She wanted to take advantage of this foot traffic today. Holiday hours are starting for all the stores." He leaned close to Caprice. "We could get an ice-cream sundae and skip the parade."

"And miss Mom waving to us from her float?"

"What was I thinking?" Vince muttered.

"You were thinking that you've been at this parade most years since you were about three. But that's the whole point. It's a tradition."

"Did you ever think the De Luca family has an awful lot of traditions?"

"That's what makes a family work, son," Nick De Luca said, apparently overhearing. "You'll remember that when you start one of your own."

Caprice could guess exactly what her brother was thinking. Moving in with Roz was one thing, having kids was quite another. However, to Caprice, contemplating the idea of having a baby was something she wanted to consider in her near future. She and Grant hadn't talked about that yet. They hadn't talked about several things they should. But they agreed on everything that was important, she hoped.

Grant pointed to the teenagers in elf costumes who were running down the street just behind the Buick. They held baskets of candy canes and were giving them out to children along the way.

Grant's arm went around her waist. "Our first Christmas parade together."

"You know, I really should start a journal or a log or something."

"Like a diary?" he asked.

"I've kept diaries on and off over the years. I'll find a special book to start writing in. I'd rather write it by hand than on the computer."

After the high-school band played a rousing rendition of "Jingle Bells," Caprice had to laugh at the float that came behind them.

"Look at the Perky Paws float. Dom and Dulcina are on it. They didn't tell me they were going to be in the parade."

Her father explained, "Perky Paws is carrying Dom's business cards for the pet-sitting service, so they asked him if he'd join them on the float. He pulled Dulcina into it."

Someone had gone to a lot of trouble to make life-sized papier-mâché dogs and cats that sat on the flat bed wagon. Greta Hansen, who owned Perky Paws, stood at a case that held her specialized cookies for dogs. They looked good enough for a human to eat. Dom and Dulcina held baskets with dog and cat treats. There was a beautiful cat and dog mural painted on the side of the float, and Caprice spotted the young man who she suspected was the artist: Danny Flannery. Danny was a teenager she'd helped during one of her murder investigations. He had painted beautiful murals at Ace Richland's home. After Caprice had staged a local house on an estate and Ace Richland had purchased it, they'd become good friends. Caprice had suggested Danny's work to the rock star. Ace had funded Danny's schooling.

Apparently, Danny had come home for the Thanksgiving weekend. He was running around the truck with a basket holding dog and cat treats and giving them out to anyone who held out their hand. He was a good kid who was going to have a great start because Ace was helping him.

When Danny saw Caprice, he waved and ran up to her.

"How's school?" she asked him.

"I love it. I'll show you some of my paintings over the holidays."

"Sounds good to me," she said.

A horseback-riding group came through on six beautiful chestnut horses, all decorated for Christmas. Their tails were braided with red and green ribbon, as were their manes. The riders wore red riding jackets and black jodhpur pants.

Businesses who wanted the publicity built floats too, including Denise Langford's real estate office. When the high school's float came by, there was a huge sign on it advertising Career Night the following week. Each of the teachers held a sign with a possible career choice. Her mother held the sign that said *Interpreter*. Kids who were headed off to college needed to know all of the possibilities they could choose from.

"Your mom looks forward to this every year," Caprice's dad told her.

"Tradition," she said with a look at Vince who just rolled his eyes.

Grant asked, "Do you want to walk to the end of the parade run? The dogs could use the exercise and probably so could we."

They all agreed that would be a great idea. The end of the parade run converged in the community park. There, Santa would move from his sleigh on the float to the cabin where he would begin to hear the kids' long lists of everything they wanted for Christmas. Caprice, Vince, their dad, and Grant could watch the rest of the parade from the park. It was a prime viewing point and usually crowded.

After they reached the park, they found a spot by a tall oak behind some children. They could see over their heads. The kids looked back and forth between the parade and the three dogs who were sitting there watching too.

About twenty minutes later, Caprice could hear the sound of sleigh bells and the music playing "Here Comes Santa Claus" as Chris's float came down the street. He was settled on a sleigh that an area farmer lent the town each year for the parade. After snowfalls, he actually took neighbors on rides across his fields. On the other hand, the huge sleigh near Santa's cabin was one that had been built for decorative use only.

"I'd like to talk to Chris if I get the chance," Caprice said. "Do you want to wait?"

Vince shook his head. "I have paperwork to put together for the house closing. Since it's vacant, I can close on it next week." He gave Caprice a hug, nodded to her dad and Grant, and he was off.

"Chris isn't going to be ready for Blitz until he's

settled in the cabin," her dad said. He addressed Grant, "Do you want to let the dogs run in the dog park?"

"Sounds like a good idea." Grant leaned over and gave Caprice a quick kiss. It might have been quick, but it did everything a kiss should. She was still smiling when the two men walked off with the dogs.

She approached the float with Chris's sleigh. He was in full beard and costume and looked just like Santa.

Seeing her, he waved. Then he lifted the leather strap with sleigh bells he'd been jingling and stood to disembark from the sleigh onto the flatbed float. However, once he was upright, he wobbled on his booted feet.

Caprice saw right away and started to climb the steps to the flat bed. Parents and kids had gathered all around.

Caprice hurried to Chris as the sleigh bells fell to the float's floor and he put his hand to his forehead. "Are you okay?"

"Fine," he mumbled, holding onto the side of the sleigh as he lifted his leg over the side to step down. But when he did, one leg seemed to buckle, and he grabbed onto the sleigh again.

One of the parents called, "Are you drunk?"

Chris's head seemed to clear, and he pulled himself together as he stood tall and straight, the proud veteran he was. He looked directly into the man's eyes. "I'm not drunk. If you want to make me take a Breathalyzer, go ahead." Then gentling his voice, he looked down at all the kids and asked, "Are you ready to tell Santa your wishes?"

"We are," they yelled.

"Then come on. Follow me to the cabin. No matter how long the line is, I'll hear every one of your lists."

Caprice touched Chris's arm. "Are you really okay?"

"I'm fine. Did you come to see if I was ready for Blitz?"

"Dad took him to the dog park."

"Do you want to go get him? The kids love to pet him."

She'd wanted to ask him about Ray Gangloff and what the man might want with him, but now obviously wasn't the time. "I'll tell Dad you need your best helper by your side."

Chris obviously wasn't going to talk to any humans about what was going on with him, but she knew if something happened, Blitz would get help someway . . . somehow. He wouldn't let anything happen to his master if he could help it.

She waited until Chris had gone down the float's steps to the ground. Kids milled all around him, their parents standing back a bit, watching. She'd be watching closely too if she thought Santa was drunk. But there hadn't been a scent of alcohol on Chris's breath. No mint cover-up either.

Just what was happening with Chris Merriweather?

That evening Grant and Caprice were seated on her sofa, their legs on the coffee table while Patches and Lady dozed beside them. Caprice's long-haired calico, Sophia, was stretched out on the sofa back above their heads. Mirabelle, a white Persian who had recently joined Caprice's family, was tucked in beside her, her paws stretched over Caprice's leg.

It was almost 10 p.m., and she and Grant were dipping their fingers into a bowl of popcorn as they watched a romantic comedy. Contrived it might be, but it was a feel-good movie, and that's what mattered this time of year, right?

Grant's shoulder was smack against hers, and she was thinking about leaning her head onto his shoulder when her landline rang. This time of night on a weekend? It could only be family.

Grant reached for the cordless phone on the end table next to the sofa. He checked the caller ID.

"It's your dad's cell." He handed it quickly to Caprice.

"Dad?" she asked as she took the call.

"I have terrible news."

"Nana?" Nana had had a health scare last year and they all still worried about her.

"No, not Nana. It's Chris Merriweather."

"He didn't look well today. Is he in the hospital?"

"This doesn't have anything to do with how he looked today, Caprice. He was found murdered on Santa Lane. Someone pulled one of the wooden candy cane stakes from the ground and whacked him with it. A patrol officer found him lying beside the sleigh near the cabin. Mack called to tell me."

Chris Merriweather, murdered near the sleigh on Santa Lane. Caprice turned to Grant, stricken, so glad he was there.

Chapter Five

Caprice's heart hurt as she witnessed the devastation on her father's face. She and Grant had driven over to her parents' house. They'd brought Patches and Lady simply because pets could give comfort. She'd known her dad was going to need all the comfort he could get.

As he sat on the sofa in the living room, Patches lay to one side of him on the floor while Lady rested on one of his feet. He was petting them both at intervals as if he really needed something to do. Her mom sat next to him on the sofa, and Nana had settled in the armchair. They were all in shock.

Her family had known Chris and Sara Merriweather for years. The news of Chris Merriweather's death had been a monumental blow.

"I just can't believe he was murdered," her father said. "Chris had a heart of gold."

"He did so much charity work," her mother added. "Most of the toys he made went to children who needed them. Sure, he sold them at craft fairs, but if he saw a needy child, he coaxed a smile from them with one of his toys." She covered her husband's hand with hers.

"What did Mack say again?" Nana asked.

Caprice's dad had told her that Mack Powalski had called him but he hadn't mentioned many details. She and Grant had just rushed over here knowing they needed to be with her parents.

"He didn't tell me much," her dad said. "He probably told me more than he should have. I'm sure he's not revealing to anyone else what the murder weapon was."

"We'll keep it to ourselves," Grant assured him. "I remember seeing those wooden candy canes all along the lane. The fact that someone used one of those probably means it was an impulsive, violent act, not a premeditated one."

"Unless they find out it wasn't one of the candy canes that was used," her father said. "After all, Mack was simply going on observation. But he's been at this a long time. The autopsy report will confirm or deny."

"Did Mack say anything else?" Caprice asked gently.

Her dad blinked a couple of times as if he were trying to remember. Then he reached down and patted Lady on the head and ruffled her ears. "He's off the case since he was friends with Chris, but Brett and Detective Jones are heading up the investigation."

"They'll figure out who did it. You know they will," Caprice said. "I don't like Detective Jones.

I think he rushes to judgment too quickly. But I know Brett is fair and only wants to find the truth."

"Brett is interviewing Mack in the morning. Mack guesses he's going to want to interview me too. Or Jones will."

"Why?" Caprice's mom asked. "You weren't on the scene."

"No," her dad agreed. "But they'll want to interview all of Chris's friends. Brett knows that Mack and I play poker with him. They'll try to figure out something from what he said recently."

"And what did he say recently?" Nana asked.

"Not much," her dad admitted. "The past couple of games he was quieter than usual, definitely didn't joke as much. He seemed to be distracted."

"Would you say he seemed tired?" Caprice asked her dad.

Her father studied her. "Why would you ask that?"

"Sara mentioned it to me. But she thought the fatigue was just the onset of the holidays, the uptick in business at the store, and Chris taking on Santa duties."

"You know Chris suffered from PTSD before it was even diagnosed as that," her mom explained.

"Had he found help for it?" Grant asked.

"He found help in his own way," her dad said. "His trip to D.C. every year with other veterans was one of his ways of confronting the emotions, I guess. Making toys in his workshop was another. The past ten years or so, I didn't see any evidence of it, but that didn't mean anything. Chris was a

private person and could hide his feelings well."
This time her father bent down and ruffled the hair
along Patches' back. "I think Blitz was a big help.
Once he rescued that dog, he seemed happier."

"Pets can often do what humans can't, not even
loved ones," Caprice suggested.

"Blitz was with him constantly," her dad agreed.

"Except for the night he stopped in at the community center," Caprice remembered. "And besides
his bruised jaw and that cut over his eye, Sara said
he had bruises around his ribs."

Her father was on alert now. "When I asked him
about the jaw, he said a box from the store on a
high shelf had fallen on him. But that wouldn't
explain the ribs."

"Not unless he fell or something like that," Grant
said.

"A fall could do all that," Nana agreed. "But you
all sound as if you didn't believe him."

Caprice gave a little shrug. "I don't know. He
didn't meet my eyes when I asked him about it and
he told me what happened. And Sara told me he
admitted he was in a fight, but he wouldn't tell her
more than that."

Caprice's dad leaned away from the dogs and
thought about it. "Maybe he'd gotten into some
kind of trouble that he didn't want anyone to know
about."

"What kind of trouble?" Nana asked.

For her father to mention it, Caprice imagined
he had something in mind.

But her dad shook his head. "I have no idea."

"Are you going to say anything to Brett about the bruised jaw and the cut above his eye?"

"I don't feel I have much choice," her dad responded. "If they want to get to the bottom of who did this, everybody has to be honest with them."

From past experience Caprice knew an investigation wasn't that easy. She knew not everyone was honest, not everyone told the truth.

Grant, who was sitting on the arm of her chair, put his hand on her shoulder. "Carstead and Jones will get to the bottom of it, Caprice. Motives for murder always come out in the end."

She knew Grant was right. She just hoped those motives came out sooner rather than later, so that Chris's family could grieve properly . . . and so that justice could be done.

"Why do you think she wants to see us?" Caprice asked her dad the following evening as he drove them to Sara Merriweather's house. They'd both gotten a call from Sara who'd asked them to stop by this evening.

He pulled up to the curb in front of the house. "She could want to see us for lots of reasons. She might simply want to talk about Chris to somebody who knew him."

"Possibly," Caprice said. "She also might want to cancel listing her house. Maybe she doesn't want to deal with Denise herself."

Denise Langford, the real estate agent who was

handling the house sale, could be quite assertive and somewhat brash at times.

"You didn't move much furniture in for this house staging, did you?"

"No. I mostly just moved around what she and Chris had and told them what they could take out. It's possible she could want me to take all the Christmas decorations away. I'm sure she doesn't feel like Christmas."

They both seemed to be thinking about that as they went up the porch steps to the door. Caprice rang the bell. It was only a moment until Sara answered. Opening the door wide, she gave them a tremulous hello and motioned for them to come in.

Caprice gave Sara a hug and held on tight. "I'm so very sorry."

Sara nodded and accepted Caprice's comfort.

After Caprice stepped away, her father took Sara's hand and squeezed it.

Just then, Blitz came running into the living room, nudged against her father's side and rubbed his head along her father's coat.

Her dad dropped down to the dog's level. "I know you miss him too." Her father scratched Blitz's ears and rubbed him under his neck. The dog basked in her dad's attention.

"Come on in to the living room," Sara said, "and we'll talk. Would you like tea, coffee, anything to drink? I already have tons of food from friends and neighbors. If you'd like a piece of cake . . ." She trailed off.

Caprice looked at her dad and then shook her head. "We're fine."

Once they were seated, Caprice said, "I know this day had to be a difficult one for you." She unbuttoned her poncho and let it slip from her shoulders onto the chair. Her dad did the same with his coat. Any other time, Sara would have been scurrying around, taking their coats, hanging them in a closet. But she looked totally desolate. There were circles under her eyes, and her face had taken on a sallow complexion.

"Today was awful," she admitted. "I had to make a few arrangements with the funeral home. Yet I couldn't make specific arrangements because I don't know when they'll release Chris."

Sara made it sound as if Chris were a prisoner rather than a body in a morgue awaiting autopsy.

"Who are you dealing with in the Kismet Police Department?" Caprice asked.

"Two of them," she said tersely. "A Detective Jones and a Detective Carstead. They made us all feel like suspects. Detective Jones questioned Deanne as well as Ryan and Serena. They had us there for hours. He asked them about everything, from drugs to boyfriends."

Deanne, at twenty-five, was unmarried and worked in York at a spa and pool dealership. Ryan who was twenty-eight was still trying to figure out what he was good at. He'd majored in communication in college. Right now, he was working as a salesman in a phone store, which wasn't the career path that his parents had envisioned for him. According to Sara, he kept insisting it was temporary.

"Detective Jones can be harsh." Caprice empathized. "He wants to turn over every stone, and sometimes he's a little too quick doing it. But he's looking for the truth, Sara."

"Maybe so. But Maura and Reed were questioned too, and they were angry when they were finished. They said the detective asked them personal questions about their relationship . . . about their past history. Detective Carstead spoke with them after he spoke with me. I have to admit, he was very respectful with me. But he still asked me where I was. I was here alone after Chris and I condo shopped. He even questioned me about my marriage to Chris." Sara's gaze focused on Caprice. "I know you've had some experience with investigations. Do I need a lawyer? Do my children need lawyers?"

After a glance at her dad and knowing he'd agree, she admitted, "Consulting a lawyer might be a good idea. You might need more than one lawyer."

"We have a lawyer who handled our will— Jeremiah Pickens. But he's almost eighty and semi-retired. I don't think he'd want to get involved. Could Vince or your fiancé help?"

Her dad stepped in now. "Sara, I know that would be comfortable for you because you know both of them. But neither Vince nor Grant are criminal defense attorneys. They might be willing to sit in on questioning if the detectives want to interrogate any of your family again. But I'm pretty certain they would advise you to look for a criminal defense attorney. They could possibly suggest someone in a firm with multiple lawyers because that's what you'd need."

Caprice took one of her business cards from her purse as well as a pen. Turning over the card, she jotted Grant's cell phone number and then Vince's. She handed it to Sara. "Call either Vince or Grant. I'm sure they can give you the information you'll need. I'll let them know you might call."

Tears came to Sara's eyes. "Thank you. I can't tell you how much I appreciate this. It's bad enough we're all hurting because of Chris's death, but I can't bear to see my children bullied by the police."

Caprice wondered if Sara was being overprotective. After all, this *was* a police investigation into the murder of her husband. The questions the police asked were going to be tough, and they would be looking at everyone with an intense magnifying glass.

She told Sara, "Just try to keep in mind that you or your children might have a clue as to who this murderer is. That's what the police are trying to gather—all the clues they can to put the puzzle together. If you think of it that way, maybe it won't seem as much like a personal affront when they ask their questions."

Sara ran her fingers through her usually perfectly coiffed hair. Now it was a bit disheveled. "I know you're right. It's just"—she stopped, gathered herself, and then went on—"it's just I have to concentrate on *something*. Protecting my children is easier than facing what happened."

Blitz had seated himself beside her dad. He

nudged against her father's knee, and her dad laid a hand on the dog's head. It was as if he knew exactly what this conversation was about.

Sara moved closer to the edge of the sofa seat and watched Blitz and her dad. Then she gave a little nod as if deciding something. "I have a request," she said.

"Anything," her dad assured her.

"You might wait until you hear it before you say that," Sara advised him. "I'd like to know if you would take Blitz. I know you get along well. He obviously likes you and you like him. I just can't handle Chris's dog now and none of my children want him."

The surprise on her dad's face was obvious. He'd never expected that request. He looked down at Blitz, and Caprice could see the sense of loss he felt over Chris's death. But she could also see he felt great affection for the dog. Blitz was well-trained. He and Chris had gone to obedience school even though the canine had already seemed to know the basics. But taking on the commitment of a pet wasn't something to do lightly. Her father had to think about work and home and how her mom might react to the idea.

Facing Sara he said honestly, "I do like Blitz, and he likes me. But I can't make a commitment like that unless I check with Fran first. Do you mind if I make a call?"

"Go ahead," Sara said. "If you'd like to wander into the kitchen to do it, that's fine."

Her dad stood and went into the kitchen, Blitz following close at his heels.

"They make a good match," Sara said with certainty. "How do you think your mom will feel about it?"

"She's an animal lover, but it's hard to say. As you know, having a dog is like having a child to take care of. Any pet you love is like that, really. With her teaching position, she wouldn't be involved in Blitz's care as much as Dad would."

"I know," Sara nodded. "Chris hated to leave Blitz alone. He was with Chris, you know, when he was killed."

"I didn't know that."

"Well, he wasn't exactly *with* him. Blitz was closed up in the Santa cabin. Chris had left him in there when he'd gone outside apparently to meet whoever it was. I can't imagine why he did that. It's not as if Blitz would have run off somewhere. It's not as if Blitz wouldn't have protected him. It just seemed to be a very odd thing to do."

That did seem odd, Caprice thought. For some reason, Chris hadn't wanted Blitz to interfere. Or else had he wanted to protect Blitz? Pretend the dog wasn't along with him?

Her father had returned to the living room, and he gave Sara a small smile. "Fran's not at all sure about us having a dog, but she's seen how Caprice handles and copes with having Lady and the same with Grant and Patches. My work schedule has eased up, and I'm not in the field as much as I'm in the office now. I reminded her of that, and the fact that Chris took Blitz to work. I really can't see why I can't do the same."

"So you'll take him?"

"I will. We'll love him and see he gets the best

care possible. I even have a brother who's a pet sitter. So when I get in a pinch, I can call on him."

"Not to mention me, Grant, Nikki, and Vince," Caprice added. "You've seen how I juggle. It can be done."

Sara stood and brushed a wrinkle from her black skirt. "Thank your lovely wife for me. Tell her I'll call her when I get a few minutes . . . when I feel like myself again."

"I will tell her. And you take your time. Your grief will go on long past this murder investigation. The investigation could make your grief stop and start as you have to concentrate on other things. Just know that eventually you'll get through it."

"To the acceptance stage?" Sara asked, almost sarcastically.

"It seems impossible now, doesn't it?" Caprice asked. "And I don't think we can ever accept losing somebody we love. But maybe we can be at peace with it."

After Sara thought about that, she asked, "You know Father Gregory, don't you, Caprice? I'm going to ask him to handle the service and the Mass."

Father Gregory was a good guy. He'd helped Bella and Joe put their marriage back on track. He was also her and Grant's advocate for their annulment. He was trying to smooth the waters for them. They'd had many conversations with him about that . . . and marriage.

"Chris didn't go to church," Sara admitted. "But he'd talked with Father Gregory about his PTSD several times. I don't think he told him what happened over there. I don't think he told anyone. But whatever Father Gregory advised him helped Chris sleep easier at night."

Caprice knew Sara meant what happened in Vietnam. She was glad to hear that Chris had talked to Father Gregory about some of it.

"Tell me something, Sara," her father suggested. "Do you think you'd like Blitz to come visit at any time? Not now but maybe in a month or two, or when you miss him."

"That's possible. It's also possible I'll miss him when I'm here all alone at night and the boards creak and I get scared. But I have to learn to deal with it on my own. Still, if I get freaked out, it might be nice to have him here now and then."

"All right. Then I'm going to suggest that you keep Blitz's bed that was upstairs next to yours. Keep his water and food bowl. We have extra bowls that we use when Lady and Patches visit. We also have an extra bed, but I think Blitz might need a bigger one. I'll take care of buying him that for our house. Then he can go back and forth if you like. I'm not telling you I don't want full custody, but I am telling you I think you'll miss him and maybe need him near you now and then. And that's okay with me."

Sara stood and rushed forward to give Nick a hug. "You are the nicest man. Chris knew how to pick good friends."

"I hope I was as good a friend to him as he was to me. Chris was there when Vince and I would butt heads, especially when Vince was a teenager. Somehow Chris made me see reason, and I could stay more even tempered and deal with whatever the problem was. And with my girls, the best advice he gave was *Let your wife handle them.*"

Sara actually laughed. "That's what he did here. He handled Ryan. He let me handle Deanne and Maura. We were all so off-kilter after the questioning that we didn't rally as we should have. Tomorrow we'll talk again. Then we can make the decision as a family about calling Vince and Grant."

"That's probably a good idea," Nick said. "Is there anything else we can help you with? Do you want to keep the house up for sale?"

"I do. We'll see if we get any offers. Chris and I had decided on a condo we liked. It really doesn't make sense for me to ramble around in this big house. I'll let Denise know as soon as I make a clear decision."

Her father gave Caprice a nod.

She stood and said, "We'd better go. You need to get some rest. We'll see if Perky Paws is still open and pick up the supplies we need on the way home."

"Is Blitz a good car rider?" her dad asked.

"He's the best," Sara answered. "He likes to watch out the window. But on long trips he just curls on the seat and falls asleep. Chris would always stuff pillows around him instead of using one of those halter seatbelts. But that will be up to you."

After hugs all around, Sara fetched Blitz's leash and her dad attached it. Then they went to the car with Blitz easily heeling by her dad's side.

At the car, Blitz stood by the backseat door and waited for her dad to open it. Then he jumped in up on the seat and stared at them through the window after her father closed the door.

"Mom's really okay with this?"

"As okay as she can be with something new. Give us a night or a day or two and I'll let you know."

After they'd gotten into her dad's car, Caprice buckled up. "Sara told me that Blitz was with Chris the night he was killed. The police think Chris locked Blitz in the cabin while he went out to meet whoever it was at the sleigh. But that doesn't make sense. Blitz is friendly. I've never even heard him growl. So why wouldn't Chris take him with him?"

"Unless he didn't want the distraction," her dad suggested.

"Possibly. Or possibly Blitz knew the person and liked him too much."

"Or Blitz didn't like the person and could be a threat."

"Just because he was closed in the Santa cabin doesn't mean he was there the whole time. He could have been with Chris and seen the man who murdered him."

Now that was something to think about. She wondered if the police were thinking about it too.

The following morning, Caprice drove her Camaro into the flow of traffic on White Rose Way. Since the holiday parade, the downtown area of Kismet was busier. Tourists came to flit in and out of the stores, have lunch at the Blue Moon Grille, and maybe stop at a Christmas tree farm between Kismet and York. Downtown Kismet had charm that was rooted in its early 1900s heritage. Most of the buildings, built with red brick, were accented by white trim around the windows and under the eaves. Many of the shops displayed oval signs hung on wrought-iron brackets. Caprice passed the old school building, where Vince lived, that had been renovated into condos. He'd soon be moving.

She smiled when she saw the wreaths hung on the lamp posts on both sides of the street. Stores like The Nail Yard, a manicure center in Kismet, had decorated their plate glass windows with red and green holly garlands and twinkle lights. She thought about stopping at Secrets of the Past but everything that had happened weighed on her. And she couldn't think about holiday fashion, even in a retro style, today.

Driving by Vince and Grant's office, she parked across the street from Novel Ideas, the downtown bookstore. Kiki Hasselhoff who owned the store had become a friend recently. She was in her sixties and a member of the Kismet Chamber of Commerce.

After Caprice tucked her Camaro into a parking space, she fed the meter and dashed across the street to Kiki's store. The day was pleasantly cold in the forties, but she knew the weather could turn on a dime and the Pennsylvania winter could begin.

A few shoppers were scattered between the displays of books and holiday gift ideas. She had a DVD about enhancing owner and dog relationships that she could lend her dad, but she wanted to pick up a book too. It would give him something to focus on other than Chris and his family.

Caprice spotted Kiki near one of the back shelves with an e-tablet in hand. She was possibly checking inventory. Caprice waved and headed to that section. Kiki had placed the dog and cat and other animal books next to the self-help section.

"How are you?" Kiki asked.

"I'm okay. Sad for Chris Merriweather's family."

"That's so terrible. I couldn't believe it when I heard. Are you involved in the investigation?"

"No, but I was staging their house. Sara asked Dad to take Blitz, Chris's dog. So, I'm looking for a book on dog handling for him—something beyond commands because Blitz already has a grasp of those."

"I have just what you need. Let me show you." Kiki went to a shelf where books on dog handling were displayed. She plucked one off the shelf and handed it to Caprice. "I guess your dad is old school and likes to hold a book in his hand?"

"And turn down pages and highlight," Caprice responded with a small smile.

"That's the sign of a true reader," Kiki said. She looked thoughtful. "You know, there's been a lot of talk about Chris Merriweather this morning."

"You mean the murder?"

"Not just the murder."

"I don't understand."

"There's scuttlebutt about the historic houses on Restoration Row near your friend Roz Winslow's dress shop."

Caprice had heard there were a few houses for sale there, and that a developer was interested.

"What are the rumors?"

"That developer, Bailey Adler, wants to buy those houses and tear them down to build new store fronts."

"But those are historic houses. And they have renters in them, don't they?"

"Yes, they do. But now that Chris Merriweather is dead, the rezoning will probably go through in the developer's favor. Chris was against the project and very vocal about it. But the mayor has named a new town council member who everyone knows is *for* the project."

Caprice had been so busy with work, family, and pets that she hadn't kept up with that bit of news. She'd missed the last Chamber of Commerce meeting. Could this project and Chris's negative vote have something to do with his death?

Chapter Six

Since Caprice and Grant were spending the evening together, they decided to take their dogs to the dog park to let them romp and play. The night was crisply cold and they could see the twinkle lights on Santa Lane in the distance.

As they sat on a bench and watched Patches and Lady chase each other around, Grant draped his arm around Caprice. "Are you cold?"

"No." Actually she was plenty warm in a teal-colored faux fur midi-coat that even had a hood. Still she said, "But I like your arm around me."

Grant leaned in to kiss her and then pulled away. "Something tells me your mind isn't on Patches and Lady having fun in the dog park."

"It isn't. I stopped at the bookstore today to get a book for Dad on bonding with a dog, and Kiki Hasselhoff told me something that troubled me."

"What was that?"

Caprice related what she'd learned about the rezoning vote, and that now, since Chris wasn't on the board, the vote would go in a developer's favor.

Grant shook his head, his frown cutting deep. "When you mention *developer* and *real estate* in the same sentence, you could be talking big bucks. You could be talking a motive for murder. The question is—whose motive? The developer's? The mayor's? The town council replacement member?"

"There are always logical suspects at the beginning of a murder investigation, but this one doesn't seem to be easing in any one direction. I mean, Chris's neighbor even had a grudge against him." She quickly told Grant about Boyd Arkoff's appearance at the Merriweather house.

"Who would have thought Chris would have that many enemies?"

She gazed over at the twinkle lights on Santa Lane.

Grant must have caught her looking and, seeing the concentration on her face, he said, "I heard there's a replacement Santa at the cabin. Christmas must go on. I don't suppose you'd like to wander over there?"

"When was the crime scene released?"

"Yesterday morning. Come on. The dogs will like the brisk walk, and you and I won't mind the frost in the air."

Grant held Caprice's hand as they walked, and she appreciated the feel of his hand in hers. During the years she hadn't dated, she didn't think she'd missed being part of a couple. Maybe it felt so right now because she and Grant were the *right* couple.

As they strolled up Santa Lane and heard instrumental Christmas music playing from the loud speaker on the cabin, Caprice wondered how soon it would be until everyone in Kismet forgot someone had been murdered there.

They passed the sleigh with its presents wrapped in weatherproof gold paper and vinyl red ribbons. A row of sleigh bells on a leather strap hung on the left- and right-front corners. She had a set of sleigh bells similar to those attached to the cute cat and dog wreath decoration on her front door.

Caprice couldn't help but want to get a good look at the sleigh. She nudged Grant and they circled it. After they did, she noticed that one of the candy canes stakes was missing in the line leading up to the cabin.

Had that really been the murder weapon?

A man and a boy who looked to be about four exited the cabin. They were both smiling and the child carried a candy cane and an orange.

Caprice said to Grant, "I remember Nikki and I getting a candy cane and an orange after we told Santa what we wanted."

"Bella and Vince weren't with you?"

"Bella had wanted her own visit all by herself so Santa wouldn't get mixed up with who wanted what."

Grant laughed. "That's Bella."

"And Vince said he was too old to talk to Santa, though I think he slipped Dad a letter to push into the box."

"Why don't I stay out here with the dogs while you go in and talk to Santa? You can look around to see if anything has changed or is missing. The police might not have known what was there before and what wasn't. You helped decorate the cabin so you would."

Without hesitating, she handed Grant Lady's leash. "If you wander down the lane with them, I'll text you when I'm finished."

Grant nodded, and she stepped inside.

When Caprice had helped decorate the cabin, she'd used the same homey touches that she'd added to the Merriweathers' home—pine boughs in a vase with Christmas balls, flameless candles, Chris's toys here and there. A wooden box painted with a snowman scene sat beside Santa. The large slit in the top would accommodate any size letter. There was also a mail slot in the door to the cabin so anybody passing by when it wasn't open could drop letters in there too. The man seated in what looked like a large dining room chair wasn't as tall as Chris. He was stouter with twinkling brown eyes instead of blue ones. The Santa outfit looked a little big on him and she wondered if it was Chris's. His fake beard fit him well, and Caprice decided it could possibly withstand a tug by a toddler.

"Hello, there," he said genially. "Can I help you?"

She decided to be honest. "I just wondered who took Chris Merriweather's place."

The man nodded and then extended his hand. "I'm Neal Gladfelter, and you're . . ."

She shook his hand then explained, "I'm Caprice De Luca. Chris's family and my family are friends. He was also my client. I was staging his house to sell."

Now the man eyed her more carefully. "Caprice De Luca. Your name has been in the paper a couple of times. You rescue strays and try to find them homes."

"I do."

"But you've also helped the Kismet PD solve a couple of murders."

"I like to think I was of some help."

"Are you going to solve Chris's?"

"No. I mean . . . I don't know. I'm sure the police are already on it."

"I'm sure they are too. But did you come here looking for clues?"

As she glanced around the cabin, she couldn't see anything out of order or anything that was missing. "I helped Chris set up the cabin this year. Since it's so near the murder scene, I wondered if it was involved. But nothing seems to be amiss."

"It was like this when I came in. There are those scratches on the door."

Caprice whirled around to study the inside of the door. There were scratches there, scratches as if Blitz had been trying to get out. To help his master? She turned back to Neal Gladfelter. "What do you do when you're not playing Santa?"

"I'm an accountant," he told her with a wry smile. "I also know the mayor. When he said they might have trouble finding a replacement Santa, I volunteered. I'm going to try to do more than just listen to wishes."

"I don't understand."

"I'm in a good place financially. When I give to a charity, I like to see what good my dollars do. If a child comes in with a wish list and the family can't possibly afford what he or she wants, maybe I can make it happen. A little boy came in earlier who desperately wants a jungle gym for his backyard. His parents don't have the funds and everyone is sad. But before they left, I told them I might know someone who would donate a jungle gym. They had to be talked into it because of pride, but they were grateful. From what I understand, Chris used to do the same kind of thing. He twisted an arm or two to make gifts happen for these kids."

"So you knew Chris?"

"Not personally. But the business community in Kismet is small enough that word gets around."

She knew that was true just by being a member of the Chamber of Commerce.

After Caprice talked to Neal for a few more minutes, she bid him good night and stepped outside. No one walked Santa Lane. The Christmas music should have kept the dark night pleasant, but night was night and dark was dark, and this was an isolated spot without people wandering about.

She didn't know which direction Grant might have gone. She was about to text him when he came jogging up the path from deeper in the park with Lady and Patches running beside him. He stopped when he reached her. "I just got a call from a contact at the D.A.'s office. The autopsy report on Chris came in."

"Did they figure out the murder weapon?"

"The paint and the type of wood proved he died of blunt force trauma from the candy cane stake. But that wasn't the surprising part."

"A surprise with the autopsy?"

"Yes. Chris had an inoperable brain tumor that

would have probably killed him within six months to a year."

Caprice felt as if someone had socked her in the stomach with one of those candy cane stakes. "Oh, my gosh. You know what? The day of the parade, Chris was acting odd. He seemed dizzy, and one of the parents accused him of being drunk. I wonder if that was part of the condition . . . if it had been happening often. Does his family know about this?"

"They do now. Mack informed them."

An inoperable brain tumor. Had that had something to do with his murder? It was probably the reason he wanted to move himself and his wife into a senior living facility. Just what would Sara do now?

Seeing her dismayed expression, Grant took her hand. "Let's go back to your place," he said. "We'll light a fire and try to forget about all this for a while."

But how could anybody forget an inoperable brain tumor . . . and murder?

Caprice was so glad she had work to concentrate on the following day. She had left Lady at home with Mirabelle and Sophia while she took this drive to Hanover to talk with a possible client. This evening she and her dad were going to visit Sara to see if she needed anything. But for now, Caprice was ready to concentrate on a contract for a new house staging.

The Pigeon Hills lay between Thomasville and Hanover. From the history she'd read, the Hills were composed of the oldest type of rock—volcanic rock belonging to the Catoctin Formation. She'd done research on the area when Charles Kopcek had contacted her. His house was located off High Rock Road and she knew she'd pass Pulpit Rock. This was nearly the highest elevation in the Pigeon Hills, at 1,240 feet. Vince had told her about a winery in this area. Their wines were made with fruits grown from local family and friends—black and red raspberries, strawberries, and blackberries. The grapes they used were also grown locally in York County and northern Pennsylvania. Supposedly, early surveyors owned parcels of land in York County. One of them was named Joseph Pidgeon, a surveyor from Philadelphia County. The Pigeon Hills were supposedly named after him, even though the spelling wasn't the same.

As Caprice drove along the winding road, she knew she could thank Chris and Sara for recommending her to Charles Kopcek. Chris had seemed to know everyone from the janitor at the local school to Charles who owned a home-security systems company.

After another half mile, Caprice found the lane that turned down to the Kopcek property. Caprice had seen many photos of this estate, but this was the first she was visiting it in person. Sara had told her it was peaceful, and she could see that. Yes, the elms and maples and sycamores were bare of leaves now, but thirty-foot pines lined the drive on both sides. When she'd read the stats on this home, she'd marveled that it was originally a log home but had been rebuilt. Just from looking over the property from afar, she decided on a theme if her client agreed: Mountaintop Style.

Parking at the double car garage, she marveled again at the solitude of the place, like the feeling of being alone with no one else around for miles. That was a rare feeling for her when she had family and pets around her most of the time.

Going to the door, she knocked. The wide, wooden door was opened immediately and a tall man with silver hair stood there, smiling at her. He looked to be in his late fifties.

"Mr. Kopcek?" she asked.

"That's me," he said, inviting her inside with a gesture of his hand. "And you're Caprice De Luca?"

"I am." She gazed around the house that she knew was 4,500 square feet. The living room was spacious with its seating area built around an immense floor-to-ceiling stone fireplace. The exposed wood beams, the beautiful flooring, the shiny appliances and quartz counter she could spot in the kitchen were much more impressive than mere photographs had been.

"You have a beautiful home."

"I know we do," he said, inviting her toward the sofa. "But my wife and I have decided to make a move now before we get too old to care if we do it."

From her notes, she remembered, "Your wife is a lawyer?"

"Yes, she is. She insists she can find work wherever she goes."

"The Merriweathers told me that you want to settle out West."

Sitting on the edge of the sofa, excitement sparkled

in his brown eyes. "Not settle, exactly. I'm originally from Wyoming. But I met Debbie when she was on vacation right before I went into the service. She was from here. After I was discharged, we decided to set up housekeeping here, and this is where I started my security company. But the older I've gotten, the more I've wanted to go back to my roots. Yes, we sort of live on a mountain top here, but I want to return to a real mountain top, hopefully near the Big Horns. There's a call for home security everywhere now, and not only home security, but computer security. I'm into both. I'm going to sell my business here and open one there."

"Have you found a property in Wyoming?"

"I have my eye on three, actually. But I'd like to wait until we get a nibble on this just so I know where I am financially."

"I understand. Why don't you give me a tour? You've already talked with Denise Langford, correct?"

"Yes, I have and she's appraised the house. But I don't know if we can get top dollar, and she insists with your help, we can."

"Let's take a look."

A half hour later, Caprice was still impressed. "Your house on its own merit should invite top dollar. But its location, and especially that view from the bedroom balcony, will be a wonderful selling point. Right now, you have good quality furnishings. However, with your permission, I'd like to make them a little more rustic, add more suede and leather and wrought iron. I'd like to declutter a bit too. Would you consider renting a storage unit for a while where you could store what you wouldn't be using?"

"If it means selling the house quicker, sure, I'll do that. And you can style it any way you'd like. We'll be leaving this behind, so it doesn't much matter. Now that we've made our decision, the right Wyoming ranch is just waiting and neither of us can wait to move."

"The market has picked up, and with an open house and the right publicity, you could possibly get an offer before Christmas." Caprice took out her phone and checked her calendar. "I can fit you in for an open house on Saturday in two and a half weeks. How does that sound?"

"That sounds wonderful. Denise told us you're a miracle worker when you set your mind to it."

Caprice wasn't exactly sure what that meant, but she soon found out.

Charles Kopcek asked, "Do you have time for this now?"

"If I sign a contract with you, I'll keep to the terms and move quickly if that's what you want. I have an assistant and other temporary help I can call in. Do you have any doubts about hiring me?"

"Not doubts, exactly. I have your portfolio, the houses you've staged and the ones you've sold. I've heard about Ace Richland and his estate, how he liked the way you staged the house and how he bought it, and how quickly that sale moved. Can I speak plainly?"

"Of course, you can."

"I also understand you've been involved in some

murder investigations, and you're an advocate of
animal rights and rescue."

"That's true."

"I suppose that's why I'm questioning whether
you can fit us into your schedule. Especially now,
with Chris Merriweather's murder. Debbie and I
were shocked when we saw coverage on the news.
Will you be involved in the investigation?"

"I doubt if I'll be involved. The police have that
under control. But my family is friends with the
Merriweathers, and we'll help them any way we can.
That's just part of life. My work and staging your
house is totally separate. As I said, if you agree to let
me write up a proposal and I contract with you to
do the house staging, I will keep to the terms.
That's how I've gained the reputation I have."

He was studying her now with a practiced eye
that told her he had a good sense of people's character. After all, Chris had told her Charles had been
in the service. This man knew about home and
computer security. He had to be a good judge of
character.

"Would you like me to meet your wife before
you make a decision? I can make an appointment
with her."

His cheeks grew a little ruddy. "To be honest, she
had already decided to hire you, simply according
to your résumé, your website, and asking around
about you. She has friends who belong to the
Country Squire Golf and Recreation Club. They
speak highly of you. After talking with you today,
hearing your comments and your suggestions, I
agree we should hire you."

"You might want to see my proposal first," she advised with a smile.

He chuckled. "I suppose that would be a good idea."

"I have your e-mail information," she said. "By tomorrow evening, I'll e-mail you my proposal. After you and your wife have a chance to look it over, just give me a call. If you decide to contract with me, we'll start right away."

"Do you really think we could get an offer before Christmas?"

"Of course I can't promise that, and neither can Denise. But she and I both know the best places to advertise a property like this—newsletters to get the word out, e-zines to post photos in. We would do our best for you, Mr. Kopcek."

He nodded and extended his hand. "Send me your proposal. I look forward to seeing it."

Caprice pulled into her driveway, pushed open her door, and climbed out ready to brace against the cold air. Cold or not, Lady needed to be walked. Brisk exercise would do both of them good, especially since Caprice hated to go to the pool at the gym in the wintertime—wet hair, cold wind, chills. *Brrr*. Walking Lady seemed the better alternative.

Caprice took a few seconds at her front door to appreciate the decorations. A garland with twinkle lights stretched around the frame of the rounded-top door. Cut out of metal and painted brightly, a yellow tabby sat beside a beagle in the center of a wreath. Caprice had attached sleigh bells to the decoration so they jingled when the door opened. Smiling, she unlocked the door and tapped in the security code to turn off the system.

Lady sat in the foyer staring at her as if asking, *What took you so long?*

"I was only gone two hours. I bet you didn't even eat all the kibble in your Kong ball."

Lady came over to her and sat in front of her.

Caprice crouched down and gave her a good rubdown including a belly rub. "Let me say hey to Mirabelle and Sophia, then we'll go for a walk."

If there was one word Lady understood better than others, it was *walk*, but *treats* did run a close second.

Mirabelle was lazily stretched out on the sofa, on her side, totally relaxed. Such a different cat than when Caprice had first brought her home. Her previous owner hadn't given her much attention, let alone the basics. Now, well-loved, Mirabelle meowed in greeting. She didn't rise to her paws, however. She waited for Caprice to sit beside her and slowly stroke her beautiful white fur. "I guess you're the princess and Sophia is the queen."

Hearing her name, Sophia, who was seated on the top level of the turquoise carpeted cat tree, meowed herself, a very different meow than Mirabelle. It was sharper and had a conversational quality.

"I know you want to know where your tiara is. You won't even wear a sparkly collar." Actually, Sophia wouldn't wear any collar. A long-haired calico, her beautiful white ruff stood out around her face like decorative apparel.

Deciding that Caprice had given Mirabelle quite

enough attention, Sophia climbed down another level of the cat tree, scratched on the carpeted post, and hopped down the rest of the way. Crossing to Caprice on the sofa, she wound about her legs, looked up at her, then jumped up onto the arm of the sofa.

Caprice stroked her silky fur. "Have you two had a good morning? My guess is you didn't entertain Lady all that much."

Both cats meowed in unison as if protesting that they indeed did.

Lady cocked her head at Caprice as if to say *Don't believe a meow of theirs.*

Caprice laughed. "Come on, Lady, let's get your leash. After our walk, I'll give you all lunch." She shook her finger at the two felines. "In the meantime, you two behave."

They'd been known to have their squabbles but nothing nasty, just bothersome. They liked to annoy each other now and then, just like kids.

Lady trotted with Caprice out the front door and waited until she set the alarm again and locked the door. Then they started their trek at a brisk pace around the block. In the winter, the yards looked so barren. But not for long. Many residents of her neighborhood decorated with Christmas lights, Santas on the roof, snowmen in the yard, a Nativity scene on the porch. She and Lady had a blast exploring when decorations started appearing. But today, Caprice admired the pines, the ivy that still had some green leaves, the rose bushes that hadn't quite given up to nighttime winter frost.

As they walked, Caprice couldn't help but think

about her new client. He was selling his business. She suddenly wondered if Brett Carstead had ever considered running a security company instead of being a detective. He'd have more normal hours. He could have a real life. Not that a detective couldn't, she supposed, but he'd have to have the right significant other. Could Nikki be the right life partner for him? Her sister hadn't talked about Brett lately, and Caprice wondered if they'd stopped dating.

Everyone at the Kismet PD would be on top of this investigation since Chris was the chief's army buddy and good friend.

Suddenly Caprice remembered Sara saying that Chris hadn't been the same after he'd come back from his yearly trip to the Vietnam Memorial in D.C. Perhaps it was time to talk to someone about that. Maybe even Mack.

Caprice and Lady had walked along her side of the street for about three blocks, turned around, and started down the other side of the street. Even dogs liked changing scenery.

They were almost back home, passing by Dulcina's house when Dulcina's front door opened and she stepped out onto the porch. She'd grabbed a sweater and flung it around her shoulders. "I have news," she told Caprice.

"What kind of news?"

Dulcina had a smile across her lips that told Caprice it was something good. "Your Uncle Dom has asked me on a real date."

"You look pleased."

"I am. We're going to see *The Nutcracker* at Hershey Theater. I'm excited, but nervous too."

"Why nervous? You and Uncle Dom get along great, don't you?" she asked with an arched brow.

"We seem to. But he told me he hasn't dated since before his marriage."

"You know what that means, don't you?" Caprice asked. "He'll be as nervous as you are. Just relax. When he brought you to our family dinner, all went well. You had a good time at Thanksgiving, didn't you?"

"I did and at Nana's birthday party."

"Then why should this be any different?"

"Because we're going to be alone. I bought a new dress."

"And I'll bet he'll buy a new sports jacket."

"I'm just worried. Things didn't work out with Rod. I keep thinking maybe it was my fault. Maybe I wasn't warm enough with his girls. Maybe I didn't try hard enough."

Dulcina's last romantic relationship hadn't gone well, maybe because she'd compared it to a marriage which she'd considered perfect.

"Do you want a little advice?"

"Sure. You're engaged. You have the right to give it."

Caprice laughed. "I don't know about that, but I do know one thing. Just try to be yourself. Don't think about what's going to happen next. Just enjoy being with my uncle, soak in the performance, talk about whatever comes to mind. If you act naturally, he will too."

Dulcina nodded. "That's good advice. Do you want to come in for coffee, and say hello to Halo and Miss Paddington?"

Caprice looked down at Lady. "Do you think Sophia and Mirabelle can wait a half hour for lunch?"

Lady, who wasn't a barker, gave a soft ruff. "That's a *yes*," Caprice told Dulcina and climbed the porch steps with Lady.

As soon as her pets had lunch, she'd start working on the proposal for Charles Kopcek.

After that, she'd call Sara Merriweather to make sure she was up for a visit tonight . . . to see if she needed anything. Caprice was pretty sure Sara would need the comfort of a friend more than she needed another casserole. On the other hand, a quart of minestrone soup—Nana's recipe—couldn't hurt.

Chapter Seven

That evening, Sara let Caprice and her dad into her house, giving them both tight hugs. Caprice had brought along a container of minestrone, and Sara stowed it in the refrigerator. After they all sat in the living room, Caprice could still see the tears brimming in her eyes. She was dressed in a black, long-sleeved dress that had navy around the collar and the hem. She wasn't wearing any jewelry and very little makeup. That was very much unlike her. The blue smudges under her eyes attested to her lack of sleep.

She said simply, "It was another rough day."

Caprice's dad nodded. "I can only imagine. Is there anything we can do for you?" he asked with the kindness that Caprice had known all her life.

They'd laid their coats on a nearby chair, and now Sara looked at them and said, "I should hang up your coats," but she didn't move to do so.

Caprice said, "That doesn't matter. Have you been alone all day?"

"Oh, no," she said with a shake of her head.

"Deanne, Maura, and Ryan have been here. I made them all go home before supper. They mean well. Maura answered the phone all day."

Sara suddenly asked Caprice's dad, "Did *you* know Chris was sick?"

Her father shook his head. "I had no idea. Did anyone know?"

Sara looked dejected. "Not that I know of. I feel so guilty because I didn't catch it. How am I going to live with that?"

Her dad met Sara's gaze. "You're going to have a list of *if-onlys* and *what-ifs*, and you can drive yourself crazy with them. From what Caprice tells me, with Chris wanting to downsize to move into a retirement village, he was trying to prepare both of you and make life easier. From what I understand, the tumor was inoperable. There was nothing you could have done."

Sara wasn't buying it. "We could have looked into experimental treatments. I could have searched the Internet for doctors who wouldn't have thought the tumor was inoperable." After a pause, she said, "Tell me you're going to keep Blitz. I need to know he'll be with someone who loves him as much as Chris did. The kids don't want a dog, and the truth is, I don't either."

Caprice knew *she'd* feel much differently about that. She'd want to keep her husband's dog to have a part of him with her. But Sara seemed totally removed from Chris and his love for the animal. So Caprice didn't judge.

"Blitz has already become my good buddy. Yes, I'll keep him," Nick said. "Chris was my friend, and it's something I can do for him. Besides, I've wanted a dog for a long time."

Suddenly the front door opened and Sara's daughter, Deanne, came in. She had the same classic beauty as her mother. When she entered the living room they all exchanged greetings. Then she went over to the sofa and sat beside her mother. After she shrugged out of her coat, she put her arm around Sara. "How are you doing, Mom? I couldn't stay away because you need someone to look after you. Did you eat supper?"

"I wasn't hungry."

Deanne looked at Caprice for help. "Can you tell her she has to eat? She didn't eat lunch even with all those casseroles in the refrigerator."

"Maybe a salad later," Sara assured her daughter. "Or some of the soup Caprice brought."

But Caprice understood that Sara was saying that just to calm Deanne's worries.

"I'm not going to let anything happen to *you*, Mom," Deanne promised with vehemence. "If I'd done something about that call that Dad got from Hopkins—"

"What call?" Sara asked, instantly alert.

Deanne looked as if she needed to cleanse herself of guilt. "It was before Labor Day. I had stopped in at the store and was talking to Dad in the office. He had his cell phone lying on the desk. It beeped like it usually did, and I looked down at it. The number that came up on the screen said it was from Johns Hopkins. I handed the phone to him and he went outside to take it. I didn't think much of it at the time. I had an appointment and had to get going, so I left. I should have asked him about it the next time I saw him. I should have." Her voice choked, and Caprice felt sorry for her.

Sara put her arm around her daughter. "If he didn't want us to know, he didn't want us to know. I'm beginning to realize that. I knew he'd been so tired. He seemed more forgetful than usual, but I just thought it was stress. We all missed signs. But we can't blame ourselves for that if he was trying to hide his condition." Sara nodded to Nick as if he'd been right about that. She could see it with her daughter and maybe now she could see it for herself.

Deanne took a tissue from her pocket, dabbed at her eyes, and wiped her nose. Then she stared directly at Caprice. "You've looked into murder investigations before, haven't you?"

"Usually I get caught up in them inadvertently," Caprice responded, afraid of where this was going. "You don't have to worry about the police investigation. I'm sure Mack will keep everybody on their toes. He was your dad's friend, and he won't let him down."

"That might be true," Deanne admitted. "The chief's a good guy. But there's bureaucracy and rules for them to follow. What would you do if you were looking into this?"

Her father gave Caprice a warning look, and she knew what that meant. But she also had to be honest with these women. "I'm sure the police are doing this, but I would look at anyone who had a motive to hurt your dad. Do either of you know of anyone who had a grudge against him?"

Sara was quick to say, "Boyd Arkoff had a grudge.

He was mad because Chris called the police on him. I suppose they could have argued and Boyd lost his temper."

"Did you mention Boyd to the police?" Caprice asked her.

"Yes, I did. And I told them that you were here when he threatened Chris."

"I think Boyd's all bark and no bite," Deanne said. "But there *is* someone who had a big grudge."

In spite of himself, her dad was all ears now too. "Who was that?"

"Bailey Adler," Deanne proclaimed.

"The developer," Caprice murmured.

"Yes. He's sneaky. He tried to date me and convince me to persuade Dad to vote his way. If he was that manipulative, maybe he'd resort to murder."

Caprice asked, "Did you mention him to the police?" She knew they'd all been questioned.

"Yes, I did."

"I have a question for both of you," Caprice said. "Sara, you said that when Chris came back from D.C. this year, he seemed different. Have you talked with the friends he went to D.C. with?"

"No," Sara responded. "I didn't even think about doing that. Mack couldn't go this year. You met Ray Gangloff and the other buddy of his who went was Harrison Barnhart. But I don't know what good it would be to talk to them now."

Maybe it would serve no good at all, but Caprice still wanted to know why Ray Gangloff had wanted to see Chris the day of the open house. She also wondered why Chris's mood had changed after that trip.

Caprice couldn't help herself when she asked,

"Do you have their numbers? If you'd like, I could talk to them. I doubt if I'll turn up anything, but if I do, I'll hand any information I get over to the police."

"I have their numbers on my phone," Sara said. "It's in my purse in the kitchen. I'll go get it."

After her mom had left the room, Deanne said, "Thank you."

"I haven't done anything," Caprice assured her.

"No, but one less thing she has to do right now is a burden off her shoulders. She was never fond of Dad's army buddies, so talking to them isn't something that would help her right now."

As she promised, Caprice would talk to Harrison Barnhart and Ray Gangloff. But first she wanted to have a talk with the chief, who was probably Chris's best friend. What better place to start?

Caprice was getting ready for bed that night when her cell phone played. Mirabelle was already sacked out on her bed, sprawled lengthwise over one of the pillows. Sophia stared at her from on top of the antique, yellow armoire hand-painted with hummingbirds and roses. She only jumped onto the bed after Caprice was in it. Unlike the felines, Lady was wide awake, nudging a ball toward Caprice's foot, just in case she wanted to kick it for her.

Picking up her phone, Caprice said to her canine, "Playtime is over, baby. It's time to settle down." Stooping over she patted Lady's bed and Lady stepped into it, but slowly, as if not sure she was ready for downtime.

As Caprice sat on the side of her bed and saw that Nikki was calling, Lady cocked her head, watching. After all, Caprice might decide to pick up the ball and roll it for her.

"How was your visit?" Nikki asked without preamble. She'd known Caprice was going to see Sara tonight.

"Sad," Caprice answered. "With grief, there's absolutely nothing you can do except let time pass. I really didn't know how to comfort her."

"And with the murder," Nikki added, "her grief might be on hold until some questions are answered. We know about that, don't we?"

"We do from the families of other victims. Not firsthand, thank goodness. I'm going to talk to Mack tomorrow."

Nikki was silent for a few seconds, but then she said, "You know he's off the investigation."

"Which doesn't make a lot of sense since he probably knew Chris best. He's been a cop long enough that he can be objective."

"Those are the rules, Caprice."

"Some rules were made to be broken. There's no reason he can't talk to me about his friendship with Chris."

"I suppose not. As usual, Brett's being closed-mouthed about it. Though he did say he's going to talk to you eventually, since the Merriweathers were your clients."

That didn't surprise her. She'd much rather talk to Brett than Detective Jones. "How are the two of you doing?"

"I like being with Brett. I think he likes being with

me. But this murder investigation could tank our relationship, for sure."

"Because of the long hours he's going to put in at the station?"

"No, that's part of his job. And the truth is, his job isn't a problem for me. It's his attitude. I don't mind the late nights and the canceled dates because I understand that his work is important. But he thinks I deserve better than that. I guess he thinks I deserve better than *him*."

Nikki sounded a bit forlorn, and that meant she really liked the detective.

"Do you want me to talk to him?"

"Of course, I don't. This is between the two of us. If he's going to walk away because he thinks I can't handle his job or because he thinks five years down the line I won't be able to handle his job, that's *his* problem. But I'd rather know it now rather than later."

"If you try to protect yourself, he won't know how you feel."

"I'm plain about how I feel."

"Maybe he needs some time to see that you'll stick by."

"That's what you'd do, give him time?"

"That's what I did with Grant."

In the silence, she knew her sister was thinking about that. Finally, she said, "I guess you did, and it worked out for you. But that doesn't mean it will work out for me. Maybe I'm not as sure of my feelings as you were. Maybe I don't feel I know Brett inside and out, upside and down yet. If he can't open up, I don't know if I want to stick around."

"For what it's worth, I think he's a good man, Nik."

After a pause, Nikki asked, "So you're going to just march into the police department and ask to talk to Mack? That's going to be kind of obvious, don't you think? Maybe you should go see him at home."

"If I go visit him at home and somebody notices, that could be even worse. But you *have* given me an idea."

"I hope it's a good one."

Caprice laughed. "I'll make a batch of Christmas cookies. You know how Mack loves cookies, and I'll take a tray so everybody can enjoy them. It's just my little holiday visit to the police department."

"Smooth," Nikki said, a little wryly. "But it might work. Because you became involved in other murders, I'm sure everyone wants you to stay away from this investigation."

"I'm sure they do, too. That's probably why Brett hasn't called me in yet. I'm just going to nose around a little bit. Sara deserves some answers sooner rather than later. If I unearth anything, I'll tell Brett."

"And you'll probably see him more than I will."

"Nikki . . ." Caprice warned.

"I know, I know. Be optimistic. Write down an affirmation and repeat it. Got it. I'll talk to you after your visit to the police department."

Caprice smiled as she ended the call. She was glad Nikki was her sister.

She gazed around the room at Lady with her head on her paws in her bed, one eye open, and at Sophia ready to jump on the foot of the bed as soon as Caprice put her legs in, and at Mirabelle snoring softly. Then she looked at the engagement ring on her finger that told Caprice she'd soon be marrying the man she loved. She was thankful for her life. She knew in her heart she'd do everything she could to help Sara and her family. That was just what the De Lucas did.

Caprice climbed out of her van in the Kismet police department's parking lot and stopped before she opened the door to retrieve the cookies. On its side, the van was painted with swirling psychedelic colors and a few large flowers. Turquoise lettering read CAPRICE DE LUCA REDESIGN AND HOME STAGING. When she married Grant, she would have to consider keeping her name for professional reasons. Something else they needed to talk about.

Opening the side of the van, she took out the tray of cookies and headed for the building. It had started out as red brick. Over the years, the bricks had worn and mortar had cracked, so a few years ago, the bricks had been repointed and sand blasted. The double glass door at the entrance had replaced the wooden door. One thing about the building that was unique was the bright white cupola on the peaked roof.

She went up to the police officer inside at the front desk and raised the cookie tray. "A Christmas treat for everyone. Can I put it in the break room?"

The police officer, John Platt, had seen her at crime scenes. He grinned at her. "I'm sure those cookies are a thousand times better than the coffee we'll have to go with them. They'll be gone in five minutes." He went to the door that led into the hallway where interrogation rooms and offices were located and opened it for her. "Just to let you know, we're being set up to videotape interviews. It's an advancement we never would have expected. But with the cases we've had in the last couple of years, it seems the right thing to do."

"Thanks for telling me." She wasn't a pariah to everyone on the police force, just Detective Jones. Hopefully he'd be out and about, and she wouldn't run into him.

She deposited the cookies in the break room and before she had the tin foil off the top, two officers were there, smiling, grabbing a napkin and a couple of cookies, and heading back to wherever they'd come from. She certainly wouldn't have to worry about the cookies getting stale. She was debating whether to put the tin foil back on them or not when she heard someone else come inside. She turned to see the chief.

"Just the person I want to see," she said honestly.

He shook his head. "And here I thought you had completely altruistic motives by bringing us cookies."

"If you grab a few, can we talk?"

"Since I'm off the Merriweather investigation, I suppose there's no harm in that. You didn't want to talk about the investigation, did you?"

"Of course not," she said in the same vein. And she lowered her voice. "I want to talk to you about Chris."

He gave her a warning look. "Personal stuff about my friendship with him?"

She nodded.

Crossing to the table with the tray, he grabbed a napkin, three snickerdoodles with red sprinkles, and said, "Follow me. This is a friendly almost-uncle-to-almost-niece visit, so let's keep a low profile."

Her father and Mack Powalski had gone to high school together. Although her dad had been a freshman and Mack a senior, they'd run into each other and gotten along. Mack was drafted into the army out of high school. Chris, who had already been to college and was four years older, had been in a platoon with him.

As Mack settled in the chair behind his desk and laid the cookies with the napkin on the desk, Caprice sat across from him in a hardwood chair. "Did you hear Chris's funeral is on Saturday?" he asked her.

The day after tomorrow. That meant Chris's body had been released. "No, I hadn't heard. I'll let my family know."

Again, Mack just nodded then concentrated on eating one of the cookies. He already had a mug of coffee on his desk and he took a few sips before he focused his gaze on her. "What do you want to know?"

Where to start? she wondered. "Sara said that Vietnam changed Chris. They married before he was sent over?"

"They did. They married as soon as they graduated from college. The draft lottery happened, and he had a low number and he was sent over."

"Sara said you didn't go on the trip to D.C. with Chris this year."

"No, I couldn't make it. I really wanted to, but Martha's mom was sick and we went to spend a few days with her. Chris and I were supposed to get together to talk about his trip to D.C., but life kept getting in the way. Or my job. As you know, murder investigations have kept us busy this year. Lots of paperwork to go with them. Lots of decisions to make for a small PD."

It was better not to be too intense with Mack, to let the subject wander a bit before she got back to other things she wanted to know. "Officer Platt told me you're going to initiate videotaping."

"We are. It's a step forward. In the long run, it should save us time and personnel hours, but there will be a learning curve just as there is with anything new. Some of the older officers will probably buck against it."

She didn't bring up Detective Jones' name, even though he certainly wasn't old. Yet she had the feeling he was set in his ways. "I wish there had been security cameras near the Santa cabin," she said.

Mack shook his head. "I think it will be a long time before the town council agrees to budget money for any security cameras in Kismet. I wouldn't mind a few myself, but there are lots of old-timers who think that means Big Brother is watching. So, we'll see how that shakes out in the future. Remember, you can't ask me anything about the investigation, and it's not as if I know anything because I'm off the case."

He might be off the case but she saw the glint in

his eye. He knew exactly what was going on, even if he couldn't work the interviews and stay on top of the officers himself.

"All right. So, I have a question not directly tied to the investigation. Do you know who beat up Chris?"

At that question, Mack looked shocked. "What do you mean 'beat up'?"

So maybe he didn't know *everything* about the investigation. Maybe the detectives were keeping information from him. She was sure her dad had filled them in.

"My dad asked Chris for some help with set construction at the community center for the Christmas pageant. Dad asked him to stop in the Sunday evening before he was murdered. Chris did. He had a cut high on his forehead and his jaw was bruised. When Dad asked him about it, he said he'd been in a storeroom at the store and a box had fallen down on him."

"So why do you think he was beat up? That's a plausible story."

It was a fact that Mack deduced *plausible* from *implausible* on a daily basis. "Yes. It was plausible. But then Sara told me that she noticed bruises on Chris's ribs. She was worried about him because he wouldn't go to the doctor. Bruised ribs don't account for a box falling on him."

"Not unless it was a heavy box. Not unless the box knocked him to the floor."

"Chris is a sturdy guy . . . *was* a sturdy guy," she corrected herself, feeling a tightening in her throat.

Mack must have seen her emotion. He was silent,

as if thinking over what she'd just said, willing to stop playing devil's advocate. Suddenly he looked troubled. His usual poker face reflected some inner thought that troubled him.

"What?" she asked him.

"I ran into Harrison Barnhart at Grocery Fresh after Kismet's holiday parade. Martha had asked me to pick up a few things for supper on my way home."

Caprice didn't know where this was going so she asked, "Had Harrison Barnhart been at the parade too?"

"He had. And when he swiped his credit card at the checkout line, I noticed he had bruised knuckles."

"As if he'd socked someone's jaw, or maybe punched them in the ribs?"

"I didn't think much of it. Harrison is an outdoor kind of guy, likes to fish, boat, hunt."

"Did you interview Harrison Barnhart?"

"I'm off the case, remember. I'm pretty sure Brett did the interview. He happened to leave it lying on his desk, and I looked it over. There wasn't anything there about an altercation with Chris. Then, of course, would Harrison mention it if it would give him a motive for murder?"

Wasn't that just the question of the year?

Ten minutes later, Caprice left the police department. Mack's phone had buzzed and the mayor was on the line. She knew her interview with him was over, at least for today.

In her van once more, she decided to call her dad to tell him about the funeral. He answered on the first ring.

"Hi, honey. What's up?"

"I was just at the police station to talk to Mack, actually to deliver Christmas cookies. He told me Chris's funeral is on Saturday. I wanted you to know."

"Thanks for telling me. You don't happen to have any extra Christmas cookies do you? I ran out of Nana's biscotti."

"Are you at the office?"

"Nope. I'm home today. I thought it was better if Blitz settled in here, you know, got used to his surroundings. I'm glad the weather's cold for him right now. I suppose in the summer I'll have to keep him in air conditioning. That coat of his is something else. I feel like I should be in Alaska roaming the tundra with him."

"I don't think Mom would be happy in Alaska."

"I don't know how happy she is having a dog in the house."

She could tell her dad just needed to talk. "I'll stop at home, grab a tin of cookies, and bring Lady along. That will give Blitz some company."

"Sounds good. Don't bother to knock," he teased.

A half hour later, climbing the steps to the side porch, holding onto to one of the pillars styled like a rope, she realized this house grounded her. It held so many reminders of the love she'd always known that had prepared her for her adult life . . . that had prepared her for her marriage to Grant.

She didn't knock.

She opened the door that led into a foyer and

unfastened Lady's leash. Lady bounded through the living room and took a left onto the sun porch that was used more on sunny winter afternoons than any other time. Sun poured in the casement windows as her dad sat in an armchair with a book on his lap. At his feet, Blitz stood, shook himself, and greeted Lady, nose to nose. They rounded each other, sniffed at tails, then clambered into the living room.

"Don't go too far," Caprice warned them. At that, Lady ran through the foyer, Blitz close on her heels. She knew they'd probably make a round of the kitchen, a couple of circles around the dining room table, then come back to the sunroom.

Her dad lifted the book that he was reading— *Set Design.* "I think Bella needs all the help she can get."

Caprice had to smile at that. "How's Blitz settling in?"

"He's eating, drinking, and seems to have energy when we go on walks. But he usually won't let me out of his sight. If you bring Lady over more often, that should help."

"I can do that if you don't mind having two dogs to babysit."

"I'm working at home in the library for a few days. I can assemble crews and assign jobs from here. That will give Blitz a chance to settle in and me a chance for some quiet time. Grieving is lonely, but it usually has to be done alone."

She had never lost someone really close to her, and she didn't want to contemplate it. Yet she knew her dad had to. "Mom understands. You can talk to her. I was too young to realize what grief meant when Grandpa Tony died. The same with Mom's parents. I can only imagine the sense of loss."

Her father put the book aside and folded his hands between his knees. "It's not only loss for *now*, but it's loss for the future. No more poker games with Chris. No more late nights drinking beer. For Sara and her family, they'll miss him at every important event. If Deanne gets married, there will be that hole."

"I was really surprised Sara didn't want to keep Blitz. Yes, he'd be a reminder of Chris, but isn't that the whole point of grief, to try to hang onto someone you've lost? She let go so easily."

"Sara's just not a dog lover," her dad said. But then he added, "Chris probably talked to Blitz more than he talked to Sara. They'd married before he went to Vietnam. When he got back, even though he'd changed, they stayed married and weathered the bumps. But I think Chris always held part of himself removed. It was easy for him to play Santa and be kind to strangers' kids. The truth is—I don't know how close he was to his own children, or even to Sara. The proof of that is his secret. I can't even imagine not telling your mother if something was wrong with me, if I received a bad doctor's report. We talk about *everything*."

"I'm hoping Grant and I can do that too."

"It's so important, honey. Vows are important. Loyalty is important. Fidelity is important. But at the base of all of it, it's just how well you can talk to each other. Never, ever let the sun go down without telling each other how you feel."

"I'll remember that," she said. And she would. "I put the cookies on the side table in the foyer. I'd better take them to the kitchen."

The dogs came scrambling back to the sunroom, stopped before Caprice and her dad, sat and looked up at them expectedly.

Her father glanced at her. "They want to go for a walk. Do you have time?"

She had a feeling her dad needed her today just as much as the dogs needed exercise. Yes, she had work to do, and she'd do it even if she had to stay up well past midnight to fit it all in. But right now, she'd take this time to be with her dad.

Chapter Eight

Residents of the town of Kismet poured into St. Francis of Assisi Church on Saturday morning. There had been an early private viewing just for the family, but the funeral Mass was open to all.

The De Luca family, except for Uncle Dom who had stayed back at Caprice's childhood home with Blitz and Lady, slid into a pew about halfway up the aisle. It wasn't long until almost the whole place was filled. Chris knew a lot of people who wanted to grieve along with the family. It didn't take long until no pews were open. Caprice noticed Mack sitting on the other side of the church, and there were two men seated with him. One was Ray Gangloff. Was the other Harrison Barnhart?

Nikki must have been watching for Brett. She motioned to him as he walked in the door and nudged everyone to move over to make room for him. Brett slid into the pew on the other side of Grant.

Grant asked Brett, "Do you want to sit beside Nikki?"

"It's okay," Brett said. "I'm here in an official capacity too. It looks like half the town showed up."

Grant said wryly, "A man who plays Santa Claus has to be well-liked."

Brett returned, "Maybe. But someone had a grudge."

It wasn't long until the processional started, the organist played, and the priest, altar boys, and pall bearers with the casket solemnly strode in. The family trailed behind the casket and followed it up to the front pew. Caprice could see that Sara, Deanne, Maura, and Ryan's wife, Serena, were all teary-eyed and held tissues in their hands.

A movement of Brett's as he shifted in the pew caught Caprice's attention. Focusing on him, she could see he was watching the family carefully. Why was that? She'd have to ask him.

Soon she was caught up in the service and forgot about everything else around her. She teared-up too at the music, the words from scripture, thinking of Chris and his grieving family. After the recessional, when the pews began to empty to follow the priest, altar boys, the casket, and the family out, she stood with everyone else until the casket and the family had left the church. When she reached over and tugged on Brett's suit sleeve, Grant let her step in front of him so she could talk to Brett.

She said in a low voice, "I saw you watching the family. Why was that?"

He looked chagrinned that she'd observed him.

But then he shrugged. "Reactions can tell the truth."

"The truth about how they feel?" she asked.

His brow arched as he answered her. "Yes, and background checks are even better."

At that response, she knew he had his eye on someone. Chris's children? Their spouses? Sara? Any more questions would have to wait until they were back in the social hall after the funeral.

Standing beside Grant at graveside, Caprice spied Mack with Ray and Harrison again. They were all particularly somber. When the flag was presented to Sara, they stood at attention. Because Chris had been a veteran, a gun salute was fired. Grant took Caprice's gloved hand in his. The silence was as deafening as the gunfire.

After the graveside service, Sara and her kids decided to greet friends and acquaintances who had known Chris in the social hall at St. Francis. Since the cemetery was located only a few blocks away, it was practical to come back to the church for the gathering to listen to stories about Chris, to give comfort to each other, to have a body of friends who would promise never to forget him.

Caprice's family headed toward the Merriweathers. But Caprice had her eyes elsewhere.

Grant asked, "Are you coming?"

"In a minute," she said.

With an understanding nod, Grant joined her mom and dad.

Caprice noticed that Mack had come to the social

hall but neither Ray nor Harrison had. She beckoned to Mack to join her at a table.

He did, saying, "Thanks. It's easy to stick out like a sore thumb at these things."

"I saw you with Ray Gangloff and was that Harrison Barnhart?"

"Yes, that's right. They both had to leave."

"Good reasons to leave, rather than expressing their condolences to the family?"

Mack eyed her carefully. "They might have already done that. We don't know."

"No, we don't, but it would be good to find out, don't you think?"

"Now, Caprice—"

Yes, that was a warning note in his voice, and she ignored it. "Can you tell me anything about them? You know, personal stuff."

"Pure human interest?"

"Of course."

Mack gave her that I-know-what-you're-doing look again, but this time he answered her. "Harrison isn't married. I don't think he's ever *been* married. And Ray is at the opposite end of the scale. He's divorced. In fact, he's living at home with his parents to help them out when they need it."

Caprice knew the two men might clam up with the police, but they might also open up to *her* in the right atmosphere.

She asked Mack, "Did Chris and Harrison and Ray hang out together much? Other than their yearly trip?"

"He mentioned getting together with them now and then for a beer. Sometimes I joined them."

"Anywhere in particular?"

"Chris didn't have a whole lot of extra time, not with the store hours he kept, his charity work, craft fairs, and then this time of year playing Santa."

"But you said you did meet up."

"I saw him on poker nights. When we met up with Harrison and Ray, it was usually at Susie Q's."

Caprice had heard of Susie Q's. It was a sports bar downtown. Nikki and Vince had attended singles events there. "Is it mostly singles who go there?"

Mack thought about it. "Mostly guys who want to hang out, young couples, and maybe young girls, above drinking age of course, who want to meet guys their age. That's the circus, Caprice. Be glad you're out of it."

Mack suddenly stared at Chris's family, then a far-away look came into his eyes. "I'm having a tough time with Chris's death."

Caprice put her hand on Mack's shoulder. "I'm so sorry, Uncle Mack." She hadn't called him that for a while, but it was what she'd known him as when she'd been a child.

"A death like this makes me think: What do I want to do with the rest of my life? What do Martha and I want to do? Maybe we should forget about all the have-to's, maybe buy an RV, visit our kids across the country and spend some time with them. What do you think?"

"I think it's a perfectly good idea if it would make you happy. Would it?"

"I don't know," he responded, running his hand through his gray hair, now thinning at the part. I feel like I need to catch some bad guys in between. Know what I mean?"

"It's been your work all these years. Of course, I know what you mean. Let me ask you something. I know you're not privy to the investigation, at least not all of it, but just from the hubbub at the station, can you tell if they think it's going to be solved sooner rather than later?"

"From what I've heard so far, Caprice, it could be as hard finding the right clue as it would have been to find the right treatment for Chris's brain tumor." Now he put his arm around her shoulders. "Come on. Let's go find your family and give our condolences to Sara."

Although Caprice and her dad had spoken with Sara and Deanne since Chris's death, seeing the Merriweather family and speaking with them now still was difficult. Caprice hugged each one. They all seemed similarly affected by Chris's death. Even the men found it hard to hide their grief and their somber expressions said they missed Chris.

Reed held Maura's hand while Ryan had his arm around his wife's waist, as if by being protective of her he was gaining comfort too.

Caprice asked Sara, "How are you holding up?"

Chris's widow shook her head. "I feel like a robot, just going through the motions. After today maybe I can process it all. Choosing scripture and songs for Mass gave me something to do." She motioned to the food outlay in the social hall. "Planning this did too. I have a meeting with Jeremiah Pickens this afternoon to go over legal issues. But after that, that house is going to be way too quiet."

Caprice knew that long before Vince had become an attorney, Chris had engaged Jeremiah Pickens to handle his business affairs as well as his will.

Overhearing, Maura stepped closer. "Mom went to see the condo again that Dad liked. I went with her. I think it will suit her."

Ryan stepped in now too. "I don't know about that, Maura. Mom's memories are in that house. Dad's presence is there." He shook his head and addressed Sara. "I can't believe you're thinking about moving."

"We've been all over this," Sara said wearily. "I don't know what's going to happen with the business. I'm going to talk with Jeremiah about that today."

"You're not going to sell the business too?" Ryan looked horrified.

"I don't know what I'm going to do. The expenses with a house that size, the utilities alone, might be beyond my budget. My objective will be to get expenses down as best I can."

Maura's husband, Reed, stepped into the conversation. In his forties, he was older than Maura. His life experience was evident in his comment. "If you sell the house now, you'll have to be prepared to invest the money that doesn't go into the condo. Do you have someone to do that for you?"

"I have a list of friends' recommendations. I have to check them out. I just don't have the energy for that right now."

Reed nodded. "That's what I mean. It might be best if you hold on to the house at least until spring."

"Reed could be right, Mom," Maura said. "You really shouldn't make any major decisions right now."

Caprice certainly couldn't fault Sara's family for that suggestion because it was true.

"I don't know what I'll find when I go through all of Chris's papers," Sara admitted. "I began sorting his desk last night. I found bills he'd paid from Hopkins that insurance didn't cover." Tears came to her eyes. "He took care of the bills and the supplemental insurance. Now I have to find our policies and figure out where we stand. I just wish he had confided in me and not gone through the news of his medical condition and the prognosis all alone."

Ryan's wife Serena frowned. "You know, Sara, the way Chris died was awful. But bludgeoning might have been a much kinder way to die than a brain tumor."

Sara looked appalled by that opinion. But Caprice glanced at the family's faces. It was obvious that Reed and Ryan agreed with Serena's assessment.

Nana and Caprice's mom, who had been speaking with Maura, now stepped over to talk with Sara. Caprice spotted Grant talking to Father Gregory. Others milled about waiting to give their condolences too.

Caprice nudged her dad's arm and he nodded. "Let's get something to eat. Your mom, Nana, and Grant will be along shortly."

As Caprice started for the food table, she was thinking about what Brett had said and wondering if he did background checks on everyone in the family. She was so deep in thought that she almost ran into someone.

When she looked up, she saw who it was: Detective Jones.

He didn't give a nod or even say hello. He just side-stepped her and headed for the other side of the social hall. To talk to some of the guests? To wait until the family was free?

Caprice said to her dad. "That was a snub if I ever felt one."

"He doesn't want to acknowledge that you've helped the police department more than once."

"He doesn't have to acknowledge it, but he doesn't have to be rude about it either."

"Detective Jones is who he is. You're just going to have to accept the fact you can't make friends with everyone," her father advised her philosophically.

She didn't like that idea. She didn't like it at all.

Glancing over the array of food, Caprice chose a fresh fruit cup, then ambled a little farther down the table, selecting a ham and cheese sandwich. She added a dollop of potato salad to her plate.

Her dad, who was right beside her, picked up the equivalent of two sandwiches cut into little triangles and added generous amounts of potato salad, macaroni salad, and a spoonful of a cauliflower cheddar casserole to his plate. "Blitz and I will have to take an extra-long walk this afternoon," he said as he grabbed a handful of chips.

"Uncle Dom might take him to the dog park," Caprice offered.

"I think I'm going to be spending a lot of time

there. He's well-behaved enough that your mom could walk him too."

"Maybe you could walk him together. It could be the start of a new exercise program."

"I might suggest that. Your mom always says she doesn't get enough exercise when school's in session."

As she and her father crossed to a table, she saw him glance toward the Merriweather family again. "You know, as much as I hate to admit it, and as much as you probably don't want to hear it, Sara might be better served to wait to sell the house. Reed was right about not making decisions at least for the first six months. And from what Sara said, she's going to have to wade through Chris's finances."

Once they were at their table and seated, Caprice confided in her dad. "I think Brett's looking hard at the family."

At her dad's surprised look, she added, "In case any of them had any motive to want Chris gone. Do you know if they did? You said the other day you didn't think the kids were close to their dad. Why did you say that?"

Her father looked pensive. Then he sighed. "Brett's probably looking into Ryan's background. He had his share of problems in high school— truancy, a rebellious attitude, and even drugs."

"I never heard anything about that."

"Chris and Sara tried to keep it hushed up. They enrolled Ryan in one of those wilderness programs when he was sixteen."

"You mean where they send the kids out West for some kind of survivalist training?"

Her father's look was troubled. "Exactly. Chris

showed me the brochure. Long hikes in uncharted terrain, overnight stays in tents no matter what the weather, sessions with counselors more than once a day. In a way, they try to break the kids . . . get them to hit bottom so they have to trust someone when they come up for air. I don't know if I approve. I'm not sure Chris did. But he and Sara didn't know what else to do."

"Did it help?" Caprice asked.

"It seemed to. When Ryan came back, he was like a different kid. He *seemed* to have straightened out."

Caprice noticed her dad's emphasis on the word *seemed*.

"But?" she prompted. "What aren't you saying?"

"From what Chris told me, Ryan didn't turn to drugs again. But after he returned to Kismet, he had a chip on his shoulder toward Chris that was never resolved."

"Did he resent his dad for sending him out there?"

"He did, and he seemed to lay it all on Chris's shoulders. It was as if he forgave Sara but not his dad. I suppose he thought Chris researched it, found the program, and made the decision to send him there. For the most part, he was right about that."

"Ryan moved away from Kismet, didn't he?" Caprice inquired. She seemed to remember the fact that he'd lived in Chicago for a while.

"After he graduated from high school, Ryan went to college and hardly ever came home. He met his wife at Northwestern his senior year. They eloped to Las Vegas without inviting anyone in the family to the wedding. Then they lived in a suburb in Chicago. But they've lived in York now for a few years. They moved back here when Serena was pregnant. Ryan had just quit another job and was looking for work."

"But they don't have any children."

"Soon after they moved back here, she had a miscarriage."

"That must have been hard on all of them."

"You'd think so. I do know Chris and Sara helped them financially until Ryan found his job as manager of a phone store."

"Sara's probably going to need help with the craft store. Do you think Ryan would help her with that?"

"I don't know. Serena is working at a jewelry store at the Galleria Mall in York. Chris and Sara helped them with the down payment on a small house there."

"Why not in Kismet?" Caprice asked.

"Even though Ryan moved back here, I think he still wanted to keep some distance between him and his parents. I don't think he forgave them for whatever his experiences were out West."

"So, he might hold a grudge."

"He might."

"Do you think he's capable of hurting his dad?"

Her father took a long moment to answer. "I don't know him well enough to even guess. I'd certainly like to think it's something he wouldn't even contemplate."

"But in the heat of the moment—"

"Even in the heat of the moment, I'd like to think

that's something that would never happen." Her father picked up a sandwich and took a large bite.

Her father's troubled expression and her fondness for Sara urged Caprice to consider making a stop at the phone store in the near future.

A short while later, her family seated at the table to enjoy the light meal, Caprice considered everyone who could be a suspect—Ryan, Boyd Arkoff, Bailey Adler, Ray Gangloff, Harrison Barnhart. Grant, who was seated to her right, leaned close to her and bumped his shoulder against hers. "You haven't touched the food on your plate."

"I'm really not hungry."

"What's wrong?"

"Just look at how many people are here. Everyone has a story about Chris: how he made their kids laugh, how he was a good friend, how he brought a food basket to their door when they needed it. Yet he told no one, absolutely no one, that he was sick. Does that make any sense?"

"We don't know for sure that he told no one," Grant said. "He didn't tell his family, but who knows who he might have confided in? Are you sad because you think he was lonely despite of all the good he did?"

"Maybe. I think as Sara said, Blitz was his best friend. I do want to talk to Harrison Barnhart and Ray Gangloff, but they left right after the graveside service. I have to wonder why. Why wouldn't they want to be here with Chris's family?"

"You're operating on a woman code."

She leaned away from him. "What's that supposed to mean?"

"It just means that you're thinking about what *you* would do, or your sisters would do, or your mom would do. But many guys don't think that way. We really don't know what kind of friendship Chris had with Ray and Harrison. Yes, they were in the service together. But did their friendship go beyond that? I know that's what you want to ask them, but I'm not sure it's going to give you any answers."

Sometimes Grant's practicality irked her, but other times she realized how reasonable he was. He did have a different perspective than she did on many subjects, and she appreciated that.

He leaned in close to her again clearly not wanting to be overheard. "While you were talking with your dad, I had a conversation with a client of mine who's on the town council. And don't ask me who, because he's my client and I don't want to divulge that."

Doggone it, she hadn't seen who he'd talked to after she noticed him speaking with Father Gregory. She'd been too engrossed in her conversation with her father. Still, it wasn't who Grant talked to but what the person said. "Did you learn anything?"

"I did. It's true that Bailey Adler was campaigning hard to have those homes torn down on Restoration Row. And Chris stood in his way. I also learned that he does have an eye for younger women, so I think Deanne was telling the truth when she said he'd tried to date her. His reasons were probably two-fold. She's a beautiful young woman, but he also wanted her to convince Chris to vote his way. My client said that Adler learned early on that when Chris took a stand on an issue, he didn't budge from it."

"If Adler removed Chris from his path, he could make lots of money. If he murdered Chris, that could have been premeditated."

"Or they could have gotten into an argument. Chris wouldn't budge. Adler was furious." Grant was silent for a few seconds and then said, "I can't believe you're sucking me into this suspect game again."

"It's not a game," Caprice said seriously.

"Don't I know it. You had a concussion not so long ago because you tangled with the wrong person. Do you think I want that happening to you again?"

She turned to Grant, reached out, and touched his jaw. "Don't go all protective on me. I know you don't want me to get hurt any more than I want *you* to get hurt."

"If you're going to continue this vocation of yours, to step into murder investigations, you really should get some cop training. I don't just mean self-defense. I mean how to be on the lookout, how to stealthily sneak in somewhere, how to stealthily sneak out."

"I can talk to Brett about it."

"He'd have my head for suggesting it. No. If you'd want to do something like that, I think you'd have to do it out of the area, on the QT."

"Would you do it with me?"

"I knew I never should have suggested it," he muttered.

"I'm sure you have some kind of program in

mind. We could go away for the weekend. It could be fun."

"At least you're smiling again," he said, touching her cheek now. "I really do have a weird fiancée when surveillance training can make her smile."

"I never said I was normal."

"I'd kiss you for that comment, but it doesn't seem appropriate here."

Sara's son Ryan suddenly whisked by their table in a hurry to stride out of the room. He looked as if a thunder cloud had overtaken him.

"I wonder what that's about."

Ryan's sister Maura rushed after him trying to catch up.

"Funerals as well as weddings bring out every emotion a family can experience," Grant said. "Some old storm might have come to light again."

"Dad told me Ryan was in trouble when he was in high school: drugs. Sara and Chris sent him to one of those wilderness training camps out West. But Dad doesn't think Ryan ever forgave Chris for sending him away."

"Another grudge?" Grant asked. "If he had a temper and Chris had a temper, and they both flared at the same time, anything could have happened."

"I don't want to believe that."

"I know you don't." Grant moved Caprice's plate away and pushed her fruit cup in front of her. Then he handed her a spoon. "The fruit's fresh and you need sustenance. Eat, please."

"You're a good fiancé."

"Just good?" he asked, waggling an eyebrow.

"You're a great fiancé." She squeezed his arm in thanks and picked up her spoon.

However, the whole time she was eating her fruit cup, she was thinking of kids and parents, buddies in Vietnam, husbands and wives. Someone had killed Chris Merriweather, and she wanted to help figure out who that someone was.

Chapter Nine

The following evening, Caprice returned home about 6 p.m. from an interview with a new client. Lady met her at the door, and even Sophia and Mirabelle came into the foyer and looked up at her as if saying, *Our supper is late!*

"Don't you make me feel guilty," she told the three of them. "I gave you snacks before I left. Sophia, you even had your dollop of cream." Sophia was one of those cats who could tolerate dairy. Her dollop of cream kept her fur healthy and her mood mellow.

After Caprice removed her coat and hung it on the antique oak stand in her foyer, she took her purse with her to the counter in the kitchen equipped with buttercup-colored vintage appliances. Opening the back door for Lady, she let her outside. She stood on the porch while Lady did her business and did it quickly. After all, she was hungry for supper.

Caprice cleaned up, washed up, fed her trio of pets, and put a square of lasagna in the microwave to warm for herself. She froze squares of it then thawed them out for quick and easy suppers. Knowing she needed to eat something healthier with it, she fixed herself a salad, sprinkled it with peach vinegar, and settled down to eat, enjoying the company of her pets.

She was just finishing up when her doorbell rang. Checking the portable monitor on the kitchen counter, she saw it was her dad and Blitz.

Quickly she went to the door and opened it. "Hi, Dad. This is unexpected. I just got home a little while ago. Come on in."

Wondering if something was wrong, she gave her dad a hug and then stooped down to pet Blitz. He rubbed against her Katharine Hepburn–style cranberry slacks and she massaged his shoulders under his furry coat. "I bet you like this colder weather, don't you?"

He looked up at her with glistening eyes. If those eyes were in a human, Blitz would be considered an old soul. There was knowing there and maybe understanding too.

"Would you like a slice of chocolate loaf?" she asked her dad. "I made a batch for Grant this afternoon. Well, one for him and one to keep here for when he's here."

Her dad shook his head and unzipped his parka. "I'm too upset to eat."

She could see that in her dad's expression and his rigid stance and the way he was already pacing her foyer. Blitz paced with him.

Lady trotted in to greet Blitz and the two of them ran around Caprice's downstairs, ending up in the foyer again. Lady had been cooped up pretty much all day, and maybe Blitz needed some fresh air too. She had a feeling her dad didn't want to be confined either.

She said, "Let me put on my coat. We can take the dogs out back and let them romp while we talk."

"It's cold out there," her father warned.

"My coat's warm." She reached for the calf-length faux fur with its hood. She patted her hip and said to Lady, "Come on, girl. Let's go out."

All Lady needed to hear was *out*. The same must have been true for Blitz because he followed the cocker spaniel to the door.

Sophia and Mirabelle, who had settled on the yellow braided cushions on two of the kitchen chairs, watched the parade go by them with barely a blink of their eyes.

Out on the porch, the dogs quickly went down the steps into the yard, ran to and fro and snuffled around the edges of shrubs.

Caprice motioned to the robin-egg blue fifties-style glider on her porch. She sat and her dad sat beside her. "Tell me what's wrong," she said.

"Sara called me. She was terrifically upset."

"She has every right to be upset."

"This is about more than Chris's murder," her father responded. "She and the kids went to the lawyer's office yesterday. Chris's will was read."

Caprice didn't quite understand. Why should Sara be upset about that? Unless—

"Is there something in the will that Sara didn't know about?"

"Oh, yes. I can hardly believe it myself, and yet in other ways I can."

Since Caprice had learned listening was a gift, she waited so her dad could tell what he had to say in his own time and in his own words.

"Apparently, Chris had his lawyer set up a trust fund years ago that she didn't know anything about!"

With her mind racing, Caprice thought about all the possibilities for that trust fund. Then her father added facts she'd never suspected.

"When Chris was in Vietnam, he had an affair."

As Caprice tried to absorb *that* bombshell, her dad went on. "The result was a son. After Chris came home, he sent money whenever he could. After he gained success with the craft store, he set up a trust fund for the boy. He's been sending checks twice a year. On his death," her father further explained, "his will directed a lump sum payment to be sent to the young man."

"Oh, my goodness," Caprice said, feeling for Sara and the rest of the family too. "What a shock."

"Sara's stunned. She can't believe it. She never had an inkling."

The dogs, checking in with their humans, came to the porch and sat in front of the glider.

Caprice absently pet Lady. "Do you think Mack knows?"

"I don't know. Your mom and Nana were at a meeting at church tonight and I couldn't talk this over with them. I didn't want to overreact or do something I shouldn't. But I do think maybe I should talk to Mack. What do you think?"

"I think it's a good idea, but we should do it face-to-face. Shall we ask him to come here?"

"Let me give him a call and see what he's up to. I'll play it by ear."

When Caprice's dad called Mack, he learned that he was just leaving the station. He told him he had something important to talk to him about and asked him to stop at Caprice's. Mack said he wanted to know what it was about, but her dad just told the chief he'd tell him when he got there.

Caprice heard her dad say, "I don't like surprises either. But I had one and I need to talk to you about it."

While they waited, Caprice made coffee and cut slices of the chocolate loaf. Setting them on a turquoise stoneware plate, she placed it on the table. The coffee had just finished brewing when Mack arrived.

The cats had since vacated the chairs and were happy lounging on the cat tree in the living room. Caprice let Mack in, and after greetings led him to the kitchen. She took his coat and hung it around a kitchen chair.

Mack faced her dad. "Now what's going on? We're not in some kind of spy movie."

"No, we're not," her father agreed. "Have a seat. There's something I want to ask you."

Mack seated himself warily but looked a little more relaxed once Caprice placed a cup of coffee in front of him and offered him a slice of the chocolate loaf.

He slid a slice from the serving plate to a dessert

dish and picked up his fork. "All right. What's this about?"

Her father said, "Sara found out yesterday that Chris had an affair when he was in Nam and he has a son."

Mack tried to keep his face expressionless but he didn't succeed.

"Tell me the truth, Mack. Did you know?"

The chief laid down his fork, apparently his appetite for chocolate loaf forgotten. He frowned. "I knew about the affair but not about the son. I've kept the secret all these years."

He stopped, looking pensive. "Maybe I made excuses for Chris. I know infidelity is a horrible thing in a marriage, but Chris—he and Sara were young when they got married. Soon after, he was sent to Nam. He never intended to be unfaithful. He wasn't that kind of man. But war and death, needing solace, not knowing if he'd live or die, led him to a friendship with a beautiful young woman. He didn't know if he'd ever see Sara again, and he fell in love with Kim. But I thought his association with her was truly over when he came home." Mack shook his head. "A son. I can't believe Chris never told me."

"It seems Chris kept many secrets," her dad said, almost angrily. "Apparently, Kim died several years ago. Their son Trung works in management in a shoe production factory in Ho Chi Minh City."

"The knowledge that Chris had a son had to be devastating to Sara. How is she?" Mack asked.

"Shell-shocked," her father answered. "I'm not sure she knows which way to turn. Her life—her marriage—has been shaken up. It's going to take her a while to find her bearings and decide what she wants to do next."

"Apparently, you've become someone she confides in," Mack suggested, giving her father a steady look.

Her dad said, "I know. I don't know why she didn't call *you* instead of me."

"Maybe my position as chief of police has something to do with that, or maybe she felt betrayed by me too. Maybe she guessed that I knew about the affair."

"It was a burden to keep that secret, wasn't it?" Caprice asked Mack.

"Yes, it was. Yet in a way, it seemed like a past life. Chris and I didn't talk about it. I thought Chris had put it behind him. I thought he was just dealing with PTSD all these years."

"Did *you* have problems with PTSD?" Caprice asked Mack.

"I did. For years. My wife was a saint. She had to go through some bad times with me, just like Sara did with Chris. Fortunately, she talked to our family physician about it, and he put me in touch with a group of guys who'd gone through something similar. That group saved me."

"Was Chris part of that group?" Caprice asked.

"Oh, no. He didn't want any part of something like that. Or maybe the reason was, what happened with Kim would have come out. He wasn't going to let anyone know about that."

"Except maybe Father Gregory," Caprice mused. "And he, of course, could tell no one."

They all sat there solemnly thinking about it.

Finally, Caprice suggested, "Don't you think Brett should know about this?"

"I can't tell him," Mack said. "I'm not supposed to have anything to do with the investigation."

"I can tell him," Caprice decided. "If he wants more information, he'll have to talk to Sara. But at least he'll have the basics."

"He's at the station now almost twenty-four hours a day," Mack said.

"I'll convince him to have lunch or coffee with me. After all, he has to take time to eat," Caprice maintained.

"He barely does. Nikki has been bringing food to his office. All the other guys are jealous."

"I'm glad she's doing something positive to stay in touch with him. I have a feeling he puts a wall up when he works like this."

"He has to, Caprice. Part of him has to stay detached. Besides, he can't go spilling everything to Nikki, and that's probably what she'd want."

"Not if he'd tell her he can't." She wished these men would stop underestimating her sister.

"Sore spot?" Mack asked.

"Not for me but for the two of them."

"Anyone involved with a cop usually doesn't stay involved long," Mack said with regret.

"Nikki's not a saint, but she has a well of understanding if Brett would just give her a chance," Caprice pointed out.

"I'm staying out of it," Mack said, pulling that chocolate loaf closer now. "When we were in Nam, I warned Chris not to get involved with Kim. That advice did no good. So I stay out of everybody's love life. That's safer for me and for them."

Caprice didn't know if staying neutral was the best thing to do or not. What if Sara had found out about Chris's affair? Would she have forgiven him? Would that have made their marriage stronger? Would the fact that he didn't have to lie to her make their bonds better? Those were questions she'd never have the answers to.

While Mack and her dad sipped on their coffee and each ate a second piece of the chocolate loaf, Caprice called Brett. She simply told him she had information that might help his case, but she didn't want to come to the station.

"I need to talk to you about the Merriweathers. I'll text you tomorrow when I can get free," he told her. "Maybe I can make it to the Sunflower Diner. Good for you?"

"Good for me. I'll fit you in whenever your schedule allows."

After she ended the call, she realized she wasn't sure what this information had to do with the murder, if anything. But it was a lead and a strong one. Now maybe they would get some answers.

Caprice wanted to meet with Brett as soon as she could, but he couldn't get free until later in the afternoon on Monday. She had to get her mind back on work anyway. She had a job to do and this one was going to be enjoyable. Her assistant Juan would be meeting her at Ace Richland's estate. They were going to be decorating the rock legend's house for Christmas. He was having a party in a week and he wanted the house to proclaim "Christmas."

Since Caprice was in and out of Ace's estate now and then, his housekeeper texted her the new code to get through his gates whenever he changed it. She punched in the code and the gates opened for her. After she drove up the drive and parked, she crossed to his front door, remembering the night she'd met Grant there—the night he'd proposed.

Instead of Mrs. Wanamaker, his housekeeper, Ace himself met her at the door, his green eyes twinkling, his spiked brown hair not quite as stiff as usual, his earring that was at least two carats of sparkling diamond catching the light. He gave Caprice an encompassing hug. They'd become friends through her efforts decorating his house and discussing common backgrounds. He was really Al Rizzo from Scranton, Pennsylvania, and an Italian through and through. They'd gotten to know each other even better through his days as a suspect in his girlfriend's murder. She'd helped clear him, and he'd always be grateful for that. Besides all that, she'd become pals with his daughter, Trista. Trista had taken a pup from the same litter as Lady and named Lady's sister Brindle.

Ace leaned away from her now and asked, "Still happy about the engagement?"

"Wonderfully happy."

"Good. I can't wait until your wedding actually takes place."

"And why is that?"

"Because I want to believe there's hope in the institution."

She gave him a shrewd look, wondering what was behind those words. But he just grinned at her. "Your assistant already okayed the deliveries of Christmas trees and flower arrangements, and the house is starting to look holiday prepared. Even more so now that Trista is here."

"She is?"

"Her mom took her out of school for a couple of days. They're both staying here while Marsha house hunts in the area."

"So that's still a possibility?"

"Very much so, according to Marsha."

"And what about you? Will you be glad she'll be in the vicinity?"

"I'll be more than glad Trista will be close by. We can spend even more time together when I'm around. The tour is taking up so much of my time now that the less traveling we have to do, the better."

"And having Marsha nearby?"

From the way they'd been acting when she'd seen them the past few times, they were more than amicable.

"We've been having lots of long conversations. Let's just leave it at that."

Juan came into the foyer then. He said to Caprice, "Give me your coat and we'll get started. You can see what I've done. Check if you want to change anything."

"You go ahead," Ace said. "I have work to finish in my studio downstairs. Trista is up in her bedroom with Brindle. I'll alert her on the intercom that you're here. She'll be disappointed you didn't bring Lady."

"With live Christmas trees, strings of twinkle lights, and garlands with berries, I just thought this time it would be better if I didn't. But I'll bring her by soon to see Trista and Brindle after we're finished. I promise."

Juan said, "Let's start with the kitchen. I used copper canisters, red velvet, and white silk flowers."

"Sounds elegant." A few minutes later as she looked around the kitchen, she said, "And it looks just as elegant. I like that Christmas tree by the door."

"Trista helped me decorate it. She has a decorator's eye."

"When I redecorated her room for her, she knew exactly what she wanted. She does have a good eye."

They moved into the dining room and Caprice suggested greenery across the top of the hutch, a huge red poinsettia with glitter for the table, and Christmas balls in a Waterford vase.

"Red and gold?" he asked.

"That will set off the china," she responded. "I think we need some of those ten-inch diameter pillar candles too. Ace probably won't light them, but they'll give off a bayberry scent and add cheer."

"How's it going with the Merriweathers' house? Are they still going to sell?" Juan asked.

"I don't know if Sara and her children know what they want to do. And she probably shouldn't make any decisions, not within the next few months anyway. It's such a heartbreaking situation. Chris knew so many people. In some ways, that makes grieving even more difficult for Sara."

"There are rumors," Juan said.

"What kind of rumors?"

"Something about an illegitimate child of Chris's."

"I can't believe information has gotten out already. Where did you hear this?"

"At the Koffee Klatch. We live in a small town, Caprice. Somebody there said they heard talk about it when they were in the phone store that Ryan manages."

Caprice shook her head. "I imagine the family's talking about it because they're so shocked. But talking about it in public with friends who can't keep their mouths shut is just going to lead to more talking about it."

"I heard something else too," Juan admitted.

What else could there be? Though she knew this is how the gossip tree worked in Kismet—one branch dropping leaves onto another, some true, some not so true. If she could squelch unfounded rumors, she would.

"A friend of mine was at Susie Q's a couple of weekends ago."

The sports bar again. That name had come up before.

"And?" she prompted, eager to get away from gossip and get back to decorating. Yet she knew Juan didn't gossip idly, and if he thought she should know something, then maybe she should.

"I heard you're involved again . . . in figuring out who killed Chris."

"No, I'm not. I mean, I'm not actively searching.

That's the police's job. Brett Carstead is on it, and so is Jones, for that matter. They're not going to let this one go unsolved. There's a lot of pressure coming from several directions. Mack can't even have a hand in the investigation because he was Chris's friend. So, they're really stepping up their game to do this without him."

"But you *are* keeping your ears open for anything important?"

She had to be honest with Juan. They worked closely together and could trust each other. "Yes, I am."

"As I said, my friend was at Susie Q's. He'd gone out back for a smoke and ran smack dab into a fight."

"Who was involved?"

"Chris Merriweather and a guy who was bigger than he was. My friend knew Chris because his picture's been in the paper. It has been every year he's played Santa, and there's publicity for his store too. So, he recognized him right away. He said Chris was getting the worst of the action. When the other guy saw my friend, he pushed Chris into the wall and left."

"Your friend didn't call the police or anything?"

"Would *you* want to get involved with the cops? Never mind. Don't answer that. He did ask Chris if he needed an ambulance. He had a cut on his head. He was holding his jaw and his ribs. But Chris Merriweather wouldn't let him make the call. He said he was fine and he walked away, or hobbled away. He was a little bent over from those blows to his ribs."

"And your friend gave no description of the guy who was beating him up?"

"Just that he was big—tall and husky like a line-backer."

That could be a description for either Ray Gangloff or Harrison Barnhart. Both were big men, and if Mack had seen bruised knuckles on Harrison Barnhart—

Caprice touched Juan's arm. "Thank you for let-ting me know. I'll be seeing Brett later today. I'll talk about it with him. Can you give me your friend's name?"

"Not without permission. So, just see what Brett says. If it's necessary, I'll ask him to come forward."

"Will do."

Just then, Trista came running into the dining room with Brindle close by her side. Brindle looked very much like Lady though her coloring wasn't quite as golden dark. Her ears were definitely lighter, but she was a beauty and sweet . . . just like Lady.

Trista gave Caprice a big hug. "Dad says I can decorate with you if it's okay. I've been helping Juan."

"He told me. That Christmas tree in the kitchen looks terrific. He says you have a good eye."

Trista, at thirteen years old, looked as proud as could be from the compliment. She wore the latest fashion: slim-legged jeans, a long sweater that came mid-calf with a bateau neck and worn over a shirt in a contrasting color. Tall and lanky, she took after her dad, not only in her leanness but in her long face, her chestnut hair, and her very green eyes. She was getting prettier day by day, and soon Ace would probably have to fight off her boyfriends or at least give them fair warnings.

"The living room has barely been started, so we can have a blast in there. What would you like to help me with most?" Caprice asked.

"I don't know if this goes with your decoration theme, but Mom let me bring along a Nativity set that she and Dad had when they were first married. Can we set that up somewhere? The figures are hand-carved and really beautiful. The stable is made of real miniature logs."

"I'm sure we can find the right place for it. Let's go look."

"I'll finish up in here," Juan said. "Then I'll come help you, or I can move on to Ace's den." He was giving her a look that said he understood if she wanted to spend some time with Trista or Trista wanted some alone time with her.

"Ace's den sounds good," Caprice said. "Just try to keep it toned down a bit in there—pine arrangements, maybe with some of that leopard ribbon, gold balls, and copper ones."

"Will do," Juan said as Caprice and Trista went into the living room. Caprice gave the room a look, keeping her mind on Trista and the job and not what Juan had just told her about Chris.

She asked Trista, "Where do you think the Nativity set would look good. How big's the stable?"

"It's about a foot and a half high."

While Brindle sniffed at boxes that Juan had

brought in that contained everything from vases to antique balls to artistically crafted ornaments, Trista pointed to the bookshelves beside the floor-to-ceiling stone fireplace. "How about on that biggest shelf in the middle? We could remove the books."

"Sure, we can. Do you need help bringing the set down from your room?"

"Yes, I could use the help. The stable is in a big box, and some of the figures are in there with it. But then there are two other boxes."

"Before we set up the stable, you might want to think what you want for a background for it. Pine boughs? Or maybe grapevine branches? Possibly a tapestry scarf underneath it all."

"The grapevine would be different, and I like the idea of a multicolored scarf under it instead of just red or green," Trista decided.

"I think I have an antique one that I got from Isaac's shop in one of the boxes. It's threaded with gold and has gold fringes."

"That sounds perfect."

As they went to the stairway and started up, Brindle ran ahead of them.

"I thought you'd bring Lady," Trista commented.

"I'll stop in tomorrow with her and the two of them can have a play date. I'll still be putting finishing touches on here, I'm sure."

"Great," Trista said enthusiastically. "Brindle gets to see Lady, and I get to see you again."

Caprice capped the girl's shoulder. "Do you like the idea of moving back here if your mom is house hunting?"

"I do, and not just to be closer to Dad."

"Why else?"

"I'm hoping Mom and Dad get back together again."

From friends and what she'd heard, that's the fantasy of most children of divorced parents. She didn't want Trista to have her bubble burst or to be terribly disappointed if it didn't happen.

"What does your mom say about that?"

"I don't talk to her about it. But she and Dad don't argue now. They've been getting along and they seem to like spending time with each other."

"They both like spending time with *you*."

"I'll tell you a secret."

Caprice caught Trista's conspiratorial mood. "What's the secret?"

"They went on a date the last time Dad was in Virginia, and when they came home, he stayed over. I'm not a little girl anymore, Caprice. I know what that means."

Trista thought she knew what that meant, but Caprice didn't want to be the one to explain to her that having sex didn't always mean love was in the air. Sometimes the two did go together. That's why she and Grant were waiting. The love was there, and the anticipation about sex would bring them even closer together.

"I know what you're going to say," Trista said. "Don't get my hopes up. But I want to hope, especially at Christmas."

Caprice gave Trista's shoulder a squeeze. "All right, honey, I'll hope along with you."

Trista nodded then ran up the rest of the steps to the second floor.

Chapter Ten

Caprice ended up meeting Brett at the Sunflower Diner around 3 p.m. The off hour was probably a good thing because there weren't many people around. She ordered hot chocolate and he ordered coffee. The hot chocolate at the Sunflower was rich and thick with lots of whipped cream, but that wasn't why she was here today.

"I'm glad you could meet me," she said.

All business, as he was most of the time, Brett said, "This isn't a social visit. I want you to tell me about your association with the Merriweathers."

She did, explaining how her dad and mom had been friends with them for years . . . concluding with her contract with them to stage their home.

When she'd finished, he checked his watch. "I really need to get back to the station. You said you had information to give me?"

She could see Brett was stressed, and she imagined his schedule over the past week. "If you don't take time to eat and sleep, you can't give the case your best."

"I'm not sure my best is good enough. Do you know how many people knew Chris Merriweather? Santa Claus, for pity's sake. Now *that's* a murder victim you'd never expect."

Again, Caprice appreciated the fact that the diner was practically empty. Brett wouldn't talk this freely otherwise. He must be tired or he wouldn't let his worry slip.

"Have you ever thought about going into private security?" she asked him.

"You mean like a mall cop?"

"No, I mean like owning your own business. I have a client. He's moving and selling his protection service. The hours sure might be better and the monetary benefit more."

"I don't do this for the money."

"I know that, and everybody who knows you knows that. It depends on whether you want the same life as you have or if you're looking at the future toward something else."

Brett narrowed his eyes. "Did your sister put you up to this?"

"The fact that you even ask that means you don't know Nikki very well. Of course, she didn't. This just came up when I was staging his house, and I thought of you."

He looked chagrinned for a moment. "Sorry. You're right. Lack of sleep." He considered what she'd told him. "Private security. You mean like protecting bigwigs?"

"Or maybe protecting homes and businesses' firewalls. I have his number if you want it."

Brett thought about it, then said, "Sure, why not?"

As she found the number on her phone and rattled it off, he tapped it into his phone.

"I know your time is limited, so I'll tell you what I learned about Chris. First of all, Juan told me a friend of his witnessed a fight between Chris and a tall, husky guy behind Susie Q's. And Mack told me he'd seen bruised knuckles on Harrison Barnhart."

"I know about the bruised knuckles," Brett said. "We questioned Barnhart about them. He said he did it on a punching bag at his gym. Does this witness have a name?"

"You'll have to get it from Juan."

Brett nodded.

"Then the other thing . . ." Caprice hesitated, then went on, "Sara Merriweather seems to be depending on my dad a lot so she told him about this."

Brett nodded again.

"When the will was read, there was a surprise. Apparently, Chris had set up a trust fund."

"Who for?" Brett asked, looking intrigued.

"When Chris was in Vietnam he had an affair. He has a son, Trung, who lives in Ho Chi Min City. He's been sending funds there ever since he returned from Vietnam. At one point, he set up a trust fund. On his death, a lump sum payment goes to the boy."

"And his family knew nothing about this?"

"Nothing."

"But others did?"

"Mack knew that Chris had fallen in love or lust or whatever while he was over there, but he didn't know about his son. If he had, he might have told

you about that. As it was, an affair like that. . . .
He didn't think it had anything to do with the
present day."

"But it could. What if someone found out about
it and was blackmailing Merriweather?" Brett supposed. "What if a member of his family found out
about it and didn't approve of the will, or the trust
fund, or the money being sent over there? This
could be about money or it could be about morals."

And she knew what else Brett was thinking. "And
it could be about betrayal." Caprice took a sip of
her hot chocolate.

Leaning back, Brett smiled, took a sip of his
coffee, and seemed to relax a bit. "Chris Merriweather knew a lot of people, but this information
gives us a whole new aspect to pursue. I'm glad you
called me."

"I've always given you any information I thought
would be important to you. Don't look so surprised."

His brow furrowed. "The truth is, Caprice, I've
never met anybody like you and your family. At first
I didn't believe you were on the up and up . . .
thought that you had some ax to grind. And your
family? You've got to admit, they're a lot to take in."

She laughed. "Don't I know it. But we just want
what's best for each other. Most families do."

A shadow crossed his face that told her maybe
that wasn't true for his family. Did Nikki know his
history?

Finally, she asked, "You and Nikki. Is that going
anywhere?"

"If I give it a chance, it might," he muttered.

"She is what she seems, Brett. If she begins to care for you, you couldn't have anyone better watching your back." She knew she had to put it in terms he'd understand, not mushy stuff.

He took another couple of sips of coffee. "Maybe so, but I don't have time to think about it now. I've got to get going."

"You don't have to think about it full time," Caprice advised him. "But when you're driving from here to there, to and fro, give it a few thoughts. I'm sure Nikki is."

"Point to you," he said with resignation. "Grant Weatherford's going to have to stay on his toes with you."

Then he nodded his head to her as if he respected that, put a few bills on the table to cover their drinks, and left.

Caprice liked Brett Carstead. She just wished he could come to grips with whatever was prohibiting him from caring about her sister.

Caprice didn't want Sara pressured to feel she had to include her house on the Historic Homes Tour. She suspected a face-to-face meeting about it would be best. Sara had had a little time to think about whether or not she wanted to put the house up for sale, and whether she wanted to open her house to the public after such an awful, private thing had happened to her.

The day had turned blustery, and Caprice was glad when Sara opened her door immediately and invited her inside. Her daughter Deanne was with her, Caprice realized, as Sara took her coat. Caprice could see into the kitchen where Deanne was seated at the eat-at counter having a mug of something. Caprice suspected that Sara was keeping her family close, as should be the case at a time like this.

After Sara hung Caprice's coat in the closet and invited her into the kitchen, Caprice could see platters of desserts lining the counter.

"People are still bringing food," Sara said. "Customers from the craft store and everyone else who knows us, or knows me."

It was a hard shift to make from becoming a couple to a widow.

Deanne stood and asked, "Coffee or tea? We have both."

"Coffee is fine," she responded, knowing she needed it because she'd be working late tonight.

After some chit-chat about a predicted early snow and Sara inquiring how Blitz was doing, Caprice said, "Everyone will understand if you don't want to keep your house on the Historic Homes Tour. I don't want you to feel pressured in any way."

"You're kind to say that, but I know the Kismet Chamber counts on a certain number of homes for admissions, and I don't want to renege on a commitment."

"But Mom," Deanne protested, "everyone's going to be talking—not only about Dad's murder, but about his illegitimate son. Do you want that? Do you want people gossiping in your own home?"

"It might not be my home much longer," Sara said. "I think the best thing for me is to do what your father wanted: move into a condo where I don't have any maintenance to take care of or lawn duties. His workshop doesn't matter now that he's gone."

Caprice could hear the anger in Sara's statement, maybe bitterness too, and an edge of betrayal. How else would a wife feel if she'd learned her husband had been unfaithful and had a child, that a whole history of his had nothing to do with hers. In fact . . .

Caprice couldn't imagine Sara as a murderess. But what was that phrase? *Hell hath no fury like a woman scorned*. Had Sara somehow found out about the affair? Hard to tell.

"Is everyone talking about it?" Sara asked Caprice. "You get around. You hear the gossip."

"What I've heard is what Dad told me. If there is gossip, Sara, that has nothing to do with you. And in a few days, the gossips will be gabbing about something else. We live in a world of constant stimulation now."

"But Kismet is small," Deanne contradicted her. "Here people have long memories. And the truth is, I think Ryan knew."

Caprice noticed that Sara didn't dispute her daughter's conclusion. "Why do you think that?" Caprice asked.

"It could have been what his rebellion was all about," Deanne answered. "I don't know *how* he knew, but I think he did."

"Have you asked him?" Caprice inquired, thinking that was the easiest solution.

"He won't talk about it," Sara said. "And I think

Deanne is right. Something happened when he was a teenager. I thought it might have been at school, might have been drugs, might have been the gang he was running with. I mean, we couldn't get him straightened out. That's why we sent him to that wilderness camp. But I don't know what started his bad behavior. Maybe Chris did. If he kept an affair and a child from me, maybe he kept what was bothering Ryan from me too."

Deanne stirred her coffee as if she needed something to do. "When he came back from that wilderness camp, Ryan was more cooperative with Mom and Dad. But he didn't go near Dad if he didn't have to. Even when he and Serena moved back here, it was more of a compromise situation. I don't think he had any choice. He needed help again, and my parents were the ones to help him. But I don't think he liked it, and he sure wasn't buddies with Dad."

Sara looked miserable talking about it.

"Have the police discussed this with you?" Caprice asked.

"Not yet," Deanne said with a wrinkle of her nose, as if the subject would be totally distasteful.

Caprice asked, "What about Ryan?"

"I don't know," Deanne said. He's been working extra hours because of the Christmas rush. Lots of people buy phones this time of year."

Caprice felt she owed Sara loyalty since she was her client and an old family friend. She asked, "Do you mind if I talk to Ryan? Sometimes it's hard to talk to family about a situation, but it's easier to talk to someone outside the family. It might help him be more open with the detectives. If he does know anything, the police have to have that information. I know it seems far-fetched, but you never know when you'll find a clue that leads you to the murderer. If you want this solved, everyone has to be cooperative."

"I don't mind if you talk to Ryan," Sara said. "It would be good for him to open up if he does know anything. You wouldn't seem threatening to him."

"I'll go easy, I promise. I know it's a sensitive subject." She touched Sara's hand. "I'm sorry you had to find out the way you did."

"Not finding out at all would have been the best," Sara claimed.

As Caprice studied Sara's face, she couldn't see any signs that Chris's wife had known about his affair. Sara seemed ready to cooperate any way she could. On the other hand, Deanne was obviously angry at her father. Caprice could hear it whenever she talked about him, because she felt she had been duped too. Yet Caprice knew Chris was the type of man who probably never intended for that to happen.

Suddenly Sara straightened her shoulders and her spine. She said to Caprice, "I have nothing to be ashamed of. Yes, my house is going to be on the Historic Homes Tour, and yes, I'm keeping it listed and keeping it on the market. I have to change my life now whether I want to or not. So, I might as well do it in the best way for me. If people want to gossip, let them. Thanks to you, I'm going to have the prettiest house on Kismet's Christmas Historic Homes Tour."

Caprice had to admire Sara's spunk, but she also had to wonder if that's all it was, or if some part of her might be relieved she was changing her life.

As Caprice left the Merriweather home, she thought about the best time to visit Ryan at the phone store. She checked her watch and considered the work she had to finish today. Ryan might not even talk to her. It wouldn't hurt to drive by the store and see if he would. Maybe she'd get lucky.

The store Ryan managed was in the Country Fields Shopping Center. The strip malls were making a resurgence. What was old was new again.

Five minutes later, as Caprice entered the store, she almost groaned. There were lines at each cash register manned by a clerk. Apparently, everyone *did* want to buy a phone at Christmas.

Smiling at a floater, who seemed to be trying to make everyone happy as well as keep them patient, she asked, "Is Ryan Merriweather here?" Maybe he had the day off. She didn't see him anywhere in the store but he could be in an office behind one of those walls.

The clerk said, "His break. Sunflower Diner," and moved on to another customer.

Caprice rushed outside into the wind and chill. She hurried up the open sidewalk to the restaurant, wondering again why malls were going out of style. On the East Coast in the winter you'd think people would want the closed-in protection.

At the diner, she slipped inside, again glad for the off hours just before a dinner rush. She knew salesclerks received just so many breaks in their day. If this was a short one for Ryan, they might not have time to talk. At this time of day, anyone could seat themselves at the Sunflower. Caprice easily spotted Ryan, fourth booth down on the right. She went that way and stopped, peering down at him.

"Hi, Ryan. Can I join you?"

He looked puzzled. "You're the one decorating Mom's house—Caprice De Luca."

"Yes, I am."

"So, what do you want with me?" He looked more puzzled than defensive.

She motioned to the booth across from him. "Do you mind if I join you?"

He checked his watch. "I don't have much time left. Ten minutes."

"That's fine," she said. "I just want to tell you again how sorry I am about your dad."

Ryan lowered his eyes to his half-finished sandwich and his cup of coffee.

"Since your time is limited, I'll get right to the point. I'm helping to gather information that might help catch whoever killed your dad." Watching him carefully, she saw the pain in his eyes. She went on, "Your mom called my dad to tell him about the trust fund."

"That was a shock to her and to the rest of the family," Ryan admitted softly.

"But not to you?" Caprice prompted.

He finally looked up. "I don't see what this has to do with anything."

"I know you don't. But there's a reason your dad

was murdered. Somebody had a motive, and if we don't figure out what that motive was, we'll never catch the person. You do want us to catch the person, don't you?"

He looked torn but then answered, "Of course I do. Even if my dad and I didn't have the best relationship, I didn't want him dead."

"Deanne was with your mom when I talked to her. She seems to think you knew about your dad's affair. Is that true?"

"I don't know why it matters," he mumbled.

"I imagine it's hard to talk about," Caprice responded, just waiting. Sometimes listening with patience was better than pushing.

Ryan took a few swallows of coffee and set down his cup with a clink. After blowing out a breath, he said, "I found out about Kim and Trung when I was fifteen. I needed something from my dad's desk and found photos, the latest ones of Kim and Trung. I cornered Dad, and I found out the truth. I hated him for betraying Mom. And not only that, I hated him because he asked me to keep the secret. It was a no-brainer, and I didn't do it for *him*. I did it so my mom and sisters wouldn't be hurt. But I told him it was stupid to keep the photos around." Ryan closed his eyes as if seeing the whole thing in his mind. "Dad muttered something about putting them in a storage box."

Caprice went on the alert at that. Was there still a storage box someplace? In Chris's workshop? With his personal effects?

"I would guess keeping that secret is the hardest thing you've ever had to do."

"That's putting it mildly," Ryan admitted, rubbing the back of his neck. "It messed with my head. It's one of the reasons I got into drugs."

"Because you wanted to escape?"

"I guess I knew some day my mom would have to find out. When she did, our family would explode. I didn't want to be the cause of that. Yet if she found out I knew . . ."

"You thought she'd be mad at you."

"Most likely."

"But you got clean and sober."

"I did," he said proudly. "It happened at that wilderness camp. Suddenly being in those mountains, fighting for survival . . . that taught me I could do more than I ever thought I could do. I guess I made my peace with keeping the secret, but not with Dad. There was always a wall between us."

Maybe now that Ryan was talking to her about this, he could talk to his mother too. "What about after you moved back here? Did anything change between you and your dad?"

"No. But a couple of months ago he came to me and he asked me if I'd go to Vietnam to meet Trung."

"What did you say?"

"I said *no*. And now I know why he wanted me to do it. He was dying." Tears glistened in Ryan's eyes and he looked away.

Caprice hurt for the father and son who hadn't been able to find their bond again. "Ryan, I know it's too late, that you can't talk to your dad again and you can no longer figure out who you might have been together as father and son. But it's never too late to make things better. There's always something you can do."

"You mean like staying sober?"

"Yes. But also . . . you could still take that trip to Vietnam."

Ryan looked surprised at that thought.

After she said good-bye and left, she wondered if he was still thinking about it.

On Saturday, Caprice took the Historic Homes Tour with Roz. Tied up at the community center, Bella had convinced Nikki and Vince, along with their dad, to help her there, preparing for the pageant. Caprice and Roz would join the volunteers after the tour.

Although touring houses could be boring for some, Caprice enjoyed it. It enabled her to collect ideas for what she might want to do in a staging sometime . . . or in decorating. She happily soaked in the crown molding, the six-inch wide woodwork, the plank floors, the dormers, and the Victorian gingerbread. Yes, it was cold and they walked quickly for most of the tour. But as she spoke with Roz along the way, she hardly noticed the chill or the buffet of wind every now and then. She'd worn a red maxi-coat with faux fur around its sleeves and collar and huge red buttons. It was reminiscent of a seventies style. She'd worn a red felt hat too, similar to a Fedora, but this one had a strap so it didn't blow off in the wind.

Roz was her usual, elegant self in a calf-length, camel wool coat, no hat, and emerald earrings. Still well-connected at the Country Squire Golf and Recreation Club, she'd convinced many of the patrons to take the tour. The proceeds would go into the Kismet Chamber of Commerce coffers. At each home, tour goers would pick up coupons to Kismet's restaurants and stores. It was a win-win situation for everyone. At each home there were cookies, pastries, and hot beverages that encouraged the tour goers to mingle and chat and look around.

The Merriweather home was by far the best decorated, in Caprice's estimation. Sara had decided she wouldn't be present today and had enlisted real estate broker Denise Langford's help to act as hostess. After all, this tour could very well sell the house. Roz hadn't been inside the Merriweather home before and was impressed as she wandered from room to room.

In one of the parlors, they heard sympathetic statements such as, "It's such a shame what happened to Chris Merriweather" and "I wonder who could have done it?" and "I wonder what Sara will do now? The *For Sale* sign is still on the house."

As Denise came into the parlor, she heard the last comment. She beckoned to Caprice and Roz. They followed the real estate broker into a corner of the living room where no one was sitting.

With a frown, Denise said, "I had two possible

contracts on this house, and they both fell through because of the murder."

"But it didn't happen here," Roz protested.

"That doesn't seem to matter," Denise claimed with a scowl. "Murder is taboo, and no one wants it affecting their house sale unless they're ghoulish. I just hope today brings in a new contract. If not, this place might not sell until spring."

"I know Sara would like to move into a condo and get settled as soon as she can," Caprice said.

"She won't have to wait for the sale money on this house, from what I hear," Denise revealed. "Chris had taken out a hefty insurance policy."

Caprice and Roz exchanged a look. Would the police look at that as a motive for murder? They always consider the spouse first, then the other family members.

A group of women bustled in the front door, oohing and aahing over the Christmas decorations. Caprice said to Denise, "I don't want to be in the way. Is the toy shop in the back open? I'd like to show Roz."

"It is," Denise assured her. "It's not part of the tour, but in case anyone was interested in buying the house, I wanted them to be able to see all aspects of the property. Go on out. If you see anybody who's interested, shoo them back in here to me."

Nodding that she would indeed do that, Caprice gestured Roz to the kitchen, where they could pick up a couple of hot chocolates to take along and then go out the back kitchen door.

Twinkle lights blinked from the trees and bushes.

Although the winter cold prevented groups from gathering at the chairs and table on the brick patio, it still looked inviting. A miniature pine tree, decorated with what Caprice knew were solar lights, sat in the middle of the table.

"You did a great job staging this place," Roz said.

"You're prejudiced."

Roz laughed. "I suppose I am. But you sold my house with your staging. Why shouldn't I be?"

Caprice slid open the carriage door and they slipped inside Chris's workshop. Caprice's throat tightened when she thought about Chris working in here, making the toys. Many of them were gone now. She imagined Sara had donated them for Christmas. Why let them sit around when they could make a child happy?

The rocking horse was still there though, and Caprice wondered if Sara was keeping it for her new grandchild.

"I love that horse," Roz said. "I wonder if Sara would sell it to me."

"You can ask her. She might want to keep it for her new grandbaby. What are you going to do with it?"

"For now, put it in a corner for decoration. But I do want children."

"Me too," Caprice agreed. "Grant and I really haven't talked about that, and we should. I wouldn't want him ever to feel that a baby of ours would make up for the child he lost. But I think it would take him a long way toward complete healing."

"I think Vince is skittish about the idea," Roz

confided. "Every time I bring it up, he runs from the subject."

"But you're happy that you're moving in together?"

"I am. A little anxious too about living with someone again. Vince is too. And I imagine living with Grant in college was a far cry from moving in with me now."

"Do you feel the house will be big enough? I know Vince is worried about that."

"Because in the past I was used to a mansion? We talked about that. The house is plenty big. Just how much room do two people need?"

"Is your closet big enough?" Caprice teased.

Roz laughed. "Vince is letting me have the walk-in. I'm also using a closet in a spare room. We're good. But truthfully, I don't know how committed Vince is. If he was really committed, wouldn't he have let me buy into the house too?"

"Except that would be messy if things don't work out."

"My point exactly. It's as if he gave himself an out."

Suddenly Caprice heard voices just outside the door. It was a man and a woman talking.

Roz started toward the door and then stopped. She whispered to Caprice, "That's Fiona Weaver. She's on the town council."

"And I think that's Warren Shaeffer." Warren was the president of the Chamber of Commerce and had been involved in Caprice's last murder case. She and Roz stayed put and listened.

Fiona said, "Do you really think the vote will go through?"

Shaeffer responded, "Adler will probably get his way. Since Chris is dead, Adler will be able to develop his new storefronts on Restoration Row. There's big money for him in that."

As Caprice listened, Warren's answer to Fiona's question played in her mind. Was there enough motive in that money for murder?

Chapter Eleven

Ace Richland knew how to throw a party. Especially at Christmas, he went all out. His daughter, Trista, had a lot to do with that . . . and when Caprice saw Ace with his arm around his ex-wife, Marsha, she wondered if Marsha did too.

He'd asked Nikki to cater the bash for him, and she'd pulled out all the stops. She'd baked a cake shaped like a Gibson guitar decorated in red and green. Ace had mentioned a few Italian dishes in reference to his background that Nikki had provided, from ravioli to lasagna to caprese salad. Loaves of garlic and Parmesan cheese bread graced the baskets that sat atop the holly-decorated embroidered tablecloth. Other desserts included cannoli and tiramisu. For anyone who wanted lighter fare, there was chocolate gelato.

Caprice had worn a sixties-style red dress with black trim around its round neck and a black inset lining its long bell sleeves. This dress was short with a full A-line skirt that came just above her knee. Black, strappy pumps completed the outfit.

Grant looked at her now as if he'd never seen her in red before. "Have I told you how pretty you look tonight?"

She smoothed her hand down the lapel of his charcoal pin-striped suit. "Have I told you how handsome you look tonight?"

He dropped his arm around her shoulders and led her into the crowd in Ace's living room. Caprice recognized Ace's manager standing near the dais where Ace and his band would perform in a little while. She waved to his parents across the room who reminded her so much of *her* parents though a bit older. Ace's brothers and sisters-in-law were there too.

Marianne Brisbane, a reporter who covered everything from parties like this to murder investigations, sidled up to Caprice. She said, "Not to be a downer at a Christmas party, but we haven't talked since Chris Merriweather was murdered. Are you involved?"

Grant just raised an eyebrow.

Marianne smiled. "Uh oh. I guess you are, and he doesn't want you to be. Nothing new there."

"I'm not involved . . . exactly," Caprice responded.

Grant made a sound that told Marianne that he didn't agree. "She had a conference with Brett Carstead and she gave him information. I'd say that's involved."

"I've heard all sorts of rumors swirling around," Marianne said. "Is it true Chris Merriweather had a son in Ho Chi Min City?"

"That's not something you should write about," Caprice warned.

"So, it *is* true."

"That's personal, Marianne, and has nothing to do with the investigation," Caprice said more forcefully.

"Are you so sure about that?" Marianne asked. "If anyone knew about it, there could be all types of motives."

"Don't let your imagination run wild," Grant said, backing up Caprice.

"It had to be something personal," Marianne contended. "He certainly didn't keep cash in the Santa's cabin, and nobody would want to steal letters to Santa Claus."

"Are you sure?" Grant asked.

Marianne looked determined. "I know for a fact the police went through all the letters. I do stay informed. Someone got really angry with him and hauled off and hit Chris Merriweather with one of those candy cane stakes. No premeditation but lots of passion."

"Are you suggesting it was a woman?" Grant inquired, obviously interested in the reporter's take on the murder.

"I'm suggesting that if there was one affair, there could have been another, closer to home."

Caprice hadn't even entertained that thought, and she didn't want to. She'd known Chris Merriweather, hadn't she? The past history of a young soldier was one thing. Infidelity in the present was another.

One of Ace's band members waved to Marianne. She waved back. "I promised Zeke Stoltz that I'd give his sound studio some press. So, I'm going to talk to him while you think about what I've said. Just factor it in is all I'm saying."

After she'd disappeared into the flow of the crowd, Caprice asked Grant, "Do you think I should factor it in?"

"Your family knew his. What does your gut tell you?"

"My gut tells me Chris wasn't that kind of man. Let's get something to eat."

"Vince and Roz should be here. Have you seen them?"

"Nikki has drinks and snacks in several rooms. They might be somewhere else talking. We could check the parlor that leads to the pool area. I decorated out there for Ace too, along with the trees around the fire pit." She smiled. "We could return to the scene of your proposal."

"Let's do that before we leave, when we have our coats on. If no one's there, we can make out and remember."

"I'll never forget your proposal. Not ever." She fingered her ring and gazed up at him.

He leaned down and lightly kissed her. "Couldn't resist," he said huskily.

They were almost at the parlor when they heard voices inside. Caprice thought she recognized one of those voices—Boyd Arkoff, Chris Merriweather's neighbor.

She laid her hand on Grant's arm. "Chris's neighbor is inside," she said in a low voice. "He's the one who threatened Chris."

"Then we should probably turn around and go the other way."

But she shook her head. "I want to listen."

"Of course, you do," Grant muttered, but then he listened with her.

"We'll have to practice every day to do well at the audition," Boyd said.

"At your place?" one of the band members asked.

"Yeah, at my place. Where else would we go? At least now we don't have to worry about our dead neighbor. We can practice all we want as late as we want."

"How about his wife?" a band member asked.

"I heard she's going to be selling soon," Boyd responded. "She's not going to care."

"No, but new neighbors will," another band member reminded him.

"This New Year's Eve gig could set us up for the year. We could get lots of bookings from it," Boyd claimed. Then his voice went a little lower, but Caprice could still hear him. "All good things must come to an end," he decided. "Even Santa in his workshop. New neighbors will learn I don't take orders from anyone."

Caprice stepped a few feet away from the doorway and asked Grant, "Was that an admission of guilt?"

"I don't think Brett or Detective Jones would think so. Do you know if they questioned him?"

"Sara told Brett about him." She paused, then said, "I really feel like saying something to them about their attitude, as if a music gig is more important than a human life." She took a step toward the parlor as if she was going to do just that.

However, Grant took her arm, placed a hand on the small of her back, and gently guided her away. "This is a Christmas party, Caprice. I know how you feel about their attitude, and Boyd Arkoff is scum for even thinking it. But you don't want to start something at Ace's party, do you? A guy like Boyd will have karma catch up with him one way or the other."

Caprice just hoped Grant was right.

Caprice had agreed to help Bella at the community center on Monday evening with painting scenery. To her surprise, one of the volunteers there was Harrison Barnhart. Not the neatest painter, Caprice already had managed to smear red paint on her wrist and forearm. She nudged Bella, who was painting next to her, and pointed to the crew getting set up by the stable.

She asked Bella in a low voice, "Do you know him?"

Bella looked in the direction that Caprice was jutting her chin. "You mean Harry? Sure, I know him. He comes in on Saturdays to play basketball with the guys. He's really good with the older teens. Why?"

"Because he was in Vietnam with Chris Merriweather, and I need to talk to him."

Bella screwed up her face. "You're not getting

distracted, are you? We have to get these sets done in time."

"I can multitask. If you're okay here, I'll go help with the stable."

"If Nikki didn't have so many catering jobs this time of year, she could be helping too. But I'm good. This is like coloring with messy liquids. I'll get a Christmas stocking out of it yet."

"I'll help you with the fake snow after I talk to him."

"It's a deal."

Bella was a sister who always negotiated and made deals, but Caprice didn't mind. As nonchalantly as possible, she left Bella with the red and green paint, took a small can of brown from a stack in the corner, and went over to the group who was painting the stable. Harrison was tall enough that he could reach the peak of the stable without a problem. She settled next to him and in long strokes tried to paint rustic, woodlike planks onto the lower part of the plywood.

After they'd both been painting for a few minutes, she looked up at him and asked, "You're Harrison Barnhart, aren't you?"

When he gazed down at her, she said, "I'd shake your hand but I have red paint on mine. I'm Caprice De Luca."

He looked disconcerted for a minute, as if he realized that a conversation he didn't want to have was coming. "I've heard of you, Miss De Luca. Your family and the Merriweathers were friends."

She nodded. "That's right."

"And you didn't mosey on over here to help me paint the stable." He gave her his full attention now.

"Do you mind if I ask you a few questions?"

"Yes, I mind, but from what I hear, you'll do it anyway."

She gave a little shrug. "I'm only trying to help."

"Help who? Do you want to salve your curiosity or prove you're smarter than the police?" His tone was hard.

It was easy to see he wasn't going to pull any punches, so she wasn't either. "How about we step behind the stable for this conversation."

He glanced around and maybe decided he didn't want anyone else overhearing them. Symbolically, he agreed by laying his paint brush in the paint tray and moving it where no one would step in it. Afterward, he walked around to the back of the stable.

Following him with her paint brush in hand, Caprice knew they wouldn't have long to talk before they were interrupted by someone. When they were face-to-face, she began, "You asked me who I want to help. I'm hoping to help Sara. There are things she doesn't understand. She knows about Kim and Trung now."

Harrison asked, "Kim and Trung? You mean the Kim he was involved with in Nam?"

"You didn't know he has an illegitimate son? That he's been sending money to Kim and Trung ever since he came home from Vietnam?"

"No, I didn't. Maybe I wasn't completely wrong about Chris."

That comment interested Caprice, but she'd

follow up on that later. "It's hard enough for Sara to understand the affair and his loyalty to Kim and Trung. Kim is dead, you know."

Harrison's eyes looked shadowed and his expression was genuinely sad. "No, I didn't know. Do you know if Chris ever saw his son?"

"I don't know any more than I just told you. In his will, Chris left provisions for Trung."

"I see," Harrison said, getting a faraway look in his eyes, as if he were remembering times that were a world and continents away.

"You and Chris were more than buddies who fought in Vietnam together, weren't you?"

"We were . . . once."

"I need to ask you something so at least some of Sara's questions are answered."

"Go ahead," he said with a nod.

"Did something happen on Chris's trip to D.C. this year?"

Harrison looked as if he'd sustained a blow. He obviously hadn't been expecting *that* question.

While he got his footing again, Caprice went on, "Sara felt that Chris was different when he came home. Can you tell me why?"

There was laughter from a group of painters on the other side of the stable. Chattering noise seemed to suddenly surround them. Harrison glanced around as if still afraid he'd be overheard and shook his head. "I can't talk about that here."

"Where *can* you talk about it?" Caprice asked.

After Harrison gave that some thought, he responded, "How about at Susie Q's tomorrow evening around 6:30? That's a slow time there mid-week, and we'll have plenty of privacy."

As Caprice agreed, realizing their conversation for tonight was at an end, she watched Harrison round the stable and pick up his paint tray once more. He seemed like a loner. There was a removed air about him. Why was that?

And just why did they need privacy for him to answer her questions?

The next morning Caprice awoke early. Sophia, on the armoire, blinked sleepy eyes at her.

"I have a lot to do today," she told the feline, who considered herself queen of the house. "What do you want on your menu this morning? You haven't had tuna for a while. What do you think? I know Mirabelle always says *yes* to tuna."

Mirabelle who was sprawled beside her on top of the covers looked up with her golden eyes, laid a paw on Caprice's arm, as if to say, *Tuna's fine with me anytime.*

Lady, getting into the mood of the discussion, put her paws on the bed then danced back and forth.

"I haven't forgotten about you. We'll play outside until Jack Frost nips our nose." Swinging her legs over the side of the bed, she couldn't help think about her short talk with Harrison last night. Just what was he going to tell her about Chris or about the trip to D.C.? Something had obviously happened.

She thought about that as she skipped her own breakfast, fed her felines and Lady, then led Lady outside. To her surprise, there was a light coating of snow on the ground. It had already melted on the sidewalk but the frosting on the grass was pretty. Snow was always pretty until it got in the way of something she wanted to do. Lady didn't seem to mind as she snuffled in the grass and ended up with frost on her nose.

"All we need is a red hat and you'd be a hairy elf," Caprice said with a smile.

Lady gave a yip, and Caprice couldn't help but think about her dad and Blitz. Was her dad taking Blitz for a walk this morning? Just how had adopting the big white dog changed his life? Animals did change lives, usually for the better. But it was a change, nonetheless.

Today, Caprice dressed in a fifties-style A-line rose skirt with a ruffled blouse and a boyfriend cardigan. Out of her closet she pulled a color-blocked ruana in deep rose, royal blue, and black. Last night she'd loaded her van with everything she'd need for her appointments today. She was starting with a client meeting at the Koffee Klatch. Afterward, she'd be visiting a potential client for a house staging. And this afternoon, Christmas shopping and maybe wedding-gown gazing with Nikki, Bella, and Roz. Her day was packed. She'd give her Nana, who was an early riser, a call and see if she'd like Lady's company.

With Nana's *Sure, bring her over* ringing in her ears, Caprice loaded Lady into her crate in the van and set off.

At the Koffee Klatch a half hour later, her client was on time. After one double latté and plans for a surprise make-over for her client's husband's den, Caprice watched the middle-aged woman leave. As soon as she got home, she'd work up a cost estimate. The real work would come in a week or so when her client had to make decisions on colors and styles and fabric.

Caprice was taking a last sip of her latté when she spotted Sara's daughter Maura come in. She went to the counter, ordered a decaf latté to go, and headed for the door. She hadn't taken time to look around inside and hadn't spotted Caprice. Caprice couldn't let her go without asking her how she was doing. Sometimes pregnancy as well as grief could be overwhelming.

After dumping her now-empty cup, Caprice followed Maura outside, hoping to talk to her. But Maura was hurrying away. Caprice followed her around the corner to a fabric shop doorway. The shop wasn't open yet. But there was someone there with her.

Caprice's breath caught when she saw who. The man was . . . Bailey Adler. There was no mistaking that bald pate and long gray hair growing from either side of it. The two sides were banded together in a ponytail at the back of his neck.

As Caprice studied his long, pointed face and Maura's delicately pretty one, she noticed neither looked happy. In fact, they seemed to be arguing. Adler shook his finger at Maura, gave her a scowl, and then walked off in a huff.

Should she approach or not? Should she mind her own business or not?

Minding one's own business was overrated. Quickly

going to Maura, she saw there were tears on her face. "Maura, what's wrong?"

Maura looked miserable and the tears kept flowing. Hiccupping, she dug in her purse for a tissue.

"That was Bailey Adler, wasn't it?" Caprice asked as a conversation starter.

"It was," Maura said with another hiccup. "He was going to pay me to get my father to vote for the project he wants to go through. He offered me a thousand dollars to try to convince Dad, and another thousand if I delivered. I did try, but now he won't pay me the first thousand, and Reed and I need it."

Caprice put her arm around Maura. "Take it easy. Just breathe."

After Maura took a few breaths, she wiped her nose. "I don't want Reed bugging my mom right now for help. Mom has enough to deal with, especially if the house sells quickly and she has to move."

"Your mother has a lot of decisions to make," Caprice agreed, thinking what a scoundrel Bailey Adler was to take advantage of Maura.

"It's not only the house," Maura went on. "Mom also has to decide if she wants to keep the craft shop or sell it. Actually, I'd like to help her run it, but with the baby coming, I don't know how much help I can be."

"Have you brought this up with your mom?"

Maura shook her head. "There's just been too much going on, especially with all of us being suspected of murder. How can the police think any of us would have killed Dad?"

"The police have to look in every direction, but

I understand that can be upsetting." Changing the subject back to what Maura had said before, Caprice suggested, "Why don't you offer your mom help and just see where it goes? When you can no longer help physically, I'm sure there's office work Sara would appreciate having you do."

"I wish Mom would actually hire me." She sighed. "I'm going to have to have another go-around with Reed, and try to convince him buying a new place isn't the best idea right now."

"You have a lot of changes to deal with," Caprice sympathized.

"The biggest one is that I always felt closer to Dad than Mom. Sure, sometimes he seemed far away. But I felt safe around him and protected by him. That feeling of security is gone now, and I'll *never* have it back."

Caprice imagined that was so. Losing a parent had to be the most world-rocking event. She could only imagine if she lost one of hers. Actually no, she couldn't imagine it.

"Where's your car?" Caprice asked. "Do you feel okay to drive?"

Maura pointed up the street. "It's right over there."

"Come on. I'll walk with you."

When they reached Maura's car, Maura used her remote to open the door. Caprice gave her a hug. "If there's anything I can do to help, just let me know, okay?"

Maura gave her a tearful nod and then slipped into the car.

Caprice stood on the sidewalk and watched as she pulled out of the space on the side street and drove away. At the corner, she turned onto White Rose Way.

Now that Maura had left, Caprice thought about what she'd said. If Adler had offered Maura money to convince her to sway her dad's vote, who else might he have paid off? Could Adler have paid someone to rough Chris up a bit to change his vote? What if that roughing up had gotten out of hand?

She checked her watch. She'd better get moving if she didn't want to be late for her next client appointment. It was in Reservoir Heights, and it could be a hefty contract if she made the deal. This afternoon she was looking forward to seeing Bella, Nikki, and Roz and possibly trying on wedding gowns. A trill of excitement when she thought of herself and Grant getting married made her smile.

A wedding gown. Could she find a vintage one?

For the ride to downtown Kismet, Roz drove. Her luxury sedan even had heated seats. In spite of that, the women decided to combine exercise with their shopping tour. Roz parked in a public lot near the community park and they walked down Santa Lane. No crime scene tape now, of course, but one of the candy cane stakes was still missing. There were two little boys standing at the sleigh, their parents nearby. The oldest one in a red knit cap and down parka jingled the bells that hung from the sleigh.

The sound seemed to fill the park along with the boys' laughter, and Caprice wondered how long it would be before everyone forgot about what had happened here. The pretend presents in the sleigh still gleamed brightly and the red vinyl ribbon was a testament against winter weather.

The women circled around Santa's cabin, noting the line waiting to see him, and headed for downtown.

They'd been quiet on their tour down Santa Lane but now Roz asked Bella, Nikki, and Caprice, "What can I get Vince for Christmas? You know him best. I want it to be personal, not something for the new house."

Bella shrugged. "How about a fancy silk tie for when he has to go to court or see a judge?"

"Vince is a practical guy," Nikki said. "He could always use a new wallet, maybe snakeskin." They all knew price was no object for Roz.

Entering the store front area of Kismet, they passed lampposts decorated with wreaths, plate glass displays with whimsical snowmen, cute elves, or holly garlands.

Roz turned to Caprice. "So, what's your suggestion?"

"If you really want to buy him something he treasures, how about a Mickey Mantle signed baseball? He has his heroes, and he'd love something like that. He's still an avid baseball fan."

Roz's eyes lit up at the suggestion and she nodded. They'd decided to park near the community park because the bridal shop was at that end of town. Caprice wanted to look at the local shop before she ventured out farther. The Blue Garter had been Kismet's premier bridal shop for as long as Caprice could remember. As a little girl, she'd often stared at those long white dresses with satin, lace, and tulle, and wondered if she'd ever wear one. Now that possibility was looming ever closer. She knew it took months to order some styles. She didn't have months. If the annulment came through by spring, she and Grant would want to get married as soon as they could, as soon as St. Francis Church had an available date.

The gowns in the window at the Blue Garter were all strapless. Forecasting spring styles? Or were all gowns strapless now? She might be a bit old-fashioned, but she was going to have a church wedding. That meant she didn't want cleavage showing.

All of the women were studying the gowns when Roz asked Nikki, "Are you going to buy Brett a Christmas present?"

That question made Caprice turn toward Nikki, to watch her face when she answered. "I don't know yet," she said honestly. "He texted me yesterday morning and we had a quick lunch together at the Sunflower Diner. But we probably won't have another real date until Chris Merriweather's killer is apprehended. I mean, even at lunch, Brett wasn't totally there, if you know what I mean. His mind is constantly buzzing as he sorts through evidence and suspects."

"Do you know if he looked into the security company I told him about? He could buy the business, handle private security, maybe some computer security, and have decent hours."

"He didn't even mention it," Nikki said. "Which

probably means he dismissed the idea. I don't think he'll ever want to give up police work."

"And if he doesn't?" Caprice asked.

"I like Brett a lot," Nikki admitted.

"And he *is* hot," Roz said with a sly smile.

"There's that," Nikki agreed. "I think I could handle having a serious relationship with a cop as long as I knew he'd make time for us. I'm just not sure Brett's at that stage yet." She gave Caprice a knowing look. "But I'm sure Grant will put *you* first, no matter what. Come on, let's look at these dresses."

Bella was unusually quiet as she'd studied the styles of each gown in the window. She looked thoughtful as she opened the door to the bridal salon, and let Caprice precede her inside. In the warmth of the boutique, they unbuttoned and unzipped their coats and glanced around at all the gowns encased in vinyl.

"Are you still sure you want to go vintage?" Bella asked Caprice.

"I'd like to, but I think I want to lean toward satin rather than lace."

Bella nodded. "I'm not sure you're going to find what you're looking for here. Have you found anything online?"

"One or two, but they're not *exactly* what I want."

The boutique salesclerk started toward them.

"You're just going to have start trying them on to see what styles look best on you," Roz told Caprice. "I'm thinking maybe something like the forties-style dress you wore to the Valentine's Day party, only white and long, with a train."

"Now all you have to do is find it for me," Caprice teased.

Bella pulled out a gown that had sparkles around the neckline and belt.

"I wouldn't mind pearls, but I'm not into bling," Caprice told Bella.

As the clerk approached, Bella rolled her eyes. "I can tell this is going to be harder than buying Joe the perfect Christmas present. Let's get started."

Caprice hadn't realized shopping for a bridal gown would be so daunting.

Chapter Twelve

Susie Q's was one of those sports bars with the backlight from the TV doing most of the illumination. The atmosphere reminded Caprice of a bar in an old forties movie, except, here and now, a TV ruled the place. Yet the wood and mirrors, the scarred tables, the ladder-back chairs might have originated in a different era.

Since she couldn't see to the back of the bar, Caprice wandered through the tables as if looking for one, took a good look at everyone seated at the bar, then settled at a side table from where she could view most of the other tables and the front entrance. When Harrison came in, she'd spot him.

However, 6:30 p.m. came and went and he didn't walk in the door. She kept checking the bar stools in case he knew of another entrance she didn't. Still, he was tall enough and broad shouldered enough that he'd be hard to miss.

The evening business began to pick up, and she was trying to decide how long to wait past a half hour. Suddenly the front door opened and two people walked in who she'd never expected to see together.

Bailey Adler wore a long, black winter overcoat, and with him was Kiki Hasselhoff! They slipped inside as if they didn't want to be noticed and settled at a table in a far corner. Caprice didn't move. She didn't want them to notice her. What did a bookstore owner and a land developer have in common?

The Chamber of Commerce, maybe. But Caprice couldn't imagine what else. She knew a bit about Kiki, who was good friends with one of Nana's friends. Bailey Adler was an unknown quantity, except for what she'd heard about him from Maura and Deanne.

Bailey and Kiki's business only lasted about fifteen minutes. Then Bailey stood, pushed his chair back with a bit of agitation, and left. As far as Caprice could see, they hadn't even had a drink.

After Caprice put enough bills on her table to pay for her soft drink and the waitress's tip, she approached Kiki's table before the bookstore owner could leave. Slipping into the chair that Bailey had vacated, she said, "This isn't the type of place where I'd expect to see you."

Kiki looked startled for a minute, but then she gave Caprice a wry smile. "No, it's not my usual stomping ground. Let's just say I'm not a sports enthusiast."

Caprice laughed, hoping to put Kiki at ease, and that little interchange seemed to have done it. "So why are you here?"

"This is where Bailey wanted to meet. Why are *you* here?"

"I was supposed to meet one of Chris Merriweather's buddies, but he didn't show."

"You're investigating?"

"Not precisely. I'm just gathering information where I can."

"You really helped Rowena when her nephew was murdered. I can't thank you enough for that. I felt helpless. You did something about it."

"You weren't helpless. You were her best friend and stood by her. That counts." Caprice glanced over at the bar where the waitress was busy lining up drinks on a tray. "Bailey's name has come up while I'm gathering information. Can I ask why you two were meeting?"

"You can ask. When the council vote goes his way for the rezoning, he wants me to move my bookshop into one of his stores. He even offered to cut the rent for the first year."

"I have to wonder why. Don't you?"

Kiki gave a snort of disapproval. "I don't have to wonder far. I believe after that year, the rent would double and keep going up. I've been around long enough not to fall into *that* trap. I'm staying right where I am with a landlord I can trust. I as much as told him that, and he wasn't happy."

"I wonder if Bailey is wheeling and dealing because he wants to assure the city council he'll be able to rent the stores and bring in revenue. Maybe he has to have proof of that."

"That's possible. You said you were gathering information about Chris Merriweather. Chris had

warned all of us shop owners that Bailey could be
ruthless and we shouldn't fall for his spiel. Chris's
word was gold, so it *is* possible Bailey's having problems finding renters. He might have to bring in
someone from outside. I don't know if any of us
want that, and I don't know if the town council
would approve that."

The two women locked gazes and seemed to
read each other's thoughts.

Finally, Kiki said in a low voice, "You're not really
thinking Bailey could have committed murder, are
you?"

"I don't know. Could Chris's opposition be a
motive for murder?"

Kiki shook her head. "I don't know. Whenever
money's involved, it's always a possibility."

The waitress finally crossed to them to take their
orders. Kiki said to Caprice, "So how about having
a drink or coffee with me? We're both here. We can
say we rooted for our team at Susie Q's."

"What team?" Caprice joked.

Kiki patted Caprice's arm. "A team that won't
have the wool pulled over our eyes, not by Bailey
and not by anyone."

That sentiment made her wonder about Harrison and why he hadn't met her as they'd planned.
Just why didn't he want to talk to her? There was an
obvious reason: maybe he was guilty of murder.

The miniature cat sitting in a Christmas stocking
hung from one of the pine boughs on Grant's Christmas tree.

"You have great taste in ornaments," he said the following evening, coming up behind Caprice and nuzzling her neck.

She laughed. "We both have good taste in ornaments. I'm just glad you can have a Christmas tree here if I can't have one at my place. I tried that the first year I took Sophia in. She climbed it and made the whole thing shake. I don't know what Mirabelle would do, but I thought it would be better not to take any chances. Most of my Christmas decorations are hung high in places Sophia and Mirabelle don't usually go."

After snuffling around the base of the tree while they'd set it up, Patches and Lady had pretty much settled for a nap over by Grant's sofa. "They're being very good about it."

"We'll hang the unbreakable balls near the ground, though," Grant assured her. "That way if Patches decides to nose one and it falls to the floor, no harm done."

"This is our first tree together," Caprice proclaimed as if she'd just realized it.

"We're going to have a lot of firsts this year," Grant reminded her, looking as if he had something on his mind.

Caprice was silent in case Grant wanted to tell her what it was. When he didn't, she took another ornament from a box on the coffee table and then hung it on the tree.

He did the same and asked, "How's the murder investigation going?"

"Do you want every detail or just the highlights?"

"If you think the details are important, go ahead."

She caught him up on everything she'd found out ending with her stint at Susie Q's. "So, Harrison stood me up but Kiki and I had a talk. Apparently, Bailey Adler has devious ways. He offered Kiki one of the new retail spaces at a decreased rent for the first year. But she suspected he'd double it to make up for that the second year. She doesn't trust him."

"Have you ever met the man personally?" Grant asked.

"I spotted him with Maura. But, no, I've never talked to him myself."

"That's probably just as well. He's probably one of those people in a murder investigation you shouldn't go anywhere near. That's not a directive, just good advice."

She smiled because she knew Grant appreciated the fact she didn't like to take orders. "I accept all advice from my fiancé."

"Okay, so let me try more advice. Don't be too trusting with Sara."

That advice totally surprised Caprice. "Why not? I don't suspect her."

"Is she collecting life insurance money from Chris's death?"

"I imagine since Chris was trying to prepare everyone for that event, he could have upped his policy."

"But she wouldn't have known that."

"No," Caprice said slowly. "She wouldn't have.

Brett might know about insurance money, but I don't know if he'd tell me."

"Even if you're not looking at Sara as a suspect, consider anyone who could benefit from Sara collecting the money or even selling the store."

"I suppose any of the kids might benefit. But unless that insurance money was a real windfall, she's going to need an income. Retirement housing has fees no matter what she makes on the house if she sells it. Maura's interested in running the craft shop with her. I told her to talk to her mom about it. I'm not sure why it's so hard to communicate sometimes with people we love."

Grant gave her an odd look, then he took her hand and led her over to the sofa where the dogs lay. "Since you brought up having conversations like that . . ."

There were a lot of conversations they needed to have about the wedding, so she wasn't overly nervous that Grant wanted to discuss something.

". . . *we* have to think about housing," Grant continued.

"You mean, where we're going to live after the wedding?"

"Exactly. Do you want to buy a house?"

That question took her aback. "I *have* a house."

"I've given a lot of thought to this," he said. "My place only has two bedrooms. Your place has three but no place where I could have a home office to meet clients. Maybe we should find something new or build something new."

Her breath caught at the idea, and she felt near panic. The truth was, she'd never thought about selling her house. She *loved* her house. But if she told Grant that, how would he feel? She wasn't sure how *she* felt. Until she knew what she was willing to do and what she wasn't willing to do, she didn't want to have this conversation. Grant had had time to think about it. She needed time too. So, she was honest about that.

"I haven't really considered where we would live up until now. Can you give me a couple of weeks to figure out what I'd like to do?"

"Of course, I can. It's not as if we're getting married next month, though I wish we were."

"I looked at wedding dresses with Roz and Bella and Nikki."

"Uh oh. The four of you could get into some real trouble."

She laughed. "No trouble, and no dress. I didn't see anything I liked. If I want to order something, I'm going to have to do it really soon. But I don't want to rush into it. So I think I'd just like to keep looking around and hope I find the just-right dress."

"I don't care what you get married in, as long as we both stand at that altar and say *I do.*"

To Caprice, her wedding dress was important. The church and flowers and pearls and lace were important. She was beginning to realize that she'd have to adjust her thinking to fit with Grant's. She supposed that's what compromise in marriage meant. She loved Grant, so they could work anything out, couldn't they?

The bigger question was, could she give up the

house she loved to have a more spacious one with her new husband?

Exercising Lady in Kismet's dog park the next evening, Caprice realized the one thing she liked best about walking there was watching other dogs with their owners. With about an hour of daylight left, Caprice stood under a decade-old oak and tossed Lady's favorite ball, watching her run after it, retrieve it, bring it back, and plop it at Caprice's feet. In the same area of the park, she noticed a woman with a toy schnauzer walk the perimeter of both the closed-in area and then the more open area. The little dog was wearing a sweater that could have been hand-knitted for all Caprice knew. It was adorable in white and red with faux fur around the neck. The red pattern was reminiscent of a Nordic sweater. A black standard poodle wearing a red wool coat pranced by her and Lady. The dog's male handler was dressed in a black car coat with a black felt Fedora on his head. He was talking on his cell phone, and Caprice wondered if he was wheeling and dealing.

To her left, a woman who could have been in her fifties trundled by in a white and yellow down parka. She wore a dog sling around her neck. In that sling nestled the cutest little Maltese. Apparently, the pup's owner was the one who needed the exercise and the pup came along for the ride. Caprice noticed this dog was also wearing a cute sweater and a rhinestone collar too.

She checked her watch. She was supposed to be meeting her dad here at four and possibly Grant too, if he finished his appointment downtown before dark. The temperature today was around forty degrees, though it would certainly drop as nightfall swept over the town. With global warming, December could be a mixed bag in Pennsylvania. Some years the temperature stayed at almost fifty degrees. Others, they had snow.

For today, blue skies had prevailed, and although the sun was dipping toward the horizon, its rays still spread warmth. She'd worn her sixties-style navy pea coat with its gold brass buttons. Her wool camel slacks, reminiscent of sixties bell bottoms, had navy binding on the side seam. Her navy leather boots with their chunky heels could have been pulled straight off a vintage shelf. Secrets of the Past had put in the line with its retro style last year. To top it all off and to keep her head warm, she'd worn a John Lennon–style watch cap, also in camel. She and Lady had had a meeting with a dog-loving client late this afternoon, and her attire had been appropriate for that appointment as well as for this walk in the dog park.

She noticed the black aluminum fencing around the dog park had been decorated in intervals with arrangements of pine boughs. A large candy cane adorned each swag along with a red ribbon. Those candy canes served as reminders to Caprice of the weapon that had been used to kill Chris. How terrible that a symbol of Christmas now had another meaning in her mind. And whenever she heard sleigh bells, she remembered the ones that Chris had jingled as he rode in the parade. She remembered the ones that were still on the sleigh where he'd been murdered.

Lady's ears flopped as she tilted her head from side to side and looked up at Caprice expectantly. *Aren't you going to throw it again?* she seemed to ask.

"Of course, I am," Caprice assured her, scooping up her ball from the ground and tossing it in a different direction. It landed under a boxwood in a pile of dead leaves and Lady snuffled through them to find it.

All day Caprice had been thinking about everything Grant had said. Each time she thought about selling her house, her heart hurt. Yes, she wanted to start a new life with Grant, but she liked her neighborhood. She liked her house.

Shaking her head, she told herself over and over again they could choose a home together. Her home would be wherever Grant was, along with her animals. A home wasn't about plaster and walls, a bay window, or even a back porch with a glider. No, it was about a house they could choose or build together. Wasn't that the best way to start a new life . . . with something new to both of them?

Still, she was sad about the idea of leaving a house she so lovingly painted, decorated, and furnished. It suited her and her pets' needs beautifully. But apparently it wouldn't suit Grant and what he needed. She'd just have to work on her affirmations and her thinking. If she'd simply let go and stayed open to ideas, they could work it out together. She knew they could, couldn't they?

She was so lost in thought that she missed the sight of her dad loping up the gravel lane toward her with Blitz at his side. The Malamute held his head high and pranced as if he knew where he was going—which was obviously straight toward her.

Now that the dog had captured her attention, she dropped down into a crouch to greet him. "Hello, you beautiful fella. How are you doing today?"

Although Blitz was stocky and furry, he was still able to dance from side to side, telling Caprice he was glad to see her. He rubbed his head against her coat. She put her arms around him and scratched his neck. He seemed to like it so much that she kept at it as she looked up at her father.

"Hi, Dad. How was your day?"

"About the same as Blitz's," he said with a straight face.

She laughed. "Does that mean you were together all day?"

"We were. Blitz helped me put together end-of-the-year tax information."

"Did he tell you which pile each receipt went on?" She knew how her dad worked. He spread out all over the living room, using categories only he knew to sort the receipts, which he then input into the computer program.

"He was quite helpful until he swished his tail and everything went flying," her dad explained. "But then we reorganized into even better categories."

Lady came running over to Blitz, and Caprice

stood so the two dogs could say hello. "Where's your ball?" Caprice asked.

But Lady gave a sharp yip then nosed along Blitz's side as if to say greeting her friend was so much more important than fetching a ball. They rounded each other a couple of times until Caprice's dad unleashed Blitz to give him more freedom. Then once Lady had apparently caught Blitz up on what she'd been doing before he arrived, they both ran off in the direction of the ball that had gotten lost in the pile of leaves.

"How are you really doing?" Caprice asked her dad.

"I'm keeping busy. Blitz and I mourn together, then we find something to do together. Your mom is making us both one of her special casseroles tonight—ground beef, noodles, carrots, and peas. I'm sure Blitz will enjoy it as much as I will."

"If she's making Blitz food too she must be accepting him."

"She is. Who could not love a dog as gentle and special as Blitz?"

That was Chris's friend talking.

"So, how are *you*?" her dad wanted to know. "How was your appointment?"

"Mrs. Rivera signed on the dotted line. I'll be staging her house after the New Year. We had the decluttering talk, and she wants time to try to do it herself with her husband. They're going to rent a storage unit and move there what they think is in the way. They don't want to start until after the New Year, which is fine by me. I have enough to keep me busy now."

"Work or the investigation?"

"Both."

"Have you found anything out that Brett can use?"

"Possibly."

"And that means?" her dad asked.

"It means that Harrison Barnhart stood me up. I was supposed to meet him at Susie Q's and he didn't show."

"Harrison steps to the beat of his own drummer."

Caprice gave her dad a look.

Her father shrugged. "He always has. He wasn't one to take orders without question from what I understand from Mack. He often had skirmishes with his commanding officer."

"But now he owns his own construction company."

"Yes, he does, and is quite successful. He's a leader, not a follower."

"Then he must have had a reason for not wanting to meet me, but I wish he would have just told me that."

After a glance toward Lady and Blitz, her dad asked, "Did you know Harrison's brother died in Vietnam?"

"No, I didn't! Were they there at the same time?"

"Yes, they were. Gary was also part of Chris's platoon."

"That had to be devastating."

"It was. It's one of the reasons why everyone cut Harrison some slack. They still do now, even after all these years. I know Chris put up with his moods." Her dad shook his head. "I still can't believe Chris is gone."

"I'm sure that's how Harrison feels about his brother."

"I'm sure."

"Did Chris ever talk about his experience over there?"

"No. I know when women get together, old traumas and hurts might come up. But it's not like that with guys in the service, especially not those in Nam. I'm sure you did your reading of history in school. Veterans weren't welcomed back with open arms. There was such a division in this country about whether we should be there or not, whether men should serve or not. There were the draft dodgers who skipped to Canada. Even after the fact, the pardon and giving amnesty to anyone who had left was divisive more than unifying. It was a tough time, and the men came back with scars and didn't even realize it because nobody talked about PTSD then. Vietnam was a silent bond that never required words. Anyone who had been in the service over there had been in a brotherhood."

"So, Chris's yearly trips to the Vietnam Memorial . . . that was about this brotherhood?"

"From the way I understand it, from what Mack has let slip, the group would visit the Memorial, go to a bar, then watch sports replays in their hotel room. It certainly wasn't about sharing their experiences or talking about anything that happened over there."

"Yet Sara had the impression that this time was different.

"Different in what way?"

"She didn't know."

Blitz kept pace with Lady as they ran back to their starting point. Since Blitz had liked Caprice's method of massage so much, she crouched down to him again, scratching his back, along his ears, around his neck. Her fingertips brushed his collar. It was thick and wide.

She mused, "Chris hardly ever leashed Blitz. I wonder why he has this kind of collar on him. Maybe in case Sara had to handle him?"

Her father was about to answer when instead he waved over Caprice's head. "It's Grant and Patches."

Caprice stood and turned, the collar forgotten. Her fiancé looked so good in his black leather bomber jacket and black jeans. His sports boots could have been worn on a Harley. Excitement wiggled through her, and she felt like Lady when she came upon a new toy. That wasn't a great analogy. Grant was anything but a new toy. But he was handsome, broad shouldered, strong, and . . . hers.

When he unhooked Patches' leash, the cocker ran toward Blitz and Lady. Then Grant took Caprice into a tight hug and kissed her hello. The rest of the world just fell away, and Caprice liked the feeling.

Chapter Thirteen

"I don't even have time for a cup of coffee," Brett claimed when Caprice called him Friday morning. "We have suspects up the kazoo and details to follow up on."

"I can add to those details," Caprice assured him. "But do you want to do it over the phone?"

She heard his sigh. "No, I don't. How about this. I'm not that far from your house. I'm in the vicinity, and I'm in an unmarked vehicle, so why don't I just pull into your driveway. You can run out. We'll have a five-minute conversation and we'll be done."

Trying for some levity, she said, "I hope your dates with Nikki have a little more substance than that."

Obviously, he didn't think it was funny. "Caprice—"

"Fine."

"Three minutes, then I'll be there," he said.

Brett was definitely a take-no-prisoners, forget-the-frills kind of guy. That was okay with Caprice. After all, she wasn't dating him. But she had to admit, Grant had been a little bit that way when they'd first reunited again too. *Reunited* was kind of a funny word for the separate lives they'd led. He'd established his law practice with Vince back then, and she'd swung from a home-decorating business into a home-staging one. Who would have thought their paths would have intricately crossed again? She was so glad they had.

From the moment Caprice slid into Brett's car, he was giving her that cop look . . . his just-the-facts-ma'am face.

"Have you heard anything about Bailey Adler's machinations?" she asked him.

Apparently, he hadn't because he narrowed his eyes. "Do you have hearsay or facts?"

"You need to get more sleep."

"Seems to me Nikki told me that too. Facts, Caprice."

She launched into what Kiki had told her ending with, "She said if she signed on for a year, he would lower the rent. But she was sure after the year, he'd double it."

"But she doesn't know that for sure."

"Bailey's done it before. It's a pattern. Don't you look at patterns?"

"You know we do. But I can't just go looking at his finances. I'd need that little thing called a warrant, and for that I need probable cause."

"That's *your* problem. I'm just telling you what I know."

"And it's just giving me more leads to follow up, not anything concrete."

"Look, Brett. You and Nikki need to go take a

walk together in a woods or go Christmas shopping. You need to chill."

He leaned his head back against the seat and took a deep breath. "What good would a walk with Nikki do me? Or Christmas shopping?"

"You know perfectly well that in a high-stress job you need a means to de-stress. Nikki could be your de-stresser."

He opened his eyes and cut her a glance. "I'm sure she'd love that idea."

"Do you really know what she'd love?"

He sat up straight and his shoulders squared. "Let's get back on track, Caprice."

"Okay, back on track. Did you find anything out from the video footage of Chris's store? He did have a security camera, right?"

"We had a week's worth of loop before he was murdered."

"And did you see anything?"

"This is an ongoing investigation—"

"Get over it, Brett. You gave me information before and I've given you information. Give and take. That's what this is about, isn't it?"

"No, it's about solving a murder, and you're not supposed to be anywhere near it."

"If you don't share with me, I'll just keep the information I have to myself. I'll figure out who did it."

"If you do that, I'll arrest you for obstruction."

"You wouldn't."

"Try me."

In the mood he was in, she believed he would. He wasn't getting enough sleep. He was frustrated he couldn't figure out who the murderer was. And he had more work than he knew what to do with.

"I understand, Brett, I really do. But you can't keep going on like this. You'll be a lonely man with nothing but paperwork on your desk and a killer on the loose."

"You do know how to sweet-talk a guy. I hope you do better than that with Grant."

"When he needs to take a hard look at what he's doing, I tell him the truth."

Running his hand up and down the back of his neck, Brett admitted, "We're understaffed. This is another murder in Kismet—in a town that used to be quiet. Once upon a time the police department only had to worry about DUIs and jaywalking. Yes, we're updating with video equipment for interviews now, but that doesn't mean the police department is up to snuff on staff or the latest investigative methods. So, when you seem to be able to help us with nothing more than a smile and a couple of questions, it really gets everybody's goat."

"Maybe you should try a smile and gentler questions."

"I'm not even going to respond to that one." He gave her another probing look and then said, "There wasn't much on that video. The only thing that was on it was an argument Chris had with his son-in-law."

"And you talked to Reed about it?"

"Sure, I did. But he said he was trying to convince Chris to loan him money and he wouldn't. We already knew that. Chris's wife and his daughter were up front about that too. They've been open through the investigation."

And it seemed that Reed had been open too. Had he been? Could there be more to that story? Caprice had the sudden burning desire to go looking at used cars.

There was no better day than today to visit the car lot. She actually had two places she wanted to go: Kismet Motors and Seal and Send, the packaging center where Ray Gangloff worked. After all, she did have a package to mail to her Aunt Marie. Her aunt appreciated a particular treat Caprice made—cranberry and white chocolate cookies. She'd send them overnight so her aunt would know she was thinking about her.

She wished Aunt Marie would come home for a visit, but her aunt's life in New Mexico was very different from life in Kismet. Marie was an artist who made everything from jewelry to sculptures. She preferred a solitary existence with a few friends. When she came home, she said she always felt as if she had family overload. She was her father's younger sister, and Caprice had often thought about traveling to New Mexico to visit her and the sights. Maybe that was something she and Grant could do together.

She knew she had an ace in the hole as far as visiting Reed's car lot. What car salesman wouldn't want to take a look at her restored yellow Camaro? He was a man and he was interested in cars. Bingo. As for why she was there? Well, just maybe she needed a new work van. She didn't, of course, but he didn't know that, and there was no harm in looking.

The car lot was situated on the north side of town off Walnut Street. Before she left the house, she spent time brushing her two felines—separate brushes, of course. They wanted no part of smelling like each other. Mirabelle liked a gentler stroke than Sophia did, and Caprice let her stretch on the sofa to do the grooming.

When she said, "We're done," Mirabelle blinked at her, rose to a sitting position, and then proceeded to wash herself. Sophia gave Caprice a look that said, *I'm not being groomed the same place she was groomed,* so Caprice went to the oversized dark fuchsia chair and patted the seat. Sophia gave her a small meow as if that was acceptable and leaped to the chair.

Caprice held the brush up. "Back or tummy?"

At that, Sophia lay on her side as if to say, *Some of each, please.*

During all this, Lady lay by the coffee table watching.

Caprice told her, "I can't take you with me, but I don't expect to be gone long. When I get home, we'll go for a walk. Then we have to settle down to work."

As Caprice drove to Kismet Motors on the north side of town ten minutes later, in her mind she'd ticked through everything she had to do the rest of the day. She had two house plans to stage and another living room—dining room combination to redecorate. At seven, she'd be video conferencing with a new client. And at some point, she had to get serious about Christmas shopping. She liked to frequent the local merchants rather than big box stores or online shopping sites. She was working on the perfect gift for Grant.

Kismet Motors had two entrances. She pulled in one of them and parked in a space near the office. She knew her Camaro would probably attract attention. As soon as she climbed out of her car, there was a salesperson dressed in a red parka approaching her, not looking as if he wanted to be out in the weather.

She just smiled at him sweetly and asked, "Is Reed Fitzgee here?"

The salesman frowned. He looked to be in his fifties, with gray hair and a ball cap. "He's inside, just wrapping up a deal. Is there anything I can show you?"

"No, I've spoken with Reed before, and it's really best I deal with him." Through the murder investigation she'd helped with, she'd learned just how far half-truths would go.

Instead of being sour about it, the man opened the door to the showroom for her and she walked in with a *thank you*. Then she said, "Do you have a business card? I'd be glad to give it out to my friends who are looking."

Quickly he unzipped his parka, pulled out a card from an inside pocket, and grinned at her. "Thank you, I appreciate it."

Caprice guessed this was either a second career

for him or a part-time job to make money on the side. She would pass out his card if she had the opportunity.

Against one wall, opposite the plate-glass windows, were situated three cubicles and a closed-in office. Reed Fitzgee was shaking hands with a young male in his mid-twenties. They both looked as if they'd made a fine deal. Caprice heard Reed say, "The car will be ready for you by four o'clock this afternoon with detailing and an extra shine."

The young man pumped Reed's hand again, then with a wave passed by Caprice and left the building.

When Reed glimpsed her standing there, he came forward with a puzzled expression. "Miss De Luca, isn't it?"

"Caprice," she said with a friendly smile.

"Did Sara send you?"

Now why would he think that? But then again, Sara was their only connection. "No, she didn't, but she did recommend your car lot."

He gazed out the plate-glass window where clients usually parked. "Is that your yellow Camaro?"

"Yes, it is."

He whistled low. "I could have a buyer for that in a minute."

"Not going to happen," she told him honestly. "My dad and my brother have put a lot of hours into that car, not to mention other mechanics and repairmen, and even an expert on Camaros. No, I'm looking for something more mundane. I have a van I use for work. I have my logo painted on the side and all of that. I need it for carrying cargo from my storage compartment. But it's ten years old, and I'd rather update before I have to, if you know what I mean."

"Oh, I do. You don't want to be caught unawares."

No, she didn't. Not in any circumstances. "Do you think you have anything that would be suitable for me?"

"Let me get my coat and we can go take a look. There are a few possibilities. You caught me here on a good day. After tomorrow I'm out of town for a couple of days—car auctions."

After he donned a leather jacket, he motioned for her to go ahead of him and they walked to the door. He opened it for her and they stepped outside. As they started walking around the corner of the building, he said, "Trucks and vans are back here."

She followed him then caught up and kept pace. "I know Sara's excited about Maura's pregnancy," she said conversationally. After all, she didn't want him to think this was an interrogation, even though it was.

Reed ran his fingers through his sandy blond hair that he had styled straight back from his forehead. The wind tried to pick it up but couldn't because it was gelled. His fingers cut little channels in it but didn't really move it. In spite of the stylized hair, he really was a handsome guy.

When his blue eyes met hers, he said, "We're excited about having a baby, but as Sara probably told you—she seems to tell all her friends—things are tight for us right now."

She didn't want to deny or confirm what Sara

might have said. "I do know what you mean. Costs are rising every day. I can only imagine how challenging raising a child might be. Financially, I mean."

He nodded. "It's not just a matter of wanting to provide for a child as it grows."

"I understand there's tuition for pre-school now," she acknowledged.

"There's that," he agreed. "Montessori is still one of the best schools for challenging gifted children. We can only hope our child will be gifted."

"That's a big expectation to put on a baby." She kept her tone light.

"Possibly. But even if a baby is average in learning capability, there are ways to increase that learning potential. I've been reading up on it. The Montessori style, the philosophy of a child learning at his or her own pace, is probably the best. Add in the student-to-teacher ratio and chances for success are huge."

He studied Caprice for a moment as they stopped in a line of trucks and vans. "Did you ever hate going to school?"

"Is this true confessions?" she joked.

"No, but what I'm getting at is that there are children who procrastinate, who get sick, who hate going to school. I had a teacher in third grade who made my life miserable. Did you have any of those?"

Caprice shrugged. "I did have one particularly taxing teacher in second grade who expected me to sit still and not ask questions. My mother had several parent-teacher conferences with her until she became a bit more tolerant. But, yes, I hated school for those few months. I felt humiliated and wanted to withdraw."

"Exactly. And that kind of experience leaves its mark. I never want that to happen to a child of mine."

"So, you want to provide the best you can."

"I want to provide the best the family can. Don't you think family should stick together?"

Wasn't *that* a loaded subject? Did he mean the whole family should share the financial burden of each family member? That was almost a commune concept.

"So, for instance, you believe Maura's brother should help fund your child's education?"

"No, nothing like that," Reed said. "But my parents are no longer living. There isn't family we can count on on my side. But Chris and Sara Merriweather were successful. I didn't think it was too much to ask that they help out a bit. But Chris was adamant that Maura and I should do it on our own, whether it was school for the baby or college fund or a better place to live."

"You know, don't you, that if you love this child, that's what's most important of all?"

"That's a given," Reed said. "But sometimes love isn't enough."

She wondered if Reed had had a deprived background, if his family had been poor, and that experience had shaped the ideas he had now. But she really didn't want to make this an interrogation, and he'd pretty much just admitted to what he'd told the police.

"You probably know that Sara asked me to find out what I could about what happened to Chris."

"I don't know what she thinks a nonprofessional can do. You could get yourself into trouble."

"You mean with the killer?"

"Oh, I wasn't even thinking of that. I was thinking more that the police would resent it and maybe try to shut you down."

"That's always a possibility. I just wondered if there's anyone you know of who might have had a grudge against Chris." Again her tone turned lighter. "After all, Santa Claus couldn't have many enemies, could he?"

"Even Santa might have stepped on a few toes," Reed admitted.

"Do you have someone in mind?"

"You know the police didn't ask me that question."

"They didn't?"

"No, they just wanted personal information. They wanted to know if Maura and I fought, if she intervened when Chris and I didn't agree. Things like that."

"I see," Caprice said, knowing detectives explored relationships to get to the bottom of motives. "Sometimes the detectives do have a particular track they're pursuing. But who do you think had a beef with Chris?"

"His neighbor did, for one—that Arkoff fellow. Chris made it plain he thought the guy's music was atrocious, and he didn't want to hear it through his windows. He even had the police chief call him."

"I heard about that," Caprice said. "I was even there when Arkoff came over and threatened Chris."

Reed nodded. "Sara told us about that, and I know she told the police about him."

"There was someone else?"

Reed nodded toward a silver van that looked almost new. As he took a key fob from his pocket and flicked the remote, the side doors opened. "What do you think?" he asked.

She imagined he was still sizing her up, deciding if he could trust her. She looked inside where the back-seats folded down providing a large cargo space, then up front to the two leather bucket seats. "Nice," she said. "It looks comfortable for the driver yet has lots of cargo space too. I often take my dog from place to place and keep her crate inside the van."

Caprice actually stepped inside and had a look around. She ran her hand over the front seat and the console between the seats.

As she emerged outside again, Reed asked, "Do you want to take it for a spin?"

After all, who knew when her present van would conk out on her? "I'd like that."

"Why don't you sit inside the van while I get a li-cense plate. And I'll need your driver's license to make a copy. Procedure."

She opened her purse, took out her wallet, and slipped out her driver's license. Then she handed it to him.

After he took it, he hesitated a moment then re-vealed, "I stopped at the craft shop one night to talk to Chris. Sara wasn't there, and the clerk pointed me to Chris's office. So, I went to the back of the store. The door was almost closed, but I could hear arguing inside. When I peeked in, I could see that real estate developer—Bailey Adler. He was shaking his finger at Chris and Chris's face was red. I decided that wasn't the best time to talk to Chris, so I left. But both of them looked angry enough to come to blows. I thought about telling the police about it, but I didn't hear anything specific so what could I say? That Chris and Adler were arguing? It's the police's job to investigate, and I'm sure Adler's name came up with the way Chris was blocking his attempt to buy those buildings downtown. They'll find out that Adler was an enemy. They didn't need to hear it from me."

Reed was an intelligent guy, and in this case, his feelings were like so many other people's. Don't get involved if you don't have to. Don't turn the spotlight on yourself. Furthermore, his final conclusion was probably right. Many people were mentioning Bailey Adler's name now in reference to squabbles with Chris, so the police would be looking at him. But charging him with murder was something else entirely.

Caprice thought about everything Reed had said while he went to fetch the license plate and copy her license. Nothing new there but a father's concern for his baby, and his own ideas on how he thought a family should help. Ideas made the world go 'round. The best ideas advanced it for that generation and generations to come. She could see some of Reed's points about schooling and about family. But she could also see it might be hard to convince a whole family to pool together to raise a child.

* * *

An hour later when Caprice pulled up at Seal and Send, it was hopping with activity. The parking area around the store was full. Since she'd seen Ray Gangloff in Chris's workshop the day of the open house, she knew what he looked like. Speaking with him could be a good idea and it could be a bad idea. It was hard to know until she tried it. She just felt approaching him here was better than trying to approach him privately. After all, look what had happened with Harrison.

Going inside, she spotted Ray easily. He was a tall, lean man and stood out with his shaved head. Since Seal and Send was a private mailing service that mailed FedEx and UPS as well as U.S. Post Office packages, it had several clerks on duty. They added and subtracted personnel as the season called for. This was their busiest season, and there were four lines, four registers, four sets of scales. Caprice supposed Ray had quit being a postal carrier—which had been his occupation after Vietnam—because he was older, the routes longer, and the winter weather tough on aches and pains. Working at Seal and Send definitely made more sense for a man of his age.

Besides her Aunt Marie, Caprice was sending packages to Grant's parents too, with cookies and fruit bread she'd baked. If she could, she'd send his dad cannoli because he'd liked them so much when they'd visited. But that was impossible. She could take her Nana's shells along and make the filling if she and Grant visited his parents in Vermont. She would really like to do that.

Ray didn't pay her any notice until it was finally her turn and she was standing before him, her packages on the counter.

He nodded. "Miss De Luca," he said.

"Hi, Mr. Gangloff."

He picked up the first package, weighed it, sized it, and asked her how she wanted to mail it. She chose a private carrier, hoping that would be quicker than even Priority Mail. As he was readying that package, she asked, "I'd like to talk to you about Chris Merriweather. Do you think we could do that privately? Maybe on your break?"

He closed his eyes for a moment and then he shook his head. "I have no idea when I'll get a break. We alternate, and it depends on the flow in and out of here. So that doesn't work for me."

She didn't get perturbed but just asked, "What would work for you?"

"Not much, Miss De Luca. I don't see any reason to discuss what happened to Chris."

"Would you mind if I came to your home?" She could be pushy when she had to be.

"Look," he said a bit impatiently as he slapped the sticker onto the package, "I live with my elderly parents. Honestly, I don't want them involved in any of it. *I* don't want to be involved in any of it."

Caprice wondered if he had something to hide. He certainly was acting like it. "Chris was your friend, wasn't he?"

"I thought he was."

Just what did that mean?

He took her second package, the one that was going to Grant's parents, and sized it up. While he was doing that, she slipped her hand into her purse and pulled out a business card. As soon as he finished with the second package, he asked, "Is there anything else I can help you with today? Stamps?"

She said, "No. Not now." Then she held out her business card to him. "I'm trying to figure out who wanted to hurt Chris. If you think of anything that might help me, please give me a call."

He studied the card and then he studied *her* again. With a sigh, he slipped the card into a shirt pocket. "Have a good day," he said.

She knew she shouldn't hold her breath waiting for his call.

Chapter Fourteen

The Mountaintop Style open house on Saturday afternoon proceeded swimmingly. Unlike most of Caprice's clients, Charles Kopcek had decided he'd like to stick around for the open house just to see the dynamics of it. And that was okay with her. Who knew? An offer could come in in the midst of the open house.

Nikki had done her magic with the food. Because of the cold temperatures and the season, she'd created several casseroles that could warm up anyone on a winter day. The chicken with onion and peppers was a hit as was the cabbage bake and beef with fennel and potatoes. Desserts ranged from red velvet cake with a fluffy white icing to individual lava cakes oozing with chocolate.

Charles was enjoying one of those lava cakes when Caprice passed the small office in the back of the house. He waved at her and then at the cake. "Your sister knows how to bake."

She laughed at the smudge of chocolate on his lip. "Yes, she does. She also knows what clients like. No, the food doesn't sell the house. It would be silly to think that. But it's a secondary type of promotion. The good smells invite people in. As they sit and chat, they can imagine themselves living in the place. Denise told me there's some interest already."

Charles nodded as if he was pleased by that news.

"I mentioned to a detective friend that you were selling your business," she said.

"Oh, I've had a few calls about it." Charles had a far-away look for a few seconds, and Caprice wondered what was on his mind. She didn't have to wait long for him to tell her. "Security is important to everyone. I installed the system in Merriweather Crafts."

"I imagine Chris's murder has you wondering if any security system totally protects."

"Exactly. Chris's home system is state-of-the-art too," he said.

"So, you're thinking the town of Kismet needs surveillance cameras?" she asked.

"They could help in public areas. If that cabin had had some kind of system, we might know who Chris met that night."

"Maybe a benefactor could see to that," she suggested.

"Maybe," Charles said with a nod as if considering that himself. He paused for a while but Caprice sensed something else was on his mind. Finally, he said, "Since Chris Merriweather died, I've wondered about a couple of conversations we had."

"About?" she prompted, eager to know.

"He wanted to know if I had expertise in cyber-investigation."

"You don't just mean Internet security, like firewalls?"

"No, I think he meant searching out background material, or maybe even hacking into somebody's website. I suppose that would include firewalls. The whole conversation just seemed kind of odd. And when I asked Chris why he needed such a person, he wouldn't say."

"So essentially he was looking for an Internet PI?"

"It sounded like that. I work at protecting people and protecting their websites. Keeping others out. That's not what Chris wanted. He wanted someone to get *in* to somewhere."

Suddenly Denise Langford was at the door of Charles's office. She looked from him to Caprice. "I'm sorry if I'm interrupting, but I might have good news."

"Someone wants to buy the house?" Charles asked with surprise in his voice.

"It's quite possible we can have a contract by the end of the day. The couple would like to know if you'd talk to them about the history of the house. Could you do that? I know it's a bit irregular, but they seem really interested."

Charles set the now-empty dish from the lava cake aside. "Of course, I'll speak with them. Just send them in here."

Denise gave Caprice a wink, and Caprice knew what that meant. Denise might have a sale and a nice commission, and Caprice would have another house to add to her résumé.

But as Denise went to find the prospective buyers, all Caprice could think about was what Chris Merriweather might have been involved in.

Instead of a house staging on Sunday, Caprice and her family and friends were helping Roz and Vince move into their new home. Her family all went to early Mass, and Grant joined them. He brought along a change of clothes, more practical for what they were going to do the rest of the day. None of them had any illusions about the hard work moving would be, but Caprice was hoping they could all have fun.

Everyone had been divided into two brigades and e-mailed where they should start the following morning at 9 a.m. Half of them, with their vehicles, would rendezvous at Roz's town house and the other half at Vince's condo downtown. The condo presented more of a problem for loading up vehicles, so Vince decided he would drive a U-Haul. Roz, on the other hand, hired a crew to pack up her town house. Her furniture had been moved to the new house the day before. Today, friends and family would be toting boxes and carrying her clothes. Roz had a *lot* of clothes. This was just another one of those instances where Roz and Vince thought and acted differently. Yet they seemingly agreed to accept those differences to make living together work.

Caprice hoped that was true. Roz had not been

born to wealth. In fact, she'd been raised by a single mom who was diagnosed with cancer while Roz was in high school. Roz took care of her mom, postponing her own plans for further education, and then had become a flight attendant. Her more luxurious life style began when she'd married Ted Winslow. But that marriage had turned into a disaster. At times, Caprice knew her friend still fought the shadows of Ted's murder.

Grant changed clothes in Caprice's spare bedroom, then he jogged down the stairs, where Lady and Mirabelle went to meet him. He was wearing blue jeans, a black Henley shirt, and sneakers. To Caprice he looked yummy enough to hug and kiss, but that would have to wait.

"Lady's looking at me as if she wants to know where Patches is." He explained to the pup, "He's with Simon. He's going to be there all day." Grant's retired neighbor often pup-sat for him.

"Since we're all helping Roz and Vince, I'll have to stop back in here several times just to make sure the animals are okay," Caprice said.

"What's your dad going to do with Blitz?"

"No one is going to let Nana carry boxes. So, Blitz is staying with her this morning. Dad thinks we should get done the toting and heavy lifting by noon or so. Then he'll go pick up Nana and Blitz. She said she'd be cooking so we all have lunch."

"It's going to be a big crowd."

"Nikki's cooking too. But in the meantime, we need breakfast. How about a couple slices of cheese bread and a cup of coffee? I'll take Lady out for a last run in the backyard."

Grant followed her to the kitchen. "You could probably pick up Lady and bring her over to Vince's too."

"I thought about it, but there are going to be a lot of people, unpacking, boxes, and confusion. I think she just might be happier here with Mirabelle and Sophia for the day. She'll be okay if I stop in."

"You're going to make a good mom."

Grant's words seem to freeze them both in place. She'd wanted to bring up this discussion, but she hadn't thought about doing it now.

She said softly, "We haven't talked about children."

"And I know that's not a topic for a quick conversation," he concluded. "But I just want you to know I'm open to the possibility. I've seen you with Benny and Megan and Timmy. You're a natural." He stopped for a moment then went on. "And I . . . I loved being a dad. So, if I ever have the opportunity again, I won't look away from my child for an instant."

Caprice knew rationally or irrationally Grant blamed himself for losing his daughter. At first, he and Naomi had blamed each other. As they'd talked through it last summer, as he had come to grips with what had happened and started a new life, he'd decided that blame wouldn't get him anywhere. Still, if he had the opportunity again, Caprice knew he'd put his child and family first. She knew, if anything, he'd be an overprotective dad.

Crossing to him, she gave him a hug. Then she leaned back and said, "I want children . . . with you."

"We haven't talked much about the wedding," he said in a husky voice.

"I know. It's hard to plan with our timeline uncertain. When the annulment *does* come through, we might be rushing and I don't want to rush. I want to enjoy every minute. The biggest thing we'll have to worry about is scheduling the wedding at St. Francis Church. If we don't have our hearts set on a Saturday, that might not be a problem. A candlelight wedding would be nice too."

"So, you don't have any preconceptions about what you want?" he asked, giving her a probing look.

She answered right away. "I want a vintage-style wedding gown. Most of all, I just want you, my family, and my friends there. That's all that matters. If we're open to alternatives for the reception venue, we shouldn't have a problem, right?"

"Right," Grant agreed then took her in his arms and gave her a long kiss.

Afterward, she backed away with a little laugh. "If I don't take Lady out, we're never going to get going. Help yourself to the cheese bread. It's on the counter. Coffee's in the pot. I'll be back in five."

As she grabbed her coat, which she'd laid over the kitchen chair, and took Lady out onto the porch, she thought about her house and what Grant had said last week. Would they be looking at houses soon?

She glanced around her yard with the shrubs and trees and plants that would fill her property with color come spring and summer. She'd planned her flower gardens with care. She enjoyed her vegetable garden. That didn't mean she couldn't have both wherever they moved.

She turned around and studied her house. She really did love this house. She sighed. Maybe she could find time to talk to Roz about it today. She would understand even better than Nikki or Bella would.

Moving Roz and Vince began in an organized fashion. Grant and her Uncle Dom had been assigned to Vince's brigade. Joe and Caprice's dad were supposed to meet at Roz's. Bella and Nikki would be helping Vince, while Caprice and Dulcina would be aiding Roz, along with Caprice's mom. The division of labor wasn't set in stone, but hopefully it would all work out for the best.

Four hours later everyone who helped move was taking a lunch break. They sat around Roz's beautiful maple table with folding chairs pulled up between the sturdy chairs that accompanied the set. Roz had decided to use disposable plates since that was simply more practical on a day like this.

Caprice really did like the house. It had multiple levels, which Roz and Vince seemed to appreciate. The kitchen looked in to a nice-sized living room, where two of Vince's leather club chairs were paired with what looked like a new sofa. The colors in their house were mainly beige, peach, and green, arranged in such a way to be both masculine and feminine. The new sofa was covered in a striped fabric in peach and beige. The two club chairs were deep hunter-green leather.

Caprice crossed to the oven to pull out another pan of lasagna. Roz was right there beside her. "I saw you looking in to the living room," her friend said. "What do you think?"

"It's hard to tell without anything on the walls," Caprice teased.

"I know we're a long way from finished," Roz admitted. "But seriously, how do you think it will all look?"

"Honestly, Roz, I think it looks great. Somehow, you and Vince have combined your styles. That's not easy to do."

Roz shrugged. "We decided what furniture in our individual places we wanted to keep and what we wanted to buy new. It all sort of harmonized."

Harmonize was a perfect word. "I'm wondering if Grant and I can harmonize."

Roz lowered her voice. "Why do you have any doubts?"

"Because I think Grant wants me to sell my house so we can buy something together. You know, start out with everything new, I suppose. He needs a home office, and that's not possible with my house. So, it makes sense we can find something to accommodate us both."

"But?"

Caprice sighed. "I'm having a hard time wrapping my mind around the concept of selling my place."

"You've put time and care and love into your home. It only makes sense that would be hard to leave. But you need to tell Grant your feelings about it."

"I don't want to put a damper on our future by refusing to give in to what he wants."

"Do you think he wants you to give in, if that's not what *you* want to do?"

"I'm not sure. It's a real dilemma for me."

Just then, Caprice's phone played from her pocket. She plucked it out and checked the screen. It was Ray Gangloff. She motioned to Roz that she was going to slip down the hall to the powder room to take the call.

"Hi, Ray," she said in the hall.

"I thought about what you said. If you want to talk about Merriweather, I'll do that."

"Where and when?" she asked, deciding to take advantage of the opportunity before he changed his mind.

"I get a twenty-minute break mid-morning."

"You want me to come to the packaging center?"

"No, not in the center itself. Can you meet me out back in the alley tomorrow, say 10 a.m.?"

An alley in back of a row of buildings she didn't know very well. But she really had no choice. If Grant was free, they could be connected by their phones. They'd done that before.

"All right, I'll meet you there at 10 a.m. I'll bring coffee."

It wasn't much of an incentive, but she hoped it was enough.

Even though it was daylight, the weather was blustery and below freezing. Winter had moved in.

There was traffic on Kismet's main streets and even tourists Christmas shopping. Caprice could surmise that from the out-of-state license plates. But the alley behind Seal and Send was deserted. Not only deserted but downright barren-looking.

Caprice wasn't sure this was a good idea and neither was Grant. He'd wanted to come along with her but she'd nixed that idea. It was obvious Ray didn't want to talk to her, not really. And having someone else along would make the conversation even more awkward or shut Ray up all together. She couldn't take that chance. Truth be told, Grant wasn't that far away. Downtown Kismet would be a three-minute drive, and he'd insisted on coming to his office so he would be within a short distance from her.

In the meantime, she had her phone line open so Grant would know exactly what was going on. It gave Grant a measure of assurance that she was safe, and it gave her a backup.

She parked on the street around the corner from the alley. She really had no choice. The alley was narrow, only wide enough for one car or a garbage truck to drive through. It was a one-way thoroughfare, right now littered with bags from the bakery, one from a fast-food establishment, and a coffee cup from the Koffee Klatch. It rolled across the alley.

She jumped when a vehicle backfired. Her nerves really were frazzled, and she wasn't sure why. Probably because Ray Gangloff was a big guy, and she was meeting him solo. She'd gotten out of tight spots before because of a self-defense course she'd taken. Maybe if she had a refresher, she'd feel more confident. Or maybe she should take up kickboxing.

The door to the back of the postal shop rattled and then opened, and Ray stepped out.

She smiled and hoped that smile wasn't too uncertain. "Thanks for agreeing to talk to me," she said, handing him a coffee from the Koffee Klatch. "I just put a touch of milk in it."

He opened the lid, took a sip, then motioned to the alley. "Sorry we're meeting back here, but my time is at a premium. This won't take long because I don't have that much to tell you."

She wondered if what was coming would be any help at all. Just the fact that Ray said he didn't have much to reveal made her wonder if he did. That shuttered look in his eyes told her—almost as much as Harrison not showing up for their tête-à-tête— that these men stayed private and kept thoughts to themselves. They didn't talk easily, especially about things that had to do with each other. As her father had said, they had an unspoken bond.

She wanted to finger her phone to make sure it was still where it was supposed to be, to make sure the screen said what it was supposed to say, but she knew she couldn't do that. The warmth of her coffee cup seeped through her gloves, and she was grateful for the heat. Already her fingers were getting numb from the cold.

"Can you tell me what happened on your trip to D.C.?"

Ray didn't speak immediately, and she wondered

what he was sorting through in his head. What had happened? Because obviously something had.

"It wasn't that anything happened," he maintained.

With that statement, Caprice sensed he was lying, but she couldn't call him on it because she didn't know. "Then why did you agree to meet me?"

"Nothing happened, but Chris's behavior was a little off."

"A little off. You mean because of his brain tumor? Was he dizzy?"

"No, nothing like that. He just seemed preoccupied, and he was on his laptop a lot."

"So, he brought it along? Was that usual?"

"Actually, no, it wasn't. I mean, we had our smart-phones. When I asked him why he brought the laptop, he said he was looking at real estate sites and viewing house videos was easier on the laptop. I knew he and Sara were putting their house up for sale, and at first, I didn't think much about it. Maybe he was doing comparison stats or looking at those condos he had his eye on. But he acted funny about it."

"Funny how?"

"He closed the computer whenever one of us got close."

"So, you didn't see anything?"

"Actually, I caught a glimpse. It looked like he was in a chat room."

"A chat room on a real estate site?"

"That's not what chat rooms are usually about," Ray confirmed tersely. "But I don't know for sure. You said you wanted to know if anything happened that was unusual. *That* was. Maybe you can follow up on it somehow." Ray checked his watch. "I've got to get back inside. Christmas rush and all that."

"Thank you," she said, knowing a person really could catch more flies with honey than with vinegar— or maybe with coffee rather than with probing questions.

"No problem," Ray said, then opened the door and went back into the postal store.

However, when he did, Caprice knew he was hiding something. Call it woman's intuition or whatever you wanted, but she was sure. She told Grant as much after she fished her phone out of her pocket.

"Did you hear all that?" she asked him.

"I did. What do you think?"

She walked toward her car. "I think something else happened in D.C. that he's not talking about, and Harrison doesn't want to talk about it either. I'm not going to get anywhere with them if they don't want to open up."

"I think you're right. So, what are you going to do?"

"I'm going to call Brett. Maybe this information will help him in some way. You just never know."

"You don't have anything concrete."

"No, but I think Brett's beginning to trust my instincts."

"He has instincts of his own."

"I know. So, if we match them up, maybe we can solve this."

"You mean maybe *he* can solve this."

"Of course, that's what I mean."

Grant gave a little chuckle. "Don't think you can fool me by placating me."

Grant didn't let her get away with anything. "I would never think that."

"All right. I wish I could see you tonight, but I have papers that have to be filed in the morning."

"I'm going to be helping Bella at the community center."

"Bella can be a slave driver," he said with a touch of humor.

"She can, but she knows how to get things done. Call me when you get home tonight."

"I will. I love you."

"Love you too."

When she ended the call, Caprice was smiling. Unlocking her car she slipped inside, glad to be out of the wind. She started it up and fired up the heater. With her phone still in her hand, she found Brett in her contacts and dialed his cell.

"Hi, Caprice, what's up?" he asked.

"I just spoke with Ray Gangloff, Chris's buddy."

"We talked with him," Brett said in a quick tone, as if she thought he wasn't doing his job.

"I figured you did. Did you talk to him about his trip with Chris to D.C.?"

"I know they went on one, but he didn't elaborate on it. I poked around a bit, and he said they went down one day, stayed in a hotel that night, and came back the next. Just a guy trip."

"Maybe so," she said, "but I think something happened on that trip. He's not saying."

"And that's what you called to tell me?" Brett sounded exasperated, as if his time was too valuable for vague suspicions.

"He mentioned something else," she was quick to say. "Chris took his laptop along, and Ray said that was unusual. Sara said you have Chris's computer. Did you find any clues on it?"

"Caprice—"

"I know, I know. You can't give me specifics. Did you find real estate sites?"

"Is this going to be twenty questions?"

"Not if you answer the first one."

She heard him sigh. "Some."

"What about chat rooms?"

There was a longer pause this time. "If I tell you anything—"

"I'll keep it completely confidential, I promise."

"Except for Grant, except for your dad, except for—"

"Stop! How about this: what if I guess? You can tell me if I'm wrong."

"And how is that different from me telling you if you're right?"

"Do you give Nikki this hard a time?"

He relented and chuckled. "Sometimes. Go ahead, guess. But I might not react at all."

"Chat rooms usually have nothing to do with real estate sites. Chat rooms could have something to do with porn."

"Wrong, at least in this case."

"One more guess then. A chat room is where people hook up."

Brett said nothing.

"Have you questioned Sara about what you found?"

That question he obviously felt he could answer. "I did. She knew nothing about it. She did suggest that her daughter Deanne might have used Chris's computer."

"Ah-ha," Caprice said. "That means it was a singles' website."

Brett gave a grunt that might have meant he shouldn't have said anything.

"Am I right?"

"You're not wrong."

"Did Sara seem upset?"

"You'll have to ask her. I have to ask the questions, and I have to follow where the clues lead."

Which meant that Brett could have put doubts in Sara's mind about Chris.

"Did you question Deanne?"

"I did."

"Are you going to tell me what this website was, or do I have to ask Deanne?"

"Let's talk hypothetically."

"All right, let's," she agreed.

"Say I wanted to date somebody other than Nikki."

If he was hoping to get a rise out of her, she wasn't jumping at the bait.

He went on. "I just might put up a profile on LetsGetTogether.com. I'm told it's not as popular as it once was, but there's still lots of traffic on it."

"Thank you," she said.

"For me wanting to date somebody other than Nikki?"

"You don't have time to date *her*, let alone go trolling on a singles website."

"Touché. We're on it, Caprice."

She bet they were. But that didn't mean she couldn't be on it too.

Chapter Fifteen

That evening, the volunteers at the community center were finishing up the sets for the pageant. Caprice had washed out her last paint brush and was almost ready to call it a night. But she wanted to talk to Vince, who was moving scenery to the storeroom. She'd called Deanne earlier to have a talk about the LetsGetTogether singles' site.

Deanne admitted she had subscribed and had posted a profile on there, but she hadn't used it for about a year. In her words, "That site's old news."

After their conversation, Caprice investigated the website. In order to register, she had to pay a hefty fee for a three-month cycle to see beyond the front opening page. That's why she'd decided to talk with Vince, to see if he knew anything about it. After all, before he dated Roz, he'd been a serial dater.

She caught up with Vince in the storeroom as he moved around the set flats. They'd be transported to the theater tomorrow and set up.

"I need to ask you something," she said to him.

He stopped pushing a fir tree flat into place and gave her his attention. "What do you need?"

"Did you ever use the dating website LetsGet-Together.com?"

He gave her a wary look. "Yes. Has Roz asked you if I'm on the prowl again or something?"

"Goodness, no," Caprice denied immediately. "She trusts you."

"I sure hope so," he said. "Especially since we're sharing a house now."

"How's it going?"

"It's going okay. I keep expecting a shoe to fall. You know what I mean?"

"Are you tiptoeing around each other or are you acting normal?"

"You mean, do I leave my socks and underwear on the floor? Yeah, I have, and she didn't seem too startled by it."

Caprice laughed. "Then you're moving to a higher level."

"Once I began dating Roz, I didn't renew my subscription to LetsGetTogether."

One of the younger fellows in his early twenties, who had come into the storeroom area, must have overheard their conversation. He asked, "Are you talking about LetsGetTogether? You two on there? Any success?"

Vince said, "I used to be. *She* definitely isn't. She's engaged."

He took that in. "I'm registered on there. What a waste of money! I had two dates, but they didn't pan out. One was a total airhead. The other one kept going on and on and on about how much she wanted to leave Kismet. So why would I want to date her?"

"Are you still registered on the site?" Caprice asked. "I was just wondering what the site was all about, but I can't get past the front page."

"You want to see?" The young man held out his hand. "I'm Gerald by the way, and I'd date you in a minute."

Caprice had to laugh at that. "There's a bit of an age discrepancy," she said. "And as my brother mentioned, I'm happily engaged. But I would love to see the site."

"I've got my laptop with me. Be right back." He pointed to a work table over at the side of the room. "I can set up on there."

Five minutes later he was back, his laptop booted up, and the LetsGetTogether website front and center. "You have to put in long passwords," he said. "Supposedly that helps make it more secure, along with your username." He tapped the button and went to his profile page. He said, "See? You put up a photo and fill out a profile. They have a form that sets it up. In that profile, I just say what I'm looking for in my significant other. Of course, everybody enhances. I know some of the women airbrush their photos."

He pointed to a contact button. "Then if somebody's interested, they just click on that icon." He did that and an e-mail form came up. "A girl who wants to date me just types in what she's looking for or something cute and then it gets sent to my e-mail. I can scan it and either accept it or ignore it. If I accept it, then we can share contact information."

"So, you share your actual e-mail address?"

"Heck, no. I just set up a Gmail account. I use my real name, but lots of people don't. They use fake names. But there's another way to go besides e-mail. You can message back and forth on a personal message board. It kinda looks like a chat room."

Caprice realized that must have been what Ray had spotted Chris doing. Well, either *doing* or *observing*.

"Is there a list of user names anywhere? A list of members?"

"Nope. Everyone just has usernames until they reveal their real names at private contact. But once you subscribe, once you're a member, you can go through all the profiles and see the user photos."

"Do you mind if I just scroll through these while you finish up whatever you were doing?"

"I thought you were engaged."

"I am. This is research."

"For a college course or something?" he asked.

"Let's just say it's for a special class," Vince interjected. "She's gathering input for a friend."

"Oh, I get it. You want to tell your friend if there's anybody hot enough on here worth dating. Just remember my profile."

Gerald left Vince and Caprice in the storeroom.

"He's much too trusting with his laptop," Vince grumbled.

"Maybe he doesn't have anything on here of import," Caprice suggested as she scrolled through the profiles. There were pages and pages of user photos. The site had been up and running for a few years. Not all the profiles were active. "This is probably what the police are already doing."

"I'm going to finish moving the sets around so they fit together well enough. Just yell if you need me."

Refocusing on the screen, Caprice noticed most of the faces in the profiles were younger ones. She'd been paging through them for about fifteen minutes when she suddenly saw the icon up in the upper right. It read *Over Fifty.*

She didn't know exactly what that meant, but she thought it could mean age so she clicked on it. She found herself looking for Chris's face or maybe Sara's. Could Chris have found out she was stepping out on him?

She spent at least five minutes on the age group, scrolling faster and faster. She'd scrolled past a photo when she suddenly stopped and returned to that profile. Something there triggered recognition. The photo was of a much younger, or touched-up, Bailey Adler. His user name was Valentino.

Like in Rudolph Valentino? That made her want to laugh. Rudolph Valentino was a silent-movie sex symbol. Bailey Adler was definitely *not* a sex symbol. Is this what Chris had been looking at on the site? Could he have found dirt on Bailey Adler? Is that what had gotten him killed?

"Hey, Vince," she called, "come here and see what I found."

Girls night in was something that Nikki, Caprice, Bella, Nana, and her mom did now and then. With everyone so busy with Christmas coming fast, this seemed the perfect time to take a breath, play some

Christmas carols, and decorate the tree in her childhood home. Caprice's dad had a meeting at the Knights of Columbus. He didn't mind missing out on tree decorating and definitely not on the women's conversation. Tonight, Caprice sensed something special in the air, and she wasn't sure what it was. Maybe it was just the coming of Christmas, the thoughts of her wedding, and the warmth she felt when she was with her family.

As they sat down to a meal of lemon-pepper cod, lemon pasta, steamed broccoli, and a Chinese cabbage salad, Caprice felt Blitz nudge her leg as he settled beside her under the table. Lady had gone over to her mom.

After they said grace, Caprice aimed a look at Nikki. "I can't believe you don't have a catering gig tonight this close to Christmas." It was less than a week away.

"I do have one," Nikki said. "It's an office Christmas party. But my assistants are handling it. I went over for the setup, and I'll check in after I leave here. But they know what they're doing."

"It sounds like you're on a roll," Bella said.

"And why aren't you working at Roz's tonight?" Nana asked. "I would think she's busy this time of year too. Holiday dresses and Christmas presents."

"My custom orders have picked up for Christmas," Bella explained. "So, I spend less time working with Roz. She understands. And there are many women in Kismet who would die to have a job in her shop. With the Christmas pageant, I had to cut back on something, and Joe and I are doing okay."

"And how about you?" Caprice's mom asked

Caprice. "How was your house staging over the last weekend?"

"We got a contract. My client was extremely happy. They're hoping to move to Wyoming soon after Christmas. Now if he could just sell his business, but I think he's in talks about that too."

"Brett and I discussed it," Nikki said. "Not as future plans. We aren't anywhere near that. But he likes working for the Kismet PD. He says maybe in the future he'd think about security and a private firm of his own. But not now."

"I'm glad he's open to the idea," Caprice said. "This fish is great, Mom," she added.

"It's so easy too after a day at work," her mother admitted. "It's one of our favorite meals, and your dad likes lemon anything. So lemon pasta goes over well too."

"The tree looks beautiful as always. Do you think Dad will like it?"

"You girls did a fine job. We've been saving ornaments as long as we've been married. The ones you made us bring back so many memories. You and Grant will have to start ornament traditions of your own."

Conversations wound about the table, fast and slow, emotional and businesslike. They were all independent women, even Nana. With each other, they felt completely free to express their opinions, whether it was about politics, religion, or the state of Kismet's economy.

Bella said, "I heard the Historic Homes Tour brought in a nice chunk of change for the Chamber of Commerce. They're taking requests for town improvements. Don't forget to submit some."

"I suggested a few video cams on the streets," Nikki said.

"I can see Brett is influencing you," Caprice joked, yet remembered her conversation with Charles Kopchek.

"I suppose he is. I mean, after all, look at the murders that have occurred here. Maybe video footage would have helped capture the killers sooner. Not that you aren't doing a fine job, Caprice," she said with a wink.

"I really never intend to get involved," Caprice said. "But when I know a suspect personally or the murder victim, I just can't seem to help it. I know Grant would prefer I didn't."

"You not only have a logical mind, honey, but an intuitive one," Nana said. "Using those gifts is part of your makeup, and maybe a calling too. Did you ever think of that?"

"A calling to solve murders? That's never been one of my goals. I've never visualized anything like it."

"No, but it's happened," her mom agreed. "And I know Grant and Dad and I want to keep you safe. But we also love you and understand your need to help, just as Nikki understands Brett's desire to be a police officer."

"What are we going to do after dinner?" Caprice asked. "Watch Christmas movies?"

"I thought we'd try a new cookie that Nikki's serving at the office party tonight. It's called a Chocolate

Peppermint Blossom. What do you think? Instead of eating dessert, we can make them and taste test them."

"That sounds like a fine idea," Nana agreed. "We can make a double batch. Bella can take some to Joe, and Nikki and Caprice can take some to their beaus. Chocolate always benefits a relationship."

They all laughed.

Bella pushed her chair back. "Before we start all that, we want to talk about something else."

Caprice looked from one of them to the other. They all seemed to be sharing conspiratorial looks. "Why do I feel left out?" she asked.

"Because we've all been discussing this and we want to know what you think. Now just hold that thought until I come back, okay? My messenger bag is in the library."

Her messenger bag was in the library? They spent all their time in the living room with the decorations and all, and in the kitchen, but not in the library. What was Bella up to?

"Nikki?" she asked.

Nikki just shook her head. "Be patient."

"Patience isn't one of my stronger virtues."

Nana said, "That's why God is putting situations in front of you to test it constantly."

Her mother chuckled.

"What's up, Mom? You'll tell me the truth."

"You'll know the truth in a few minutes," her mother responded with an enigmatic smile.

At first, Bella took a piece of what looked like cardboard and set it in front of Caprice. On that cardboard, she'd pasted photos of Nana and Papa Tony on their wedding day.

"What's this?"

"Let me ask you something, and I want you to be truthful."

"I'm always truthful with you."

"That's what I'm counting on. Do you like Nana's wedding dress? I mean, do you like it enough that you'd want something like it for your own?"

Caprice looked at Nana. "I'd love to wear that style. It's beautiful. Did you keep it?"

"Oh, honey. Back then we didn't have the means to clean wedding dresses or to preserve them. The satin just fell apart after all these years."

"Then I don't understand."

Now Bella presented Caprice with another piece of cardboard. On it was taped a sketch. "What do you think of this? It's a take on Nana's gown with satin, lace insets, ruching, and a flowing train."

The design had a late-forties vintage vibe, and Caprice absolutely loved it. "Any woman would be beautiful in this, and it's exactly what I've been looking for. Where did you find it?"

"I didn't find it," Bella said. "I designed it. And, if you'd like, I can make it for you. This would be my wedding present to you. What do you think?"

Caprice was overwhelmed by the idea and so touched. She knew the work Bella did and how fine it was. She couldn't help the tears that flowed from her eyes as she hugged Bella. "I love it and I love you. Are you sure you have time?"

"I have a few months, and I'll be concentrating on this one dress."

"You deserve it, *tesorina mia*," Nana said. "And your mom and Nikki and I will find you the perfect veil and accessories to go with it. They will be our Christmas present to you."

In turn, Caprice hugged each one of them. Even the dogs got into the act, nosing in between them all. "I can't believe you're doing this for me," she said. "I didn't know exactly what I was going to end up with, but never anything as beautiful as this. I can't wait to tell Grant."

"But you can't show him," Bella warned.

"No, I won't show him. I want him to be surprised when I walk down the aisle in a few months. This is really going to happen, isn't it?"

"As soon as you receive news his marriage is annulled, you can plan the wedding. You'll have your dress, and I'm sure we can find bridesmaid dresses and mother- and grandmother-of-the-bride dresses till then. You can't pick your venue until you have the date, but if necessary, you and Grant can find some place unusual for the reception. I'm sure Father Gregory can always fit in a ceremony."

"We're going to do the workshop for marriage preparation after Christmas. Then we'll be all set." Caprice felt as giddy as a little girl, as special as Cinderella, and loved by family, friends, and Grant as any woman could be. Before she started blubbering all over the sketches again, she said, "Let's make those chocolate cookies."

Chocolate, peppermint, and coffee by the lights

of the Christmas tree seemed the perfect way to end the evening. And she wasn't going to think about murder, not for another second tonight.

The following day, Caprice arrived home near lunch time. She pulled into her driveway eager to pick up Lady at Dulcina's and greet her felines inside. She had an afternoon of work on the computer, and she was determined to accomplish it all before the Christmas pageant tonight. She'd had an appointment in Baltimore, where she'd won a contract to stage three model homes. Roland Vaughn had shown her the plans and the lots, and told her the homes should be finished by April, depending on the winter weather.

When she swung her legs out of the car, the kick pleat on her slacks hit the running board. Her fitted royal blue coat matched the color of the slacks, and her kitten heels had been perfect for the tour of the model homes. But the suit coat wasn't as warm as her other winter coats. She hurried across the street eager to pick up Lady and go inside her own home to warm up and feed her felines treats simply because she'd missed them. She'd exercise them later with the laser light. They didn't see it as exercise because they loved chasing the little red dot. It was something she could give Dulcina's two felines for Christmas.

After Dulcina opened her door and waved Caprice inside, Miss Paddington, the four-month-old tortoiseshell kitten, along with Lady, came running to greet her. Paddy's mom, Halo, ambled in slowly at a more dignified pace.

Dulcina laughed. "That's your welcoming committee."

Caprice crouched down to give Lady an ear rub, Halo a stroke along her back, and Paddy a tummy tickle.

As she stood again, Dulcina said, "I just walked Lady about fifteen minutes ago so you don't need to do it again right now."

"Thank you so much. I'm sure she enjoyed her morning with you. Maybe you can come over for lunch tomorrow as repayment."

"No repayment's necessary, you know that."

"Then just come for a gab session. You can tell me about your date with Uncle Dom."

Dulcina blushed a little. "*The Nutcracker* at the Hershey Theater was wonderful, and your uncle . . ." She blushed even deeper. "We had a nice time."

"I'm glad. You deserve to have lots of nice times."

"I'm looking forward to coming with him to your family's house for Christmas dinner."

Caprice gave Dulcina a hug, hoping her friend's friendship with her uncle evolved into more.

Five minutes later, Caprice was on her way back home, with Dulcina promising to come for lunch the next day. Lady trotted by her side as they hurried up the walk, the wind becoming stiffer.

"It's supposed to snow later tonight," she told Lady. "I hope that doesn't happen until after the pageant."

Lady's ears flopped as she cocked her head, first

one way then the other, as if she agreed with Caprice. Then she waited at the door for Caprice to unlock it.

However, Caprice froze when she studied her door. The leather strip of sleigh bells that had been attached to the cute cat and dog wreath was missing!

She looked all around the small porch and over the side rail into the gardens. But she knew it couldn't have blown away. The leather strip was attached to a brass ring and she'd securely tied that ring to the bottom of the Christmas decoration.

A little sign in the side garden proclaimed the house was under an alarm system. That in itself should help ward off intruders. She studied the doorknob and the lock. No scratches. It didn't look as if it had been tampered with. Did their neighborhood suddenly have a Scrooge vandal tampering with Christmas decorations? Maybe stealing the strings of lights?

She'd have to check with her neighbors and find out if they had anything missing.

With a little trepidation—because Caprice always expected the unexpected these days—she unlocked the door. Then she tapped in the code to turn off the security system. In the foyer she said to Lady, "Stay," and the dog did. She knew her commands.

Caprice listened. She didn't hear a sound except the furnace going on and warming her house. Then she heard another sound.

Sophia's meow.

As she stepped into the living room, she saw Sophia on her perch on the top shelf of the cat tree, back arched and stretching. Mirabelle lay upside down on the sofa as if she were a person, two paws swinging in the air.

Caprice smiled, knowing all was right with her world. The felines would never be so relaxed if an intruder had been inside.

She patted her hip and said to Lady, "Come." Lady did, putting her paws on the sofa to annoy Mirabelle.

Caprice's gaze swung back to her closed door and she wondered again what had happened to her sleigh bells. Just what she needed . . . another mystery to solve.

Chapter Sixteen

"Oh, no, my wings are falling off," Megan cried as her wings did exactly that. It was a moment when, as lead angel, she was supposed to be announcing something very important.

Beside her mom in the audience, Grant on her other side, Caprice was close enough to the stage to see tears well up in her niece's eyes. "What's she going to do?" Caprice asked.

Grant murmured against her ear. "You can't run up there and embarrass her."

"But she's going to *be* embarrassed—"

However, as Caprice spotted Bella on the sidelines of the stage starting toward her daughter, Megan must have seen her too because she shook her head, swooped down with her arm, grabbed her wings, and nudged the shepherd in front of her. She whispered something to him, and he moved behind her holding up the wings.

Megan went on with the announcement she was supposed to make as chief angel.

Her arm against Grant's, Caprice felt his chuckle. "She's definitely her mother's daughter," he said.

Caprice had to laugh too. Megan was going to find her place in the world just fine as she grew up.

The pageant, all in all, went off without too many more hitches. Some of the children fumbled their lines, and a few missed their cues. Nevertheless, because of Bella's attitude and the upbeat temperament of the other volunteers, everyone had fun and put their hearts into what they were doing.

At the curtain call, the children and Bella received a standing ovation. Bella blushed and bowed, and Caprice could see she was in her element. She loved being with kids, and she was masterful at using her creative skills.

After punch and cookies in the lobby of the theater—the kids' moms had baked and donated several varieties of cookies—Caprice had a chance to catch up with her parents as well as her sisters and brother. Uncle Dom was there too. They'd all been enthusiastic about supporting the children in this event. Caprice ran into many people she knew, from clients to high school classmates to her neighbors.

Caprice's dad said, "We have to get home to Blitz. I don't want to leave him alone too long."

Since Caprice's mom didn't roll her eyes or make a comment, Caprice realized her mother was settling in with the dog too.

Nana gave Caprice an extra-long hug and whispered in her ear, "You make sure you take time for you and Grant. Don't let this murder investigation and your work eat it all away. Christmas is a time to come together."

Caprice never minded getting advice from Nana. She couldn't think of one time her Nana hadn't been right on the mark.

Lingering to speak to people they knew, Caprice and Grant congratulated Bella again as she gathered the kids and Joe. He was holding little Benny who was asleep in his arms.

"Tomorrow the cleanup work starts," Bella said. "But Joe's taking the day off to help move the sets to somebody's barn. They'll be stored there until next year."

"Are you going to do this again?" Caprice asked.

"I don't know. We'll see what the coming year brings," Bella said.

Caprice and Grant walked Bella and Joe and the kids to their van, gave them all hugs, and said goodbye. Nikki was the only one who hadn't made the pageant tonight because of double catering gigs. Everyone understood that.

A light snow began to fall as Joe pulled out of the parking lot and headed home. Caprice and Grant had driven their own cars because Caprice had arrived early to help with dressing the kids. Now he walked her to her car, his arm around her. She should be cold with the temperature around thirty-two and snow falling. But one look at him and she didn't feel the cold. She just felt his love.

They had approached her car from the passenger side. As they rounded the hood, they were intent on each other and not much else. Grant wrapped his arms around her and gave her a huge kiss.

After he pulled away, he said, "I'd like to stop over for a while, but I should get home and pick up Patches from Simon's."

"I know. Lady's with Dulcina. After I bring her home, I still have a proposal to get ready tonight." Though as she said it, she remembered what Nana had said. "Maybe tomorrow night after the town council meeting you can come over. The vote will be taken at the meeting for the rezoning of those houses on Restoration Row."

"Why don't I bring Patches over before the meeting, and she and Lady can keep each other company."

"That sounds like a good idea. The meeting shouldn't last long."

"Or we don't have to stay for all of it," Grant said with a wiggle of his brow.

Caprice laughed and kissed his cheek. "You are so right."

They both turned toward the driver's side door of her Camaro. Grant started to say, "You be careful driving in this snow—"

He stopped mid-sentence and Caprice saw why.

"What are they?" he asked, puzzled.

Caprice could see that the sleigh bells from her door decoration were now hanging on the car door handle with a plastic twist tie. Snow was accumulating on them. She stepped closer and spied something wedged underneath the bells. A Ziplock bag. She pulled it out and as she did, she saw the note within.

In black marker on lined paper were the words *Stop asking questions or your sleigh bells will never ring again.*

Grant read it over her shoulder and asked, "Are you going to call Brett or am I?"

Her hand shaking, Caprice pulled her cell phone from her purse, found Brett in her contacts, and tapped his number. Soon she was going to have to put him on speed-dial.

Fortunately, she reached him. When he was on a case, that phone hardly left his hand. She explained what she'd found.

He asked, "Can you go back in the building?"

"They're about to close up."

"Don't touch anything. I'll be there in five."

As good as his word, Brett pulled into the lot five minutes later. There were only a few cars left, and he pulled up beside hers. When he got out, she could see he was wearing a black fleece-lined windbreaker. He jogged over to them, prepared with evidence bags and latex gloves.

"Sorry to keep you out in this weather," he said.

"We stood under the overhang at the theater until we saw you coming," Grant said. "We're fine."

Brett pointed to Caprice. "She's *not* fine." He looked at the snow-covered door handle as well as the bells and the note. "No chance we're going to get prints off that handle in this weather." He carefully collected the rest of the evidence and held it up. "But with this we might get lucky. Do you have a clue who did this?"

"I noticed when I got back from Baltimore today that the sleigh bells were missing from my front door. Those are my bells."

"Whoever it is wants you to know they're watching and they can get close—to your front door. I don't like it. You've ruffled somebody's feathers, probably the killer's."

Grant was grim-faced. "Are you trying to scare her?"

"Sure, I'm trying to scare her. She has to let this alone." He pointed his finger at her. "I want you to keep your family around you and enjoy Christmas."

"Not much chance any of us are going to enjoy it if this killer isn't caught before then," Caprice murmured, shaken more than she wanted to admit.

"You're right about that. All I need is one good lead. But I'm taking time for Nikki too. Did she tell you I'm meeting her for coffee early tomorrow morning at the Koffee Klatch? I have to have a hefty caffeine fix so I might as well have her company while I'm doing it."

Apparently, he was trying to take some of the sting from his earlier words and reassure her about his relationship with her sister.

"With her working tonight, we haven't had time to talk," she said.

"Well, when you do, she'll tell you I'm invited to Christmas dinner. I just hope I can make it."

"I hope you can too. I'm sure nothing would make Nikki happier."

Brett said gruffly, "Now get out of this weather. Go home, have hot chocolate, and make sure your security system is turned on. Got it?"

"I'm going to go home and get Patches and come over and stay at your place tonight," Grant told her.

"You are *not*," Caprice protested. "I'm a big girl. I'm not going to let anybody scare me or make me afraid to be in my own house."

Grant and Brett exchanged a look.

"What if I just want to come over, have a sleepover, and make you breakfast in the morning?" Grant asked reasonably. He lowered his voice and whispered in her ear, "I promise I'll be a perfect gentleman and let you work and make up my own bed in the spare room." They'd made a pact that they wouldn't have sex until their wedding night, and they were sticking to it.

Brett nudged her shoulder. "Take him up on his offer. You give *me* enough advice. Take mine."

She saw the worried look in Grant's eyes and knew he'd be concerned about her all night if she didn't do what he asked. So, in a way it did make sense, and she would love having him there.

"You two are ganging up on me. But before we turn into snow people, I agree."

"Thank goodness the De Luca women have *some* good sense," Brett muttered as he waved at them and jogged to his car.

As Caprice opened the door and settled in her driver's seat, Grant leaned over the window. "I'll be there as soon as I can."

"I'll make hot chocolate," she promised him.

He winked and shut her door.

When Caprice came downstairs the following morning, she smelled coffee and bacon and scrambled eggs. Grant had already let Patches and Lady outside and was cooking breakfast.

He opened an arm to her as he flipped the bacon. After he kissed her, he said, "I don't like the reason

I was here last night, but I sure like waking up with you here in the morning."

"Me too," she murmured into his neck. "Everything looks and smells great. Toast with that?" she asked.

"Sure. I think I switched Mirabelle and Sophia's dishes, and they didn't seem too happy about that. But other than that, we're all good."

Caprice laughed. "Creatures of habit, just like humans. I'll give Sophia a dollop of cream before we leave."

"Are you leaving too this morning?" he asked.

"I want to talk to you about that. Do you have early appointments?"

"I was going to take Patches downtown and work until my ten thirty appointment. Why?"

"I was thinking."

He shook his head and kept silent, and Caprice imagined he knew what was coming.

"I remembered something last night before I fell asleep."

"What?"

"When I was examining that LetsGetTogether.com dating website, I remembered seeing Bailey Adler's face on it. He had a profile. He was younger but it was definitely him."

"So, what are you thinking?" Grant asked.

"I want to know if he's the one who threatened me."

"And you're going to find that out how?"

"I want to go see him. And I'd like you to listen in to make sure nothing happens to me. After all, if I see him at his office, it's a public place. I've done this kind of thing before. I'll be perfectly fine, especially if you're on the other end. What do you say?"

Although Grant was sometimes an unwilling participant in Caprice's investigation methods, this morning he agreed. "That might be the best way to go. I don't want you in danger. But I know there isn't anything the police can do unless someone moves in on you and tries to harm you. If you go see Adler, I'll park nearby and listen in on your conversation."

This morning Caprice decided to wear an eighties-style red-and-navy floral-print wrap dress. Her slim boots went almost to her knees.

Grant's gaze moved up and down her outfit. "Why so dressed up for a visit to Adler?"

"If I catch Bailey's eye, I can distract him. If I distract him, maybe he'll let something slip."

Grant frowned as if he didn't approve. But he didn't comment on her plan.

A half hour later, Caprice stood outside of the building where Adler's office was located. It was situated on the first floor of a three-story, brick row house located near the community center. There was nothing pretentious about it. There were black shutters on the windows and a plain black door with a bell and an intercom.

She tested her phone connection with Grant. "Are you there?"

"I sure am. And Patches is snoozing beside me. So, you don't have to worry about him barking."

"Sounds good," she said. "I'm going to press the bell." She slid her phone into the pocket of her dress. When she took off her coat, Grant should be able to hear just fine.

She rang the bell, not knowing what to expect. It was possible Bailey had a receptionist or someone who would screen his appointments. She didn't have an appointment. She didn't even know if he was in. But it was nine o'clock on the dot and she expected he might be.

A male voice came over the intercom and she recognized it as Bailey Adler's. "Who's there?" he asked in a clipped tone.

"It's Caprice De Luca. Do you have a few minutes to talk?"

"I'll unlock the door," he said. "I'm in the first office on the left."

As she opened the door, she stepped into a foyer. There was nothing in it but coat hooks tacked onto one wall. Taking advantage of them, she slipped off her coat and hung it on one of them. She turned to the first door on her left and saw the brass plate screwed onto it: BAILEY ADLER. No title, just his name. That's because he wore many hats, she supposed. She just wanted to find out if one of them was criminal.

She opened the door and didn't find a suite of offices. She found a single office and Bailey Adler sitting behind a huge, mahogany desk.

He stood and came around the desk.

When he extended his hand, she took it, hoping to at least keep the beginning of the meeting congenial. "Hello, Mr. Adler. Thank you for giving me a few minutes of your time."

He motioned to the mountain of paperwork on his desk. "I'll be at that all day." He looked her over, and she didn't like the way he studied her. "I know who you are. You run that home-staging business that seems to be flying high right now."

"I'm booked up, and that's a nice feeling."

"That TV publicity probably got you a lot of clients. That was a smart move."

He was speaking about the home-decorating competition in Baltimore that she'd taken part in and won. "Thank you. I suppose that even if I hadn't won, the publicity would be helpful."

"But you won, and I like a winner. How can I help you?"

Again, he was looking up and down her dress, and that look made her want to run into the foyer, get her coat, put it on, and button it. But she told herself to remain calm, breathe, and remember Grant was in her pocket.

Sitting behind his desk, motioning her to the chair in front of it, he asked with a smile, "Since you're such a smart woman, are you here because you want to invest in one of my projects?"

Here's where the whole conversation got sticky. She wasn't going to pretend she approved of his business tactics. "No, Mr. Adler. That's not my intention. In fact, I was very much on Chris Merriweather's side not to have those old houses torn down and replaced with glitzy new storefronts."

"I see," Adler said, scowling now.

"I've been asking questions, helping to gather information about Chris Merriweather's murder."

Adler's eyes narrowed. "What does that have to do with me?"

"I understand you and he were enemies."

"That's putting it a little strongly. We were just on opposing sides of an issue. That's all."

"That was an issue that could have cost you money if Chris won it."

"If you're here to accuse me of something, you can leave right now."

Whoa! A little testy, wasn't he? Had someone else accused him of hurting Chris?

"Someone has warned me to stop looking into Chris's death," Caprice said. "I guess I'd like to know if *you're* that person."

The silence in his office took on a life of its own as he arranged his face. First, she saw a blush of anger. That was replaced with a coldness that gave him a frozen expression. "And just why should I do that?"

"Because I believe you're one of the suspects. I think Chris might have dug up dirt on you so you'd stop pushing him about voting your way on the rezoning."

The darkness that shadowed Adler's eyes told her she could be on the right track. She went on. "Maybe you thought by eliminating your problem altogether, you could push the yea vote through."

"You're crazy. And you'd better not go to the police with that theory."

Caprice wasn't about to reveal that Maura already

had, because that could put Chris's daughter in danger.

"Tell me this, Mr. Adler. Do you have an alibi for the night Chris was killed?"

Adler was silent and that silence told her he did not have an alibi. His lips pressed together and then he stood. "Leave."

Knowing that Grant was probably out of his car, ready to come in and rescue her, she said, "Oh, I'll leave. But just remember one thing. The truth always comes out, one way or another. I suppose I'll see you at the town council meeting tonight. I'd wish you luck, but the truth is, I hope the vote doesn't go your way. Have a good day."

Floored now by what she'd said, Adler opened his mouth, probably to threaten her. She didn't wait to hear. She hurried out his office door and closed it firmly behind her. Then she breathed a sigh of relief. She might have shaken up a hornet's nest. The town council vote tonight could tell the tale, and maybe even reveal if Adler had anything to do with Chris's murder.

Chapter Seventeen

One of Caprice's favorite shops was Older and Better. The proprietor, Isaac Hobbs, was more than the shopkeeper—he was a friend. When she stepped into that shop, it was like stepping back into the past. She often found furniture there for her more primitive or rustic stagings. Today, however, she wasn't looking for furniture. She was looking for an antique picture frame for a photo of her and Grant that she wanted to give him as part of his Christmas present. The other part would be an afghan she'd been crocheting in shades of blue. He often commented on the one her Nana had made her, and she thought it would go well with his sofa and living room. At least until they moved in together, whenever and wherever that was.

After she'd said good-bye to Grant that morning—he'd given her a huge kiss and a warning to stay away from Adler in the future—she'd gone home to pick up Lady and make sure she had everything she needed for lunch with Dulcina. Her cocker was good about not running around Older and Better.

Lady knew Isaac always had a treat for her behind his counter.

When Caprice opened the door to the antique shop, the security bell jangled. She saw Isaac standing at his counter having a cup of coffee, studying a ledger. His business was computerized, but he was still old-school in the lists he made of pieces he was looking for and new inventory that came in.

He called to her from the back of the shop. "Look at that Queen Anne table to your left. I don't think you'll want it for staging. A little too expensive. But I think I already have a buyer for it. It's a beauty."

Caprice went to her left and saw an antique, cherry tea table that was a tilting one.

Isaac went on. "It dates back to 1770. It was made right here in Pennsylvania, possibly Chester county. It's in outstanding condition. It's been restored, but I bet I can still get around three thousand for it."

Isaac knew his antiques. Caprice was familiar with a lot of them, but not as informed as he was. "It's a beauty," she agreed.

"At that same sale, I managed to win an auction on an 1800s, primitive, Mahantongo rope bed. That's still out in my storage shed. And just wait until you see the Pennsylvania German Dutch painted wedding trunk coming in."

"Another 1800s piece?"

"Yep. It has strapped hinges and its original key and lock. If you want to see it, I can take you out there."

"I trust your word. I like that new walnut wardrobe over there."

"That was restored too. Not as well as some other pieces—1830s. I can give you a good deal on it."

She laughed. "I imagine you could, but I'm looking for something a little different today—not furniture."

"Glassware?"

He knew she often shopped for pieces of her Nana's Fostoria crystal that her mother now had in her care. The Navarre pattern was beautiful and delicate and graced the table on holidays. "No, an antique picture frame."

"Just what do you mean by *antique*? Do you want a real antique, or do you want an antique-*looking* frame?"

"Good question. It's for a photo of me and Grant to give him for Christmas."

"*Hmmm.* Do you want to hang it on the wall or stand it?"

"I imagine either would be okay. Standing would probably be more practical."

"I have a couple that might suit you. Look at that hutch over to your right, second shelf."

She went over to the hutch and lifted a Victorian art-nouveau picture frame. It was gold with a copper gilt leaf motif. "It's beautiful. But it's pretty fussy for him, don't you think?"

"That one's around two hundred dollars. Is that what you had in mind?"

"I'll know it when I see it," she told him as she often did.

He chuckled. "While you're looking, I'll give Lady her treat. Come here, girl."

Caprice wandered around. There was a pair of

oval, gold gesso frames. The price on them was four
hundred and fifty dollars. She didn't really want
a pair.

As she crossed to a side table, she lifted an art-
nouveau, carved wood frame labeled JUGENDSTIL.
That was a style popular in Germany in the mid-1890s.
The carved design that made an arch around the
top and bottom was like a vine. The ribbon design
in the middle of the top was very simple and went
with the carved work beautifully. She could see it
sitting on Grant's bookshelf at home or at his office.
She could easily insert a five-by-seven matted photo
in it, or an eight-by-ten. She checked the price. It
was reasonable for a frame beautifully carved and
in good condition.

She took it over to Isaac's counter. "I think I
found it."

"You usually do."

"That's because you have such great inventory,
and you negotiate so well. We'll have to talk about
the price on the frame."

Isaac shook his head, brought out a clean coffee
mug from under the counter and set it in front of
her. "Coffee?"

Isaac's coffee often tasted like sludge, but this
early in the morning it should be a new pot and not
so bad. She knew he liked a little company, and she
and Lady had a few minutes to give him. As she'd
often done, she went around the counter to one of
the wooden captain's chairs with the red-and-black
plaid covering. Taking off her coat, she hung it
around the back of the chair.

Lady looked up at Isaac as if she expected another treat.

"That depends on what your mom says," he told her.

Caprice told Lady, "If you have another treat, we cut down on your kibble later."

Lady made a circle around Isaac's legs as if that was fine with her.

"Oh, sure, she agrees now," Caprice said with a laugh. "She'll complain later."

Soon she and Isaac were sipping coffee from their mugs.

"I heard Megan lost her wings," Isaac said with a wink.

"How do you hear absolutely everything? Sometimes I think you're clairvoyant."

"*Hmmm.* Not so much. I do have a scanner."

Caprice lifted her brow. "And what did you hear on the scanner?"

"I just heard some chatter about Brett Carstead being called to the theater right around the time when the pageant let out."

"Chatter?"

"It's the police channel. Rookie cops talk."

"I see. And?"

"That's what I was hoping you'd fill me in on. Megan's wings? That was in a little piece online, a vlog that one of the moms does. So, no clairvoyance there. I also read that Bella did a wonderful job."

"She did."

"Are you going to tell me why Carstead was called to the parking lot when everybody was almost gone?"

"You can't spread the word on this. My guess is Brett's trying to keep it under his hat."

"He never wears a hat. Spill it, Caprice. You know I keep secrets. It's part of my line of work. Antiques and secrets go together."

She supposed there were plenty of secrets intertwined with family histories, and Isaac was probably keeping more secrets than he knew what to do with. She also knew she could trust him. She told him about the sleigh bells that had been stolen from her door and how they'd appeared on her car door with the threatening note.

"I suppose they'll test for DNA but that could take time," Isaac determined.

"Yes, it could. Meanwhile, I'm looking into a few things on my own."

"That's exactly why you were threatened," Isaac pointed out.

"I know that. But you know me. I can't just sit by. Tell me something. Have you had dealings with Bailey Adler?"

The scowl that crossed Isaac's face told her exactly what he thought of Bailey Adler. "I avoid him and his properties. Before I bought this place, I thought about renting space at one of Adler's buildings. But that man has a reputation for being a rent gouger. I learned that just from looking around at spaces and from other shopkeepers. I knew I was better off steering clear of him. I also heard he has a mean temper when he's provoked."

"I just wonder how much it takes to provoke him. That could happen tonight."

"At the town council meeting?" Isaac asked. "I was thinking of going just to see the fireworks."

"What do you think is going to happen?"

"I think Chris's replacement will probably vote to change the zoning ordinance on those properties. But I've been wrong before."

Caprice hated the thought of the historic properties becoming shiny, modern-looking storefronts that wouldn't fit in with the rest of the character of downtown Kismet.

But she wasn't sure anyone could do anything about it.

That evening, a loud buzz sounded through the town hall's main meeting room as Caprice and Grant took seats next to Roz and Kiki Hasselhoff.

Roz leaned close to Caprice. "There's so much chatter in here, nobody can hear anybody else."

The town hall was a historic building in Kismet located near the first red light ever established in the town. Its sturdy brick had seen a few facelifts. Somehow its mortar had withstood the storms, as well as the cold and heat, of the decades. The inside had been renovated and refurbished too. The building had once been heated with a wood stove and a prayer. Now vents for heat and air conditioning ran throughout the downstairs with its main meeting hall and a few offices. The upstairs was mostly storage. The character of the historic building had been maintained with its crown molding, marble foyer, and dark hardwood floors.

As meeting rooms went, this one held about a hundred people. Tonight it was packed, mostly with business owners whom Caprice recognized. When rezoning was in the works, everyone downtown was interested—from shopkeepers to developers to renters.

"What a crowd," Caprice said. "I thought everyone would be busy near Christmas and not show up."

"You showed up," Roz said. "With good reason. Everyone with a business has concerns about rezoning. My shop is in a block of commercial zoning on Restoration Row. But the block Adler wants rezoned, that's still mostly residential. There are renters in those historic buildings, and if he kicks them out and tears down the houses in order to replace them with businesses, more tax money will come into Kismet. But the residents aren't going to be happy."

Kiki said, "Tearing those houses down will ruin the character of Kismet. Because if it happens once, it will happen again." She sounded totally out of sorts about it.

A long table had been set up across the front of the room with all the town council members seated at it. The podium stood in front of that, and now the mayor took his place there. Hadley Coulter, who'd been mayor a little over a year, stood at the podium, pounded his gavel, and started the proceedings by welcoming everyone. He first went over the agenda, which wasn't a long one for tonight. Then he formally announced Chris Merriweather's replacement—Stanley Wicks.

There was a smattering of applause as Hadley introduced Stanley, but there was also an undercurrent of whispers. It was as if people were elbowing each other and murmuring that they now knew how the rezoning would go. That rezoning vote would be an open one in front of everyone assembled. But for the most part, the crowd knew where the individual town council members stood.

Caprice didn't know if Hadley just wanted to prolong the meeting or postpone the inevitable, but he gave the facts and figures on how well the Historic Homes Tour had done. That seemed a little contradictory since historic town houses could be torn down soon. But he didn't seem to see the irony in that, and that was his problem as mayor: Hadley couldn't seem to see the finer points of many things, including enhancing the budget for the police force, adding a few officers, thinking of creative ideas to bring in revenue. He seemed to be steeped in old ways and even fought the Chamber of Commerce on several issues that could possibly help the economy of Kismet. But those issues were for another day.

Hadley wore his hair practically parted down the middle with tufts of gray falling on either side. He had a long nose and his rimless glasses slid down it often. His arms were long too and so were his fingers as they clutched the sides of the podium.

He spoke into the mike and directly to the crowd. "We are now going to vote on the rezoning of the five hundred block of Bristol Row."

Just then, the back door to the hall that led in

from the lobby opened with a loud squeak. The noise was loud enough to distract Hadley.

Heads turned in the direction of the back of the room, and Caprice was surprised to see Maura walk in. She didn't take a seat but walked up the center aisle directly to the podium where Hadley stood.

"I know I'm not on the agenda, Mr. Mayor, but would you give me the chance to speak for a few minutes?"

Hadley looked perturbed, as if he didn't know what to do next. "You want to talk about your dad?" He apparently forgot the microphone was on. Everyone heard.

"In a way, I do. I promise this will only take a few minutes."

"Let her speak," someone called from a middle row. "We deserve to hear what Chris's daughter has to say. That's only democratic."

Hadley swung around to study the council members' faces. They all seemed to give him a nod. Stepping aside, he motioned Maura to the podium. "Go ahead," he said. "We all respected your father."

Maura looked shaky, pale, and not at all prepared to speak. Caprice was worried for her. Just what was she going to say? Would she just give a tribute to Chris? Or . . .

Maura began in a shaky voice that was thready with emotion. "My dad was proud to be a town council member. He voted with his heart and his gut and didn't take any town business lightly. As you know, he did everything he could to bring economic success to all your businesses." She pointed to the hardware store owner. "Clark, I know he often sent business your way from the craft store."

Clark nodded.

She pointed to Irving Bradford, the manager of Grocery Fresh. "And he always bought all of his oranges to give out from the Santa cabin at your store. If he knew a bicycle was on a child's list, he sent the parents to your shop, Roger. In the same vein, when he knew there was a needy family, he submitted their name to Everybody's Kitchen to be put on the list for free food. My dad was mostly a behind-the-scenes person, but he came forward when it counted most. That's why I had to come forward tonight."

Uh oh, Caprice thought. This meeting was about to turn on a dime. She took hold of Grant's hand and squeezed it. She imagined he knew what was coming too.

"I want to tell you about the man who pushed for this rezoning."

From a back row, Bailey Adler stood and shook his finger at Maura. "You have no right to say anything about me."

"I have every right if I'm telling the truth, and I am because I recorded one of our conversations."

"Conversations about what?" one of the town council members asked from behind Maura.

She stood to the side of the podium so she could address not only the town council members but the crowd too. "Bailey Adler offered me a bribe to convince my dad to change his vote. I'm not proud of the fact that I was going to take it . . . not because

I was convinced it was the best thing to do, but because we needed the money. But I ask you, if Bailey Adler would try to bribe me, then what else would he do? What would happen after he tears down those historic homes? Would he do what he says—limit his development ideas to those properties? Or would he try to buy up the whole next block? And just what kind of rent would he charge storekeepers? So, I guess what I'm asking you, in my dad's memory, is for you to vote against the change of zoning. Keep it a residential block. Let history live there and the renters who enjoy downtown Kismet."

She set a thumb drive in the middle of the town council table. "The recording is on there if you want to hear it. I taped it because I know what kind of man Bailey Adler is. You might want to adjourn and listen to it and postpone the vote on the rezoning."

Adler, red-faced, almost tripped over his chair as he headed for the aisle in the back of the room. Then he left, while the crowd broke out in chatter. Caprice's gaze followed him as Adler stopped at the back door. He looked at her, and then he looked at Maura. She could see he was furious, and if looks could kill . . .

He slammed the door when he left.

It was almost fifteen minutes later until everything calmed down and Hadley adjourned the meeting. He said the vote would be postponed until the town council listened to the recording. The zoning would be taken up again at the meeting the following month.

When Maura came down the aisle to Caprice, Caprice gave her a hug. "That took courage."

"The more I thought about it, the angrier I got. I talked with Mom about it this afternoon, and she agreed with me that I should do this."

Kiki and Roz both patted her on the shoulder. "We're so proud of you," Roz said.

"Adler shouldn't try to get back at you," Grant offered. "This was too public. They'd run him out of town if he tried to hurt you. Your father was respected here . . . and admired."

Tears came to Maura's eyes, and she brushed them away. "Pregnancy hormones," she said with a sniff.

But Caprice knew grief was still very much a part of her life and would be for a long time to come.

In no time at all, the crowd that had been assembled dispersed. Caprice and Grant had just stepped outside the town hall when her phone played. She dug it out of her pocket and glanced at the screen. "I could let it go to voicemail." She knew she and Grant needed some quiet time together.

"Who is it?" Grant asked.

"It's Harrison," she said with a bit of surprise.

"Take it," Grant advised her.

She did. "Harrison? You stood me up."

"I did," he said solemnly. "But I won't do it again. Meet me at Susie Q's in fifteen minutes. This time I'll be there."

"Fifteen minutes," she repeated. "At Susie Q's." She ended the call.

"You're not going in there alone," Grant told her.

"I'd like to talk to him alone."

"Fine. You sit at a table, and I'll be at the bar. I've got your back, Caprice."

She knew he did.

Chapter Eighteen

When Susie Q's wasn't busy, it seemed to have an air of the forbidden about it, maybe because the TV was turned down low, the lights were dimmer than usual, the scent of grilling burgers not as strong. She and Grant walked in together, though she didn't know if that was a good idea. If Harrison saw two of them, he might leave.

It took a few moments for Caprice to find him. He was hunched over a table for two in a back corner, obviously wanting to be separated from anyone else who came in.

Grant touched her shoulder and leaned in close. "I'll be at the bar. All you have to do is call my name."

Giving his arm a squeeze, she nodded then walked back the long room to where Harrison was seated. Unbuttoning her pea coat she didn't greet him, just slipped in to the chair across from him.

"You brought reinforcements," he grumbled.

"Grant's my fiancé. He just wants to make sure I'm safe."

Harrison seemed to think about that, then he nodded as if the idea was okay with him. "I want you to understand something," he said. "I thought long and hard about telling you anything."

"Because you don't want anybody else to know what you're going to tell me?" she guessed.

"Exactly."

"I can't promise that. To find Chris's murderer, every stone has to be turned over."

"I don't have an alibi for the night Chris was murdered. I'm probably a suspect because I knew him as long as I did. That Detective Jones went at me with a vengeance."

Although she didn't agree with Jones' tactics sometimes, she said, "That's his job."

"Maybe. But I'm not sure that what I'm going to tell you has to do with anyone else but me and Chris."

"Something happened between the two of you?" she prompted.

After he took hold of the bottle of beer on the table, he wrapped his hands around it and squeezed it hard. "You've got to realize that me, Ray, Chris, and Mack were army buddies and real friends for forty-five years."

She nodded, suddenly aware of how deeply whatever had happened had affected Harrison.

"We shared experiences no one should have to share when we were in Nam."

"You all knew about Kim?"

"We all knew Chris had fallen for her, including

my brother, Gary. Gary died over there," he said in a terse tone.

This was the first Harrison's brother Gary's name had surfaced. She was sure he'd brought up his brother's name for a reason. She listened.

"When we went to D.C. every year to the Memorial and out for drinks, the mood was never light. I mean, we weren't celebrating. We were remembering. Mack couldn't go this year. That changed the mood. Maybe that's why Chris revealed something I wish he wouldn't have."

What could Chris have told them? "About his relationship with Kim?"

"No. I think he was trying to clean his slate, prepare himself for dying, if anybody can do that. Would he have done it if Mack had been along? I don't know."

Harrison seemed lost in his memories and she waited.

"We'd gone to the Nam Memorial then out to a bar. Chris drank more than usual. False courage, I guess. When we got back to the room, he booted up his laptop for a while but then broke out a bottle of tequila he'd brought along. I thought that was kind of weird. Usually when we went back to the room we just watched sports, maybe drank some beer, ate nachos. But this was different. Ray and I had been watching TV, and Chris clicked it off. He had something to tell us."

Caprice's heart began to race, and she didn't even know why. But Harrison's voice had gone deeper. When she looked into his eyes, she saw pain that was raw. She didn't speak. She let him tell it his way.

"Chris told us about his brain tumor and its death sentence. He expected to die in less than a year. Ray and I hardly had time to absorb that when he went on. He recounted an experience from Nam. He told us about the night Gary died. Stuff I'd never heard before. It was like he was back there again on night patrol. He talked about a bunker, return fire, men huddled together, others pushing on to make the enemy retreat."

Harrison closed his eyes for a few seconds. He took his hands off the bottle and clenched them on the table. "It took me back there and into it . . . Ray too. Then Chris dropped the bomb, so to speak. He'd been side by side with Gary, separated from the rest of the squad. Gary got hit bad. Too bad to survive? Chris didn't know. But he left my brother there so he could save himself. He ran to safety and left Gary there to die. No one else saw it. No one else knew. He said it had been eating at him like acid all these years, and that's probably where his tumor had come from. It was his punishment."

Stunned, Caprice didn't know what to say. What could she say? She reached out her hand and covered one of Harrison's. His fist stayed clenched but he didn't shake her off.

"I was in shock after Chris told us. Ray was too. I wanted to kill Chris right then and there. I wanted to shout what he'd done from the mountain tops. I wanted to take away everything Chris had enjoyed over all these years that Gary hadn't—a family, a business, life. But I was numb. We all went to bed after that. We drove back the next day without talking to each other. Once I got back here, the rage really set in. I was drinking more. I was self-destructing, just like after Nam. And I knew I had to confront Chris. So I did. It was about a week before he was murdered. I went at him with my fists and he didn't fight back."

Caprice remembered Chris's bruised jaw, the cut on his forehead, the bruised ribs Sara had seen.

"You could have done worse damage than you did," she said, wanting to find out more, wanting to find out if Harrison had gone after Chris again, maybe with that candy cane stake.

"Yeah, I could have. But I didn't. Nam was war. Soldiers panicked. But Chris left my brother for dead. That doesn't mean Gary wouldn't have died anyway, but I just had to retaliate somehow. Chris had to know our friendship was over. And in the middle of that fight when I punched him, I realized our friendship was going to be over anyway, because Chris was going to die. So why should I even waste my energy in trying to make him pay?"

Caprice's hand was still on his, and she squeezed his fist. "I'm sorry, Harrison. I'm sorry you lost your brother, and I'm sorry you lost your friend. I understand why you wanted to keep this quiet, but maybe you should tell the police before someone else does it for you. The truth always comes out. The police know someone beat up Chris because Sara told them. They're surely looking for that person. And a friend of my assistant witnessed your scuffle with Chris in back of Susie Q's, but he didn't recognize who you were."

"This gives me motive, doesn't it?" he asked, looking directly into her eyes.

"It does. Except as you said—you knew Chris was going to die. So maybe not much of a motive. You and Ray were the only two people who knew."

"I won't talk to Detective Jones again."

"I know the other detective on the case, Brett Carstead. He's fair, and he knows how to listen. Why don't I call him, and you can set up something with him."

"I didn't want to cause more grief to Sara," Harrison said. "Ray and I didn't know about Kim's boy. We didn't know Chris had been sending money. He kept a lot of secrets."

"Secrets fester," Caprice said. "Let me call Brett." Harrison nodded his head and then bowed it.

After Caprice's meeting with Harrison, she felt shaken. She'd called Brett, and he'd come right over to Susie Q's without asking her ten thousand questions. She and Grant left, but she felt so unsettled and he saw that.

He asked, "Why don't we go to your parents and you can talk to your dad?"

"Do you mind?"

"I don't mind. Patches and Lady are probably sleeping and so are the cats. They'll be okay until we get back."

They'd left all of the animals at her place. "Maybe we should get one of those spy cams," she said.

He chuckled. "Along with your security system?"

"Maybe. There would be a camera in the living

room and with some of them, you can even speak to your animals so they'd come running if they hear our voices. Don't you think that would be a good idea?"

"It's something to think about," he agreed.

When he said that, Caprice wondered if he was thinking about a new house where they could have everything installed. She knew she had to talk to him about it, but she didn't want to bring it up now, not with this new development in the murder case.

She texted her dad, and her parents were expecting them when they arrived. Blitz met them at the door like a butler, and she crouched down to rub him all over. He really liked that. Maybe with that thick coat, he needed the stimulation.

Caprice's dad waved to them from the living room. "Come on in here." They'd taken off their coats and made themselves at home when her mom peeked into the room. "I'm just going to put some snacks together. You go ahead and talk."

"Are you sure?" Caprice asked her mother. She didn't want her to feel left out.

Her mom smiled at her. "I'm sure. Your dad can always fill me in if I miss something."

"So, tell me what happened tonight," her father said after her mom had gone to the kitchen. "You met with Harrison Barnhart, right?"

"We did. He's talking to Brett now. I called Brett after Harrison filled me in. It's so sad, Dad. I thought about not telling you, but I need to talk about this, and I'm sure once the police know, it's going to get out anyway."

"So, tell me."

Caprice relayed what Harrison had told her with as accurate a memory as she could muster.

After she'd finished, her father looked troubled. "There is no excuse for Chris leaving Gary behind. But Chris was a young man then. Those boys went over there not knowing what to expect, not knowing what they were going to face. I'm sure what happened there shaped his character for the rest of his life."

Caprice was sure of that too. She considered how altruistic Chris had become, helpful with everyone he met.

"I wonder if Mack had gone along on that trip if Chris would have revealed everything."

"There's no way to know," Grant said. "I don't think you're going to have to tell Mack about it. Although he's off the case, he does look over everything. He'll hear about Harrison's interview with Brett, I'm sure of that."

"Do you believe Harrison when he said he couldn't kill Chris?" her dad asked her.

"He was so torn up, Dad, and he did beat him up. It would have happened that night if he was going to do it."

"Does Harrison have an alibi for the night Chris was killed?"

Caprice shook her head. "No."

"The police are going to look at him hard," Grant said.

As if he sensed the tension and the distress in the room, Blitz went from one of them to the other, looking up at them, and waiting for a pat on the head. When he came over to Caprice, she scratched his ears and petted along his flanks. As she did, she studied his collar again, remembering her thoughts about it the last time she'd looked at it.

She ran her finger alongside of it and under it. "Do you ever take this off him?" she asked her dad.

"I haven't yet. When we take him to a groomer, we'll take it off then."

"Do you mind if I look at it?"

Her father cocked his head and studied her with puzzlement on his face. "Why?"

"Because it seems thicker than a normal dog collar." She unbuckled it and slipped it from the dog's neck.

Grant looked over her shoulder as she examined it. He pointed to the stitching. "That looks as if it's been re-sewn many times."

She pressed along the collar with her thumb and forefinger. When she reached near the buckle she said, "I think I feel something inside. It's thicker and hard there."

"Maybe it's just the lining," her father said.

She ran her finger over it again. "I don't think so. Can we take it apart?"

Caprice had often questioned things as a child, taken things apart, asked her dad unusual questions. So, he didn't blink an eye now. He just said, "Be right back. Your mom has a tool in her sewing box that will do the trick."

He went into the library adjacent to the living room. When he came back he had a tool like a seamstress used that cut off stitches without much effort. The thread on the collar was tough so it took her dad a little work to cut through each stitch. "If this collar falls apart I can buy another one in the morning."

After removing the stitches from both sides, he handed the collar to Caprice.

She pulled it apart and inside she did find something unusual. Taking it out, she held it up.

"It's a key." She studied the initials on it. "Those are the initials for the storage company where I have a unit. My padlock has them on it."

"It says *333*," she mused. "That belongs to the building that has smaller compartments. They're bigger than school lockers. Square. I've seen owners of those compartments put photograph albums and small collectibles inside."

"You could turn the key into the police," Grant suggested. "But on the other hand, all of Chris's possessions went to Sara. So, really, whatever is in that storage compartment is hers. She probably just has to show a death certificate to access it."

"Or *she* could decide to take the key to the police," Caprice offered.

"She could," her dad said. "But knowing Sara, she's going to want to know what's in that compartment before she turns over the key."

"I'd want to know," Caprice assured him.

"Your mother would too," her dad told her with a wry smile.

"There could be love letters in there," Grant warned her.

"Yes, there could be," Caprice agreed. "Even mementos from Chris's time in Vietnam. If there are, Sara needs to make a decision whether she wants to examine it all. I'll go see her first thing in the morning, and then we'll go from there."

Grant and her dad didn't protest because they knew if they did, that wouldn't do any good.

Caprice hadn't slept much at all. It was barely sunrise when she heard Grant come out of the spare bedroom. He and Patches had stayed last night. He was in a protective mode, and although she usually pushed his concern away, this time she didn't. Maybe because she liked him under the same roof.

Grabbing her robe, she shrugged it on, belted it, and met him in the hallway. Lady raced out and joined Patches there too. The two dogs ran down the stairs eager for their day to start.

Grant gathered her into his arms and kissed her. Then he studied her face. "You have dark circles under your eyes. Didn't sleep well?"

"Didn't sleep much at all. That key on my dresser is like a magnet. I can't wait to take it to Sara."

Mirabelle jumped off Caprice's bed and came out to join them. She wound about Grant's legs then looked up at him and meowed.

"She's asking me what I'm doing here again."

"Nope. She's just asking if you're the one who's going to get her breakfast."

Mirabelle gave another meow as if she agreed with that assessment.

Sophia jumped down from her perch atop Caprice's armoire. She gave a look to Caprice that asked, *What are we standing here for?* and trotted down the stairs after Lady and Patches.

"I'll let the dogs out while you make the coffee," Grant suggested.

"Maybe after breakfast we can take them for a walk. I've got this excess energy, and I can't go to the craft store before nine."

"Sounds good," Grant said, wrapping his arm around her and giving her a hug.

An hour and a half later, Grant had left with Patches to go home to work at his town house for the morning. He was leaving for the courthouse in York around noon. He'd mentioned he'd be tied up there into the evening. She'd promised to text or call him when she had any news. It was quite possible that Sara knew about the storage compartment. Maybe her name was on the contract with Chris's. But Caprice doubted that.

Caprice hadn't called her to set up a visit at her house because she wanted to see the look on Sara's face when she told her about the key. She thought dropping in at the craft store was the best way to handle it.

The store was already scattered with customers when Caprice walked in. She knew this was their busiest season. She asked one of the cashiers where she might find Sara, and the woman pointed to the office in the back. That's where Caprice headed.

The door was ajar, and Caprice stood there a minute studying Chris Merriweather's wife as she sat at the computer, tapping in information from a legal pad next to her. She had a pen stuck in her hair above her ear.

Caprice rapped lightly on the door frame, and Sara looked up. "Hi, Caprice." She put her legal pad aside and leaned back in the swivel chair. "I'm making a list of the pros and cons of keeping this place."

"Is your list leaning one way or the other?" She stepped into the office in front of Sara's desk.

"It's about even right now. I think it's going to boil down to the fact of whether or not I want to come into work every day and feel productive. Or if I want to sit in a new condo and think about everything I can't change."

"That sounds to me as if you've made a decision."

"Possibly. What brings you here this morning?"

Caprice lifted the flap on her fringed hobo bag. The peace sign charm on the strap jangled as she reached inside and took the key from a zippered compartment. She held it out to Sara. "I found this in Blitz's collar. Do you know what it is?"

Sara took it from her hand, her expression perplexed. "In Blitz's collar?" She turned it over and saw the storage facility's emblem. But her face didn't show any recognition.

"It's from the storage center. It belongs to compartment 333. Do you know anything about it?"

"No," Sara said softly, and Caprice believed her because in her eyes there was that dismay that this was just something else Chris had kept from her. "Do you think I can get into it?"

"Grant says if you take along a death certificate, you'll be able to."

Sara studied her watch, then she went to the clothes tree in the corner and lifted off her coat. "Will you go with me?"

"We could give the key to the police," she told Sara.

"Not before I see what's in the compartment. I'll call them after we've examined it."

Caprice didn't know if this was the right decision or not, but she'd suspected it would be what Sara wanted to do. Not knowing what she'd find in the compartment, Caprice realized Sara needed emotional support. "Are you sure you want me there rather than Maura or Deanne or Ryan?"

"There's no knowing what's in there. I don't want them hurt further. I'd like you to be with me."

"Then let's go," Caprice said.

Sara stopped at home for a death certificate, then met Caprice at the office at the storage center. The manager knew Caprice because she was in and out of the center often to pick up furniture and decorations from her storage compartments. After Sara showed him ID and the death certificate, he said he would place it on file and gave them permission to open the locker.

Sara followed Caprice in her car since Caprice knew the way to the smaller compartments. They both parked on the asphalt drive. Together they found compartment 333.

Inserting the key in the lock, Sara glanced at Caprice. "I'm scared what we're going to find."

"You don't have to look," Caprice reminded her.

"Yes, I do," Sara insisted and opened the lock.

Then she lifted the door on the two-foot by two-foot compartment.

Once the door was up, they could both see a shoe box. Sara lifted it out. "Let's sit in my car. It's too cold out here."

Caprice went around to the passenger side of the sedan and slid inside.

Once inside her car, Sara blew on her fingers to warm them and then lifted the shoe box's lid. Caprice could easily see letters and photos inside.

As Sara sorted them, her voice shook when she said, "These must be photos of Kim and Trung."

Caprice didn't want to intrude, but Sara held them out to her, tears sliding down her cheeks.

"She was beautiful, wasn't she?" Sara asked rhetorically. "And Trung. He was so dear."

Caprice studied the photos because it seemed Sara wanted her to. There were about twenty in all, different stages in the life of the woman Chris had loved and their son.

"I wish he would have told me," Sara said weakly.

Caprice's heart ached for her.

Next, Sara looked through letters that Kim had written to Chris. They'd been delivered to his lawyer's office. By that point, Sara's tears flowed faster as she read a few of them.

Caprice just sat by watching and listening whenever Sara wanted to speak.

Soon Sara reached the bottom of the shoe box. There she found a sheet of paper that had been folded into thirds. It looked like something a computer printer would spew out.

When she opened it, she gasped. "That's Reed," she said, looking shocked. She handed over the printout to Caprice. Caprice studied it.

It was a screen shot from a profile page from LetsGetTogether.com. The profile had been set up two years ago. The photo was indeed of Reed. His username? Mustang.

What was Reed doing on LetsGetTogether.com? And why would Chris have tucked this away? Was it something the police should know about? She'd have to investigate further before knowing that.

"What do you think it means?" Sara asked.

"I don't know. But there's a reason Chris kept it here. I'll try to get on the LetsGetTogether website and find Reed's profile. Then we can go from there. For now, pretend you know nothing about this."

"That's going to be hard, especially if I have to go through Christmas dinner knowing he had a profile on this site."

"Hopefully before then we'll figure out why Chris kept it. There's somebody I can call who's registered on the website. I can get his name and number from Bella."

Sara looked as if she'd aged ten years from the time they'd driven into the storage facility. Caprice felt so sorry for her. She just hoped this profile of Reed's wasn't something else that would bring Sara and Maura heartache.

Chapter Nineteen

Caprice considered what to do next. Turn information over to Brett? But what exactly did she have? Not much. Simply that Reed had once been on LetsGetTogether.com. Still . . .

No, she couldn't bother him again with nothing concrete. He'd stop trusting her. He'd stop confiding in her. She wanted to call Grant and talk it over with him, but he was spending the afternoon at the courthouse in York. Only one thing left to do—follow her sixth sense, or her gut, or whatever that inside voice Nana always advised her to listen to was telling her to do. She'd text Maura. If she called her, she'd have to explain. She really didn't want to go into explanations. Not yet, anyway. Not over the phone.

Caprice texted:

I have questions about Reed's trips out of town over the year. Can we meet to talk?

She wasn't sure she was right, but Reed's trips out of town to car auctions or to deliver cars to customers might have been more than that. She didn't know whether or not to expect a reply right away, but she got one.

Maura texted back:

> I have errands in town to pick up Christmas presents. Can you meet me at the park entrance at 8 p.m.?

That made sense to Caprice. If Maura was downtown. Yet the park entrance . . .

Maybe a phone call would be better than the text. She found Maura's number in her contacts list and pressed the phone icon. But the phone went to voicemail.

All right. She had to be practical about this. Grant said he'd have her back but all she could do was leave him a message. Then she did the next best thing to having Grant as her backup. She phoned her dad.

"I don't like it," he told Caprice. "The Santa cabin closes at seven. By eight, nobody's going to be around. Where's she picking up Christmas presents?"

"I didn't ask. Maybe she's parking in the public lot. It's right near the park."

"That's possible," he agreed. "Grant's in York today, isn't he?"

"Yes, and I don't know what time he'll be back. It could be late."

"I think his appointment after his business at the

courthouse has something to do with your Christmas present."

She wasn't going to get sidetracked wondering what that was.

Her dad went on, "This is what we're going to do. Blitz and I are going to meet you at the park before eight o'clock. I'll take Blitz for a walk, but I'll be able to keep my eye on you and Maura. How does that sound?"

"That sounds like a plan. I'll meet you at the park entrance about seven forty-five. Does that sound good?"

"You just go to the park entrance. I'll stay out of sight. Text me when you get there."

"It's cold, Dad."

"Blitz won't mind a bit, and I'll make sure I wear my earmuffs. Don't worry about me. I just want to make sure you're safe. I'm concerned someone might follow you there."

"I'll take a circuitous route. I'll have my mace gun. I know self-defense moves."

Her father grunted. "Thank goodness you do. Remember, text me when you get there."

"I won't forget."

At almost 7:45 p.m., Caprice parked in the public lot near the park and glanced around. She didn't see any other vehicles . . . didn't even see her dad's. But he might have purposely parked the car somewhere else to keep it out of sight. She had taken a circuitous route to the park and was sure she hadn't been followed.

She climbed out of her Camaro, glancing all around. The lights in the parking lot didn't illuminate much beyond its perimeter. The wind blew through the white pines lining the north side of the lot. It burned Caprice's cheeks and she wondered again why Maura had suggested meeting there. She specifically said at the entrance to Santa Lane.

Did Maura want to revisit memories of her father? That was quite possible. And it was better to do that when the Santa cabin wasn't occupied. Still, the temperature was dropping to freezing.

Caprice had dressed for the cold in her faux fur coat, watch cap, and fleece-lined gloves. Her suede boots were fleece-lined too. Her wool slacks hung over her heavy socks and boots. Closing her car door, she didn't lock it. What if she had to make a fast get-away? Too many drama-filled thoughts.

Taking out her phone, she texted her dad:

I'm here, heading to Santa Lane.

He texted back:

Eyes on you.

She glanced around, wondering where he could be. But she supposed that didn't matter. She had the security of knowing he was there. When she reached the entrance to Santa Lane, she walked back and forth. To keep herself warm, she jogged about ten feet down the lane toward the sleigh and then jogged the ten feet back. If Maura was picking up Christmas presents, she could get held up any number of places. Kismet wasn't used to much traffic, and there was more of it this time of year.

She checked the phone time—8:00. How long should she give Maura to arrive? Ten minutes? Fifteen?

Suddenly, almost out of nowhere, a tall, shadowy figure materialized right beside her. Her phone was in her hand. She was lifting it to text her dad when a voice commanded, "Hand me your phone."

She recognized the voice, and now she recognized the face surrounded by a black hoodie. He wore the hoodie under a fleece coat that he'd left open.

She was about to protest handing over her phone when she looked down his torso to his hands and saw something that changed everything. He had a gun. She snaked her hand toward her pocket and her pepper spray gun.

Before she handed Reed Fitzgee the phone, she asked, "Where's Maura?" Her fingers fumbled in the lining of her deep pocket where the pepper spray gun lay.

"At home, blissfully unaware of the text you sent her. She isn't one of those people who carries her phone everywhere. She leaves it on the dresser in the bedroom. I had the day off and happened to see your text come in. I'm the one who answered it. Now start walking." He grabbed her phone and ordered, "Keep your hands where I can see them. Now."

She couldn't extricate the spray gun without him shooting her or jumping her. Better to stall for time. "Why didn't you let me meet with Maura?"

Reed slid her phone into the pocket of his hoodie. "Because you're getting too close. The same thing's going to happen to you that happened to Chris, but yours will be quicker."

She snatched another look at the gun, and she saw the tube on the end of it. His gun had a silencer.

She didn't know what to do. With her glove on, the spray can was too difficult to extricate. Most of all, she didn't want her father running into the line of Reed's fire.

The surrounding silence was only punctuated by the sound of her breaths, which were coming quicker. Her mind was racing. What could she do? How could she get away? If she made a run for it, he'd shoot her. But she had to do something before her father got involved.

"Tell me why you did it," she prompted, hoping he'd brag like some criminals did. "Why did you kill Chris?"

"You talk too much, and you ask too many questions," he grumbled.

"What does it matter now? If you're going to kill me anyway, at least give me the satisfaction of knowing why you did it."

He gave a small shrug. "I was catfishing on LetsGetTogether. I met a couple of women out of town, got them to trust me, got some money from them."

"And Chris found out?" she guessed.

"Oh, yeah. He was trying to convince me to divorce Maura. He threatened to tell her everything if I didn't. He always acted so superior . . . always acted like he knew best. He told me he'd never give me another cent. He told me he'd ruin me here, and I wouldn't be able to get any work. Then he turned away as if the divorce was a done deal, ready to let that dog of his out of the cabin where he'd penned him. That dog never liked me. I didn't want him out, and I didn't want Chris ruining my life. I couldn't let him do that. That candy cane was hardly stuck in the ground. I just pulled it out—"

Like a herald of hope, sleigh bells rang . . . the bells hanging on the sleigh. She and Reed were about ten feet from it and the noise caught Reed's immediate attention. As he turned toward the jingle, Caprice's dad emerged from the other side of the sleigh and started running toward her. But before he could reach her, Blitz streaked out ahead of him. Caprice had never heard the dog growl before, but he growled now and he launched himself onto Reed.

The gun went off.

Panic tightening her throat, her heart practically stopping, Caprice feared the shot had hit Blitz or even her dad. Rushing forward, she saw Blitz's attack on Reed had knocked the gun out of his hand. It had slid under the sleigh.

Blitz growled and pulled on the zipper of Reed's jacket. His paws pushed down on the man's chest.

Before Caprice could assimilate what was happening, her father jumped on Reed too, commanded Blitz to stop, and told Reed, "You make one wrong move and I'll order Blitz to attack."

Caprice didn't think Blitz even knew what the word meant, but Reed didn't know the threat wasn't authentic.

Running to the sleigh, Caprice pulled the red vinyl ribbon off one of the gold packages and ran to her dad who'd managed to turn Reed over and pull his hands behind his back.

A siren sounded, at first in the distance, but getting closer fast.

Nick De Luca took the ribbon from Caprice, wound it around Reed's wrists, and tied it tight. "I hit 9-1-1 as soon as I saw Reed appear. They'll be here any minute." Reed began to struggle, trying to pull his hands apart. Blitz growled again as Reed attempted to lift his shoulders. Her father pressed Reed down between his shoulder blades and sat on his legs. Who knew her dad was in such good shape? Caprice was thankful he was.

A patrol car swerved into Santa Lane, lights flashing. Two officers jumped out and came running toward them. A few minutes later amid Reed's protests, Caprice and her father told the officers what had happened, pointed to the gun, explained Reed had shot at them, that he had admitted to killing Chris Merriweather, and that he'd planned to kill Caprice.

The officers took over, read Reed his rights, and then took him into custody. As they seated him in the patrol car, Caprice's dad's arm went around her and he caught her into a huge hug.

She felt something wet on her hand. It was Blitz's nose as he nuzzled her fingers. "Thank you," she murmured to her father and then bent to stroke Blitz's head. "Thank *you*," she whispered to the dog.

"Tonight you weren't just my dad's best friend, you were mine too."

"Santa Lane will be safe now," her father said, his voice husky.

"And I'll remember the beautiful sound of sleigh bells for the rest of my life," she assured him.

Epilogue

Christmas carols played softly from a boom box in the De Luca kitchen as Caprice slid a rigatoni casserole into the oven beside the ham baking there. Nana sliced homemade bread, as her mom diced carrots to toss into the large wooden salad bowl. Caprice's dad had stepped outside to plug in the Christmas lights.

When Grant appeared in the kitchen doorway, Lady, Patches, and Blitz followed him because of the great smells emanating from the kitchen.

"Are you busy?" he asked. "Or can I steal you for a few minutes?"

Caprice's mom sent a smile to Grant. "You can steal her. Everyone will be arriving soon, and there will be so many people in here we'll trip over each other."

Nana looked up from the bread she was wrapping in tinfoil and gave Caprice a knowing smile, as if she were a conspirator in whatever Grant wanted to show her.

"Where are we going?" Caprice asked Grant as he took her hand and pulled her into the dining room.

"To the library."

"Can I ask why?"

Through the dining room and into the foyer now, they turned right into the living room as the dogs followed them. Then suddenly Lady, Patches, and Blitz raced ahead as if they knew exactly where Grant was leading her.

"I want to give you your Christmas present," he said.

She stopped and held his arm, looking up at him with all the loving feelings in her heart. "You already gave me a present last night—pink sapphire earrings to match my engagement ring." She pointed to them, thrilled with them. She wasn't wearing red today, but rather a rose dress in a fifties style with a round neck, cap sleeves, fitted waist, and full skirt. It went perfectly with the ring and her earrings.

Wrapping his arm around her, he guided her toward the doorway to the library. "This is an additional present."

Once in the library doorway, she noticed the dogs nosing around a card table that Grant had set up. As they walked toward it, Caprice could see architectural plans. For a moment, her heart sank. She didn't want to confront this issue now, not on Christmas Day.

"Come look," Grant commanded her, not giving anything away.

She had to look. He was excited about it, that was

obvious. They *could* figure out where they were going to live. If these were new house plans, she would open her mind to the possibility—

But then her gaze fell on the layout. She recognized it. That was the layout of her house, except . . . there was an addition drawn onto it.

Grant ran his hand along the perimeter of the house plan, and then he gazed directly into her eyes. "I know how much you love your house. That was obvious when you didn't want to talk about where we were going to live. I knew you were holding back because you didn't want to hurt my feelings or rock the boat."

"Grant, I'm open to whatever you want to do."

"I knew you'd say that. So, I thought about it . . . a lot. I like your house too. It's terrific. It shows all the care you've put into it. So, I had an architect draw up two different versions of an addition that could be my home office. We can either add it onto the garage side of the house or onto the back and eliminate the back porch. What do you think?" He lifted the top plan to show her one underneath.

But she wasn't looking at the plans. She threw her arms around him. "I think . . . and I know . . . I love you."

They were still kissing when the front door opened and bursts of laughter and conversation floated in. Family and friends had arrived, caught up in hugs and conversations and lots of *Merry Christmases*.

Forty-five minutes later, everyone was seated around the long mahogany dining room table. The group had taken seats randomly. Grant was beside

Caprice, and Caprice was beside Brett with Nikki next to him.

After her dad had said grace and they'd started passing around the serving plates, Caprice said to Brett, "I have some interesting news."

"Your news is always interesting," he admitted wryly. "What's up now?"

"Sara Merriweather and her son Ryan are flying to Vietnam to meet Trung."

"That *is* interesting news. Good news, too, for them. Maybe it will ease some of their heartache."

"I'm glad Reed confessed to you about killing Chris, then the family won't have to go through a long, drawn-out trial."

"His arraignment will happen this week, after Christmas," Brett explained. "The charges are public record: second-degree murder, terroristic threats for the note he left on your car, and two counts of criminal attempt homicide for his attack on you and your dad."

"Sara and Maura told us you managed to piece the whole story together," Caprice said. She and her dad had visited Sara and Maura yesterday. Since she and her father had been in danger from Reed, they'd wanted to fill them in.

"Maura helped immensely," Brett said. "And that had to be hard for her. Thanks to our best techie, we were able to access Reed's deleted profile and his messaging page on LetsGetTogether."

"Maura told me you also confiscated his tablet computer and found e-mails," Caprice said.

Brett shook his head in disgust. "I can't believe what that guy was doing."

"You mean dating women other than his wife, having relationships with them, even promising them engagements so they'd lend him money?"

Sara had confided in Caprice and her dad that Reed had always been the one who'd handled finances for himself and Maura. After he'd been taken into custody, Maura had accessed charge account receipts and found out so much she didn't want to know. She'd even found a few phone numbers and called those numbers. The women he'd dated were shocked that Reed had been married. Maura had admitted she'd been blind to all of it because she didn't want to believe Reed was lying when he said he had to work late or go out of town for business.

"Reed spilled everything to us when Maura was there," Brett responded. "I couldn't believe it. It was almost as if he enjoyed hurting her. She asked us if she could sit in on the interview, and we let her, hoping we'd get more out of Reed because of it. We did. Sometimes human beings are despicable."

"She told me that Reed explained how her dad found out about his duplicity," Caprice said. "Apparently one evening Maura and Reed had invited her parents to dinner at their house. Reed had left the room. His phone on a side table signaled a notification coming in. Chris had seen Reed tap in his passcode more than once and something made him do it then. He saw a notification about an e-mail from a woman, and it was signed *Love*. After examining Reed's apps, he saw the app icon for the LetsGetTogether site. He recognized it because Deanne had used it."

"I was amazed at Maura's spunk at our interview," Brett said. "She had it in her to really goad her husband. So, he filled us in on exactly what had happened."

Caprice nodded, remembering what Maura had said. Chris had signed himself up on the LetsGetTogether site, investigated, and found Reed's profile. Then her dad had pretended to be a woman interested in dating him. Through the messages, he realized exactly what Reed intended to do. It didn't take a genius. The women he attracted were blinded by his charm and good looks and didn't realize what a scoundrel he was until it was too late.

Brett gave Caprice a steady look. "I guess you know Reed didn't expect you to be smart enough to bring along backup that night at Santa Lane. He thought you'd be as naïve as Maura and all those women he'd dated."

Nikki, who had been listening to it all, nudged Brett's arm. "You do know, don't you, that none of the De Luca women are naïve?"

With a broad smile, Brett hung his arm around Nikki's shoulders which was his first public display of affection with her. "That's a good thing," he assured her. "I like my women smart and savvy."

Nikki asked, "Women, as in plural?"

Brett looked a little sheepish. Then he amended his statement. "I like my woman smart and savvy, and *you* are both."

Grant took Caprice's hand and squeezed it. Then he leaned in close. "I think I might have to ask Brett to be a groomsman at our wedding." Gazing into her eyes, he added, "This is going to be my best Christmas ever."

"Only the first of many," Bella's husband, Joe, interjected from across the table. "Caprice, can you pass the rigatoni?"

Bella gave Caprice a wink.

Her family definitely kept her grounded, safe, and secure.

As Grant reached for the large rigatoni casserole at the same time as she did to help her pass it, she knew *he* was her best Christmas present of all.

Original Recipes

Fran's Lemon-Pepper Cod

1 cup Panko
1 tablespoon lemon pepper
¼ teaspoon salt
Pinch of garlic powder
1½ pounds fresh cod, cut into 6 pieces
1 egg

Preheat oven to 350 degrees.

Mix together Panko, lemon pepper, salt, and garlic powder in a medium-sized bowl. Beat egg in a small bowl with a fork. Dip cod pieces in the egg then dip into the dry mixture to coat both sides. Bake on a flat pan for 30-35 minutes.

Serves 4-6

Nana's Lemon Pasta

4 tablespoons butter
1 cup chopped onion
1 clove garlic, grated
1 tablespoon lemon pepper
1 lemon, juiced
1 tablespoon grated lemon zest (taken from
    lemon before juicing)
½ pound pasta of your choice (I like
    Campanelle) cooked according to package
    directions
1 tablespoon fresh chives

While pasta is boiling, sauté onion in butter in a
saucepan, then add grated garlic and lemon pepper.
Cook until onion is tender. Stir in lemon juice. Cook
on low about 2 minutes. Stir in lemon zest and pour
over ½ pound cooked pasta. Sprinkle with fresh
chives.

Serves 4-6

Nikki's Chocolate Peppermint Blossoms

2 sticks (1 cup) butter, softened
¾ cup granulated sugar (plus an additional
  ½ cup to roll cookies in)
¾ cup packed dark brown sugar
2 large eggs
1 teaspoon baking soda
½ teaspoon baking powder
¼ cup cocoa
2½ cups flour
36-40 Hershey's specialty holiday candy,
  unwrapped (I use Candy Cane Peppermint
  Kisses)

Preheat oven to 375 degrees.

Cream butter, granulated sugar, and brown sugar.
Add eggs and mix well. Add baking soda, baking
powder, and cocoa. Mix until all ingredients are
blended well and batter is smooth and velvety. Add
flour ½ cup at a time.

When mixed, form one-inch balls and roll them in
granulated sugar. Handle as little as possible. Put
balls on lightly greased cookie sheets, leaving room
to grow.

Bake 11-13 minutes until set. Let cool one minute,
then lightly press on candy. The candy will melt a bit.

Remove cookies to a cooling rack. Let cool until
candy has hardened again, then store.

Makes about 36 cookies.

In an old Victorian in the heart of Pennsylvania's Amish country, Daisy Swanson and her Aunt Iris serve soups, scones, and soothing teas to tourists and locals— but a murder in their garden has them in hot water . . .

Daisy, a widowed mom of two teenagers, is used to feeling protective, so when Iris started dating the wealthy and not-quite-divorced Harvey Fitz, she worried . . . especially after his bitter ex stormed in and caused a scene at the party Daisy's Tea Garden was catering. Then there was the gossip she overheard about Harvey's grown children being cut out of his will. Daisy didn't want her aunt to wind up with a broken heart— but she never expected Iris to wind up a suspect in Harvey's murder.

Now the apple bread and orange pekoe is on the back burner while the cops treat the tea garden like a crime scene—and Daisy hopes that Jonas Groft, a former detective from Philadelphia, can help her clear her aunt's name and bag the real killer before things boil over.

Please turn the page for an exciting sneak peek at the first book in a new mystery series from Karen Rose Smith! Look for

Murder with Lemon Tea Cakes

coming soon, wherever print and e-books are sold!

Chapter One

"Harvey, that's so kind of you to say." An almost-giggle escaped from Daisy Swanson's Aunt Iris.

Daisy watched her aunt as she set a hand-painted porcelain teapot that was steeping blackberry black tea before a man Iris had dated merely a month. Yes, her aunt was acting like a teenager, and Daisy definitely knew teenagers. Her own daughters giggled like that around guys they deemed crush-worthy. Her aunt practically twitted like an adolescent when she was around Harvey Fitz, owner of Men's Trends in the small town of Willow Creek, Pennsylvania.

Business at Daisy's Tea Garden was slowing down for the day. Willow Creek was a semi-busy tourist town set in the midst of Amish country, near Lancaster. It was a town where neighbors knew neighbors, talked about neighbors, and proved there might be less than six degrees of separation between everyone.

Her aunt's ash-blond short curls bounced as she

slid a bone china sugar bowl painted with a rose design near Harvey's cup.

"Half a teaspoon should be just right," he said, looking at the blushing older woman as if she was more important than any tea brew.

Harvey was tall and thin with a shock of silver hair still thick and long enough to give him a distinguished look. It even turned up at his neck in the back.

Daisy had to wonder if he'd had hair plugs transplanted on the top of his head. That hair looked too good for a man of his age. He had to be seventy, about ten years older than her aunt.

She needed to break into their conversation to find out how far into dating they'd gotten. She didn't want her aunt to get hurt. They hadn't known Harvey very long, and they didn't know him nearly well enough. As far as Daisy was concerned, Iris should stay far away from him because he was still married! Separated, but married.

That was trouble, no matter how you looked at it.

Keeping her ear tilted toward the couple's conversation, Daisy glanced around the business she and Iris had grown from scratch. Well, not exactly from scratch. It had been a bakery on the first floor of an old Victorian before they'd bought it. Now they rented the upstairs to a high school friend of Daisy's, Tessa Miller, chef and kitchen manager of the tea garden. They'd developed the downstairs into a tea, baked goods, and soup business.

The interior wasn't froufrou like many tea rooms, though it did have a subtle flower theme. They'd considered the fact that they wanted men to feel comfortable here as well as women. Besides merely drawing from Willow Creek's tourist trade— Lancaster County Amish country was a popular get-away destination—they wanted to draw from the professional offices in Willow Creek and Lancaster too.

In keeping with that plan, they'd decorated the walk-in "be served or buy-it-and-go" room with oak, glass-topped tables, and mismatched, antique oak, hand-carved chairs. A yellow bud vase adorned each table. The walls had been painted the palest green in the walk-in tea serving area because Daisy believed the color green promoted calming qualities just as tea did.

In contrast, the more private room was a spillover area. On specified days, it was also the room where they scheduled reservations for afternoon tea which included mutiple courses. The space reflected the best qualities of a Victorian, with a bay window, window seats, crown molding, and diamond-cut glass. In that room, the walls were the palest yellow. White tables and chairs wore seat cushions in blue, green, and yellow pinstripes.

Tessa emerged from the kitchen with a bright smile and a serving dish in hand.

Tessa was Daisy's age, thirty-seven, with rich caramel-colored hair that she wore in a braid. She always dressed like the artiste she was, with colorful and flowy tops and skirts. She wore smocks to work in lieu of the usual chef's coat. Today, in tribute to the fall weather, her smock was bright swirls of orange and rust. She set a cut-glass plate filled with cookies in front of Harvey. On the top of the other cookies perched a lemon tea cake fresh from the oven.

"My favorite," Harvey announced, picking it up and taking a large bite. "I don't know how you do it, but every one of your cookies is delicious, not to mention your scones. You *are* going to have the lemon tea cakes at my celebration this weekend, aren't you?"

One of the reasons Harvey had stopped in today was to consult with her and Iris about his store's twenty-fifth anniversary celebration. That would be a big to-do, with engraved invitations that the manager of Men's Trends had sent out. It was a large party for Daisy and her staff to cater. Besides the main event here at the tea garden on Sunday, tomorrow—on the store's actual anniversary date—Men's Trends would be serving tea and accompanying snacks to any of their customers who wandered in during the afternoon.

"We'll have lemon tea cakes at your store tomorrow too," Daisy assured him.

Harvey finished his cookie, wiped his fingers on his napkin, then gazed once more at Iris. "Will you be at Men's Trends tomorrow or do you have to stay here to hold down the fort for Daisy?"

"I'll be holding down the fort here," Iris responded.

"But you will be here to celebrate with me on Sunday, won't you?" Harvey asked. "A celebration is only a celebration if you have the people around you who matter."

Iris's cheeks reddened. She said in a low voice, "I'll be here. You matter to me too."

Warning bells went off in Daisy's head. Harvey

had not signed his final divorce papers. Trying to be realistic, she knew her Aunt Iris didn't run in Harvey's social set by any means. *His* friends played golf at Willow Creek Country Club. The women in his soon-to-be ex-wife's circle shopped in New York, Baltimore, and D.C. They might live in Willow Creek, but they were world travelers, food connoisseurs, and wine aficionados.

Her aunt was a tea aficionado.

Yet when Harvey and Iris gazed at each other, Daisy saw something genuine there. Maybe when one reached a certain age all the rest didn't matter. Maybe when one reached a certain age, one could learn to live with loss and move on.

Daisy knew she hadn't moved on from her husband's death three years ago. Thank goodness, she had her girls and Aunt Iris, her mom and dad, and her sister. Thank goodness, she'd moved back to Willow Creek and started this new venture with her aunt. Come to think of it, in some ways she *had* moved on. In others—

One step at a time.

"I'll go over the list with Harvey for tomorrow and the weekend if you want to work in the kitchen with Tessa and Eva," Iris said to Daisy.

Eva Conner, who was nearing her forty-fifth birthday, was their dishwasher and Girl Friday.

Studying her aunt, Daisy noticed Iris might be trying to get rid of her. Did this meeting of hers with Harvey really include business?

"Have a wonderful celebration tomorrow," Tessa said as she excused herself and crossed to the kitchen. Daisy was about to do the same when the front door of the Tea Garden opened, and her daughter Jazzi blew in with the end of a September breeze. A few dried leaves did too.

Unlike herself and Daisy's oldest daughter Violet who both had honey-blond hair, Jazzi's hair was black, thick, glossy, and straight. Jazzi glanced at Harvey and her aunt and the few other customers in the tea room. Then she shifted her backpack from her shoulders and swung it into one hand. She was frowning and that wasn't unusual these days. Daisy wasn't exactly sure what was going on with her fifteen-year-old.

There was a tradition in Daisy's family that all the women had been given flower names. Her mother's name was Rose, her aunt's name was Iris, Daisy's sister's name was Camellia. Daisy had named her daughters Violet and Jasmine. But Jazzi never used her full name. She preferred her nickname.

Now Daisy went toward her to greet her with a hug. Her daughter slipped out of her hold. Daisy studied the sullen expression on her daughter's face and said, "Just in time to help Tessa with a batch of scones to refrigerate for tomorrow."

"Maybe I don't feel like making scones," Jazzi returned as she ducked her pretty face and didn't look at her mother.

"Do you have lots of homework?"

"The usual."

Daisy wrapped her arm around her daughter and guided her over to a quiet corner of the tea room. Jazzi had been unreliable and rebellious lately. There could be any number of reasons for that, but Daisy suspected the main one: Violet had gone off to college at the end of August, and Jazzi didn't seem to know how to deal with her sister's absence.

"I know you miss Vi."

Jazzi shrugged. "I don't. She's not around lording it over me."

"She's not around for you to talk to or borrow clothes from or ask for advice on makeup. When your Aunt Camellia moved to New York, I felt lost without her. Our lifestyles became very different, and I didn't know if we'd ever have common interests again. Your relationship with Vi will change, but you can still be close."

"Easy for you to say," Jazzi muttered.

Daisy gave her a long look. "If you don't want to help Tessa with the dough for scones, you can work on the cookbook."

Daisy's office was located beside the kitchen, and Jazzi was familiar with her computer. This was a family business, and Jazzi was supposed to be taking over collating recipes for this year's Daisy's Tea Garden cookbook. But she hadn't gotten very far.

"That's like doing schoolwork. I'll help Tessa with the scones."

With that announcement, Jazzi spun on her espadrilles and headed for the kitchen. With her slim-legged jeans, her long tunic-style sweater, and her black hair flowing down her back, Jazzi looked older than fifteen. Daisy wished she could keep her from growing up altogether, but she couldn't. Just as she couldn't keep Violet tied to Willow Creek after college.

Daisy was about to ask Harvey if he'd like her to

brew him a second type of tea. Okay, she was nosy and wanted to know what his conversation with Iris was about. But the glass door to the tea garden was suddenly pulled open. As the bell rang, Cade Bankert strode in.

Daisy stopped midstep to gaze at him a couple of seconds longer than she should. He, too, had been a high school classmate. When she'd moved back to Willow Creek and she and her aunt had decided to look for a place to buy for the tea garden, as well as a second property for her and her girls, she'd consulted Cade who was a real estate agent. She'd always liked him. He'd taken her to their high school prom. But then she'd left for college, and they'd gone their separate ways. Whenever she saw him, sparks of male and female interest seemed to cross over between them. But neither of them had let a spark ignite, maybe because Cade had realized she hadn't been ready for that.

When Cade saw her, he smiled and headed for a table for two. She smiled back and approached him, noticing how well his charcoal suit fit his broad shoulders. His long legs stretched out under the table as if he could finally relax after a long day.

He often stopped in for a snack and a respite before going back to his agency's office for the night. She knew he worked long hours. What self-employed person didn't?

She could let Cora Sue, the middle-aged bottle redhead with a bubbly personality, serve him. However, she signaled to Cora Sue that she'd take care of their latest tea connoisseur. As she neared his table, his gaze swept over her royal blue sweater and slacks, the yellow apron with the daisy emblem for Daisy's Tea Garden stamped on the front. Cade ran his hand through his dark brown hair, putting it in some order after the wind had disturbed it.

He glanced around, noticing tables with other customers sampling Daisy's baked goods. "You're busy. A cup of hot tea hits the spot at the end of a day."

"If I remember correctly," she teased, "when we first opened the tea garden, you didn't know black tea from white tea, or what a tisane was."

"And you've educated me," he responded. "I've become a tea lover. How about orange pekoe today?"

"Coming right up. We have fresh-baked lemon tea cakes too."

"Three of those," he said with a smile. "On second thought, make that six to go. For a change, I'm headed home at a reasonable hour."

"Satisfying day?"

"Yes, it was. House sales have picked up. I have two new listings and closed on another. How about you? Satisfying day?"

"Steadily busy with lots of tourists out on a drive, enjoying the fall weather and the countryside. We do have beautiful scenery in Pennsylvania."

"Yes, we do. Did you miss it when you left?"

"I did. I didn't realize until I moved back here that Florida never really felt like home, not in the way Willow Creek does. Maybe it was the lizards and alligators. I prefer squirrels and fox and deer."

He laughed. "Or two feet of snow in the winter."

"Only some winters," she joked.

She heard her aunt laugh again. Harvey did that

for Iris, and maybe Daisy was being too protective of her aunt, the same way she was protective of Violet and Jazzi?

As she thought of her older daughter, her heart hurt a little. Vi was making her way through the maze of classes and friendships at Lehigh University. Daisy missed her. And Jazzi—she was growing up too. It was hard to believe three years had passed since Ryan died. Maybe there was a more substantial way for Daisy to move on besides checking her daily balance sheets at the Tea Garden.

She could fetch Cade that pot of orange pekoe tea and his lemon tea cakes or . . .

"If you have the evening free," she began and then stopped. Her mouth suddenly went dry. Still, she plunged ahead. "I started stew in the slow cooker this morning before I left. How would you like to come home with Jazzi and me and have a home-cooked meal?"

Cade's brown eyes didn't waver from her blue ones. "You've just made my day."

His expression told her there could be more than friendship on his mind. Had she just made a mistake?

Daisy's house was different than most—it once had been a barn!

She parked on the gravel in front of the building that had once been an equipment shed. Now it served as a detached two-car garage. Cade pulled up beside her. They'd agreed to meet there at seven fifteen and he was right on time.

"How come you asked him to dinner?" Jazzi asked from the passenger seat, curiosity in her voice.

Daisy switched off the ignition to her purple PT Cruiser and gave her daughter her full attention. "I've known Cade for years. He went out of his way to negotiate the best deal for the barn and for the tea garden property. Asking him tonight was just an impulsive decision. Do you mind?"

Jazzi gave her a one-shouldered teenage shrug. "I guess not. I have friends over. You can have friends over. I just wondered if you're . . . forgetting about Dad."

Daisy reached out and put her hand on Jazzi's arm. "I will *never* forget about your dad. I promise." This particular subject had never come up between her and her daughters. She was glad Jazzi felt so deeply about her father. Where Violet was born from Daisy's womb, Jazzi was adopted. She and Ryan had worked hard to make sure Jazzi knew she was a child of their hearts as much as Violet was.

Jazzi pulled away, unfastened her seat belt, and opened her car door. "I'm not going to hang with you guys anyway. I have a paper due in a few days."

She was out of the car before Daisy could take another breath. Just what was going on with her? Fifteen-year-old angst? Or something else?

As Cade joined Daisy and walked with her up the path leading to the house, he glanced up at the multipaned window that had once been a hay hatch where hay bales had been hauled into the barn and out. A smaller window above that one let light into the attic space. A floodlight at the peak of the roof had gone on with dusk, and Daisy could catch a glimpse of the blue plaid curtain that draped the window in Jazzi's room. The second floor was divided into two bedrooms with a bath and had suited her daughters perfectly. Jazzi had chosen white-washed furniture as well as a spread that was blue trimmed in white. Violet's room, however, was less country and more contemporary, with sleek-lined walnut furniture. The drapes and spread were hues of green.

"You know," Cade said, "I couldn't envision this the way you did. I can't wait to see the inside."

Cade had witnessed the outside makeover, with its barn-red siding and repointed and cleaned stone base. White trimmed the windows as well as the dormers. But he hadn't seen the structural changes inside. Ryan's insurance money had made this new life in Willow Creek possible. She'd always be grateful for that.

"You can have the five-cent tour. Anyone who comes to dinner gets it."

Jazzi had her own key. She'd already unlocked the wide, white front door and punched in the code to switch off the security alarm.

As soon as Cade stepped inside the barn house, he whistled. "Wow! You should do this for a living."

"Decorate barns?" she asked with some amusement.

"No, buy them and redesign them."

He was staring at the open stairway to the rear of the living room. A huge wagon-wheel chandelier lit up the area that was open to a dining area and kitchen. A floor-to-ceiling stone fireplace was a focal point on the east wall.

"Come on," Daisy said. Leading Cade into the kitchen area, she motioned down a short hall. "My room's down here."

Cade went down the hall, and Daisy knew he could see the sleigh bed.

"A Sunshine and Shadow quilt," he said when he returned to the kitchen.

"It's my mom's favorite design. When I saw it in a shop in Bird in Hand, I couldn't resist it. I put one of those bowl sinks in the powder room and my bathroom to add a country touch."

"The antique pine furniture does that too." Cade admiringly shook his head again. "You did this all yourself?"

"I did it with the help of Mom and Iris and the girls. It was a joint project. I especially wanted Vi and Jazzi involved so it would feel like home to them."

In the living room once more, Daisy tried to see the entire space through Cade's eyes. The furniture was all upholstered in blue, green, and cream. The braided blue and rust rugs had been woven by a local Amish woman.

Jazzi had run upstairs to her bedroom to drop her backpack. Daisy smiled when she noticed her two cats, who had started down the stairs. Was Cade an animal person?

"Are you going to introduce me to the rest of the family?" he asked Daisy, pointing to the stairway.

The cats apparently sensed another friendly human because they descended the rest of the stairs. Daisy motioned to Marjoram, who was a tortoiseshell with unmistakably unique markings. One side of her face was mottled like a tortoiseshell in tan, brown, and black. The other side was completely dark brown. Various colors, including orange and cream, spotted her back and flanks while her chest was a creamy tan and rust.

"This is Marjoram," Daisy said as she scooped up the cat and cuddled her against her body. The other feline, black with white fluffy spots on her chest, crossed to Cade, sat on his shoe, looked up at him and gave a small meow.

"That's Pepper," Daisy added with a smile.

"How old are they?" Cade asked.

"Probably about eighteen months. We found them last fall in the garden, hence their names Marjoram and Pepper." After another cuddle—the tortie couldn't abide cuddling for long—Daisy let Marjoram down to the floor. "Another cup of tea before I put supper on the table?" she asked.

Pepper moved from Cade's shoe, walked a circle around his legs, then crossed to a deacon's bench under a window and settled on an afghan there.

"What kind do you have?" Cade asked.

"I have an Assam that I like. It's a black tea from India."

"If *you* brew the tea, you have to give me something to do."

"Guests don't have chores in the kitchen," she told him as Marjoram joined her sister on the bench.

"Consider it a contribution," he said. "What can I do? Really."

"You can toss the salad. I'll warm up the bread."

They worked companionably together as Daisy brewed tea, popped the bread in the oven, and watched Cade slice the carrots at the island. She pulled a basket from one of the knotty pine cupboards and lined it with a napkin, preparing it for the warmed bread. It had been over three years since she'd worked beside a man in the kitchen. Ryan's cancer had taken him so fast, they'd hardly had time to say good-bye. Not nearly enough time. But she shouldn't be thinking about loss now, not if she wanted to move on.

"I really appreciate this. Home-cooked meals are hard to come by," Cade said as he set the salad bowl on the table.

The round pedestal table was oak with a distressed wood finish. The chairs were antiques that she'd found at the flea market and refinished herself. All of it had been part of rehabilitation, grieving, and starting over. For the most part, it had worked.

"Are you saying you live on my scones?" she joked. A former dietician, she was aware of eating habits, both good and bad. When Cade did stop in at the tea garden, he usually bought a dozen scones. He'd told her that he often froze them and pulled them out when he needed them.

"Of course, I don't just live on your scones," he answered, faking injured pride. "I can fry burgers and cook an omelet."

When Daisy looked at Cade, she saw the man he'd become, but she also remembered the boy he'd been. "Why haven't you ever married?"

He shrugged. "Maybe after our prom date, no other woman could compare to you."

His explanation stunned her for a moment, and before she could decide whether he was serious or not, her cell phone rang. It wasn't exactly a ring; it was a sound like a tuba bellowing.

Cade's eyebrows arched.

"It's the only ringtone I can hear when I'm in the tea garden with customers." She saw her Aunt Iris was calling. "It's Aunt Iris. Excuse me for a minute?"

He nodded. "I'll take the bread from the oven."

Daisy moved into the living room and answered the call. "Hi, what's up?" Maybe Harvey wanted to change their plans for tomorrow afternoon in his store. Maybe he wanted her to bring a particular tea.

"Harvey just left."

"You're still at the tea garden?"

"We were talking," her aunt said defensively, and Daisy knew she'd better back off with any disapproval she might be feeling.

"Were you talking about tea at his shop tomorrow or the party on Sunday?"

"Both. He finalized everything he wants served for afternoon tea service on Sunday. But that isn't why I'm calling."

Daisy waited.

"Harvey left because he received a phone call from his lawyer. It's about the divorce settlement."

"I thought all that was finalized."

"He did too. But apparently Monica made new demands, or else changed her mind about something they'd already agreed on. He didn't go into detail. He said he had to leave and take care of it. He didn't want anything to hold it up. I think he was going to see his lawyer . . . or maybe even Monica. He didn't say, exactly."

Daisy could hear the worry in her aunt's voice and the fear that maybe dreams she was beginning to weave weren't going to come true.

"Aunt Iris, what would you say if I told you I was dating a man who wasn't divorced yet?"

Iris was silent for a few moments, but then she said, "I'd tell you to be very careful. I'd tell you to keep your eyes wide open and listen to your sixth sense."

"Is that what you're doing?"

"I am. Harvey Fitz is one of the special ones. He's worth waiting for."

Daisy wasn't sure of that. She wasn't sure of that at all.